I0661801

ECHOES THROUGH TIME

Melanie Robertson-King

King Park Press

Published by King Park Press

Copyright © Melanie Robertson-King,
2025
House image: Hansuan Fabregas (Pixabay)

Poem Ghost House by Robert Frost
(Public Domain)

ECHOES THROUGH TIME is a work of fiction.
Names, characters, places and incidents are the
product of the author's imagination or are used
fictitiously. Any resemblance to actual events,
locales or persons, living or dead, is purely
coincidental.

ISBN: 978-1-990371-12-7

DEDICATION

For those who have experienced echoes through time..

ACKNOWLEDGMENTS

Thanks to Joanna Penn and Joseph Michael for their informative workshop on ChatGPT. It turned out to be a great brainstorming partner.

Huge thanks to my eagle-eyed proof/beta reader Nancy Chapman.

Special thanks to my cousin and her husband who are fluent in German and helped me with the translations.

If I've missed anyone by name, I apologize.

Special thanks to my husband, Don, who continues to support and encourage me, and provides a shoulder to cry on when things don't go well. He redesigned my website making it mobile-friendly and taken charge on the domestic front giving me time to write.

Chapter One

Nicole placed the box on her desk and sat. She stared at the battered container while she waited for her brothers to arrive in their shared office space. Most days, they were already at work by the time she arrived. Not even their diplomas on the walls, other certificates of achievement, and large framed prints of her artwork distracted her from the object next to her. The contents had freaked her out when she opened it, but the cryptic note *for Nicole* taped to the lid chilled her to the bone.

Male voices drifted in from the back of the unit housing their kitchenette, bathroom, and storage. Cooper and Connor had finally deigned to grace her with their presence. When they entered the main office, Nicole stood.

"What time did you get here, Nicki?" Connor asked.

"Ten minutes ago or thereabouts."

"You look like you've seen a ghost," Cooper observed.

"I think I did. Remember the china head doll I sketched and somehow photographed at the Kembleford Manor Hotel?"

"Yeah, what about it?" Connor asked.

"Lift the lid, then look at the picture on my screen and the page in my sketchbook."

Her brothers rounded the desk and stood on either side of her. Neither moved to open the box, so she yanked off the lid and lifted out the doll. "Look," she said, her voice trembling.

Cooper shrank back at the sight. "That's it all right," he said when his voice returned.

"Where did you find it, Nicki?" asked Connor.

"I cleaned my car on the weekend. One last thorough clean before winter, and I found this under the front passenger seat. Until then, I'd never seen this box before. How did it end up hidden in my vehicle? It's unsettling, to say the least."

Connor patted her shoulder. "Don't know, sis."

"The little girl that drowned there had no connection to Mummy, so that box shouldn't have been in the storage locker. And look at the note on the lid."

Cooper picked up the lid. "For Nicole," he said. "How would whoever got it into your car realize you're the Nicole the doll was intended for?"

"I don't know, but I can tell you it's downright creepy," Nicole answered. "I don't recognize the handwriting. If I had, it might not have spooked me so much."

"It's possible you brought it from the storage locker, and somehow it ended up under the seat? Think back to the day. Did you have to do a hard brake? If so, the box must have fallen off the seat," Cooper said.

"I know you're trying to make me feel better and I appreciate it." Nicole hugged him.

"It's like it wanted you to find it. Maybe the Kembleford Manor ghosts aren't finished with us?" Connor suggested.

"I need no more ghostly connections, thank you very much," Nicole said, "But there has to be one. The doll might be just a piece of a bigger puzzle."

"Call Dad. He might remember putting it in your car?" Cooper suggested.

Memories of how emotional Nicole had gotten at Kembleford Manor flooded back to Connor. The text message from Mitch. Until then, he didn't know there was even a boathouse there, let alone a little girl who drowned. A little girl who owned the china head doll that now sat on his sister's desk.

He pulled out his cell phone. Did he text Mitch? He was with Nicole when she had the vision of the little girl face-down in the murky water of the boathouse. Cooper wouldn't thank him for it, but Nicole might. He tapped out a message with his thumbs.

Remember the boathouse? Nic freaked out? The same doll turned up under the seat in her car.

Did he add any more? That should be enough for the man to figure out what he's talking about. If not, he'd explain in more detail. At least communicating by text message, Cooper didn't overhear the conversation, providing a moment of relief from potential disapproval.

Connor wracked his brain, trying to recall when things turned sour between his brother and Mitch. He and his sister still got along with the man; only his twin didn't. No more time to ruminate about it. Another prospective client wanted a website done, complete with graphics, Nicole's forte, and the coding which he and Cooper did.

He placed his phone face-down on his desk, sat and logged into his computer.

The three gave a short recap of their current project and the key areas they needed to focus on this week. At least this job wasn't as complicated as the *Barnsley's Bakery* one they had finished. That job was an update. Things could go south in a short time — a wrong variable here or there, a typo in a CSS file. And some clients were harder to please than others. This one was starting on the ground floor, but at least it was a simpler task than they had done.

Mitch's phone vibrated and the screen flashed Connor Holbrook's name. He pressed the hands-free button, expecting a phone call, but was a text. It would wait until he arrived at the job site, about five minutes farther up the road.

When he pulled into the driveway, he wasn't sure what to expect from this place, except the homeowner was frantic and made little sense on the phone. From the outside, the house looked in good repair. The mansard roof with three dormer windows over a full two-storey square structure seemed intact, with the original slate shingles no less.

Mitch exited the truck, pocketed his phone, and walked towards the front door, keeping a close watch for anything out of place. There was a small front porch with three steps. All the boards were solid, and there were no signs of rot. Maybe the owner wanted a renovation done. He had dealt with people who panicked over the least little thing. He rang the doorbell and waited.

As he was about to ring again, the lock scraped, and the door creaked open. A bit of WD-40 on the hinges wouldn't go amiss. Mitch would do that for free, depending on the extent of the job.

"Mitchell Kane," he introduced himself to a small woman who didn't come up to his shoulders. "You called me about some renovation work?"

"Oh yes, please come in."

Mitch stepped over the threshold and into the grand hall. The wallpaper was outdated, but a rich brown stain covered the trim, not paint. That was a positive. "So what is it you'd like me to do?"

"This way." The woman, wringing her hands, led him through the house towards the back. "In here." She opened the door to the room.

The plaster had turned a sickly yellow-brown, and watermarks spread outward in a jagged circle. A cast iron, claw-foot bathtub sat in the middle of the floor, partly buried in debris and its surface covered with it. Splintered beams poked through where the tub had crashed from, leaving a gaping hole in the room above. Mitch walked closer to inspect the damage. Chunks of plaster and broken tiles littered the floor, and a thin stream of water sprayed from one of the exposed pipes. He found it difficult not to laugh. The scene of Tom Hanks pouring the bucket of water into the tub in the movie *The Money Pit* when the bathtub fell through the floor came to him. He hoped this poor woman wasn't hurt.

"Can I have a look upstairs, Missus? I didn't

catch your last name."

"Yes, please. Right this way. And it's Anderson."

"Right, Mrs. Anderson, let's go have a look."

As they ascended the stairs, Mrs. Anderson moaned about how she struggled to maintain the home since her husband's death. "My pension doesn't go as far as it used to when I first retired."

Mitch tried to be sympathetic. It was a huge home for one person. The home's interior looked in good repair except for the bathtub, which sat in a room it didn't belong in. What caused this?

A fluffy black cat appeared from one of the rooms on this level. Mrs. Anderson scooped it up into her arms and opened a door on the second floor. "Here you go. Mind the floor. I'm afraid it might all collapse."

"You wait out here in the hall, then. I need to get a closer look." Mitch pulled his phone out of his pocket. "What the?" he muttered.

"Is everything all right in there?"

"Yes." He stared at the message Connor had sent him. It made no sense. How would that end up in Nicole's car? He tapped out a message.

Quoting for a repair. Will call u later.

The the musty scent of damp wood and mould filled the air. Its sharp stench burned his nostrils. Mitch walked as close to the hole in the floor as he dared. Each step he took squelched on the punky, soggy floorboards. He took pictures, looking down into the room below, then knelt and peered into the space between the floor and the ceiling below. Water? The lath and plaster appeared wet. More pictures. One of the bathroom pipes had leaked, and for this much damage, it had to have been leaking for quite some time.

"Did you ever notice water damage on the ceiling in the room below the bathroom?"

"The ceiling paper was discoloured. That's all I can tell you."

"Right. What about a shut-off tap for this room?"

"I'm not sure. Oh dear, what am I going to do?" She pulled a tissue from her pocket and dabbed at her eyes.

"If I don't have to, I'd rather not off turn the water to the entire house. But we need to intervene." Mitch looked around the perimeter of the room. The only shut-off was the one on the toilet. A previous contractor installed a modern sink and vanity, so he opened the doors and discovered taps under the sink. With luck, they'd turn off the water to the entire room. The water gods must have been smiling down on him because the spraying water stopped when he closed off those taps.

Mitch exited the bathroom and pulled the door closed. "I want to get a better look downstairs now."

Back in the room beneath the bathroom, Mitch scanned the remaining ceiling for water damage. It was almost impossible to tell because so much collapsed with the bathtub.

"Where were you when this happened?"

"In my garden," said Mrs. Anderson.

"At least you weren't in here. You could have been killed."

The woman paled at his comment.

He patted her arm. "You'll be okay as long as you don't enter either of those rooms. I have to get a ladder from my truck. I need to get up in the cavity between the joists, the bathroom floor, and this room's ceiling. I'll be right back."

Mitch headed to his truck and pulled his phone out before anything else. He took a few minutes to re-read Connor's message and, if needed, respond quickly.

WTF? How did that happen? Makes no sense. Kinda like this job I'm quoting.

He returned his phone to his pocket because this job quote was his immediate priority. The house, second empire style, was built in the late 1800s. Sometime between 1870 and 1899, he estimated. So it was well over one hundred years old. If they installed indoor plumbing during construction, they would have used cast iron for drainage and galvanized for the incoming water.

Mitch strapped his tool belt to his waist, removed the ladder, balanced it on his shoulder, and carried it back to the house. He wanted to examine the tub's underside.

He set the ladder up in the room, climbed until his head was in the gap, then turned on his phone's flashlight and looked around. From what he could tell, the remaining joists seemed sound. Mitch took his hammer and tapped the exposed beams. Chunks of soggy wood crumbled away. He wouldn't know how bad the damage was until he got the bathroom floor up and the ceiling pulled down. Mitch took more pictures.

When he came down from his lofty perch, he felt around in the debris close to the displaced fixture. The chunks of wet plaster gave way as he touched them. "You've got significant water damage, Mrs. Anderson. I must remove the bathroom floor and ceiling here to determine how extensive. Joists will have to be replaced. It might be worth it to have the house re-plumbed with modern materials. Do you have another bathroom you can use while this one is out of service?"

"Yes, I do. But, my word, that much work?" she asked, still holding the cat in her arms.

At least having her pet with her, made her calmer. She couldn't wring her hands, which the way she had been, Mitch was sure, she'd rub them raw.

"I'm sorry, but things will get worse if I don't get to the bottom of it. I'll crunch numbers and get back to you with a price in a few days." Mitch raked his fingers through his hair. This wasn't just a patch job. It was a full-blown restoration. He muttered, calculating the hours and materials needed to do the job correctly.

Chapter Two

It had been an exhausting labour and delivery. June had slept almost a full twenty-four hours after giving birth. She had the baby at home, since the cost of a hospital stay was beyond their means. As it was, the bill from the doctor would be enough to put her and the child in the poorhouse.

June threw the covers aside and sat on the edge of the bed. Her newborn son's cradle set in a frame to elevate it, making it easier for getting him in and out, stood next to the bed. She gazed at the sleeping baby. As she was about to lift him out, a wave of dizziness overcame her, and she had to lie down again.

The faint sounds of someone in the kitchen reached the room. A few minutes later, June's mother entered, carrying a tray with a teapot, cup, saucer, milk, and sugar. She set it on the corner table.

"I'll help you up. You need to eat and drink. Tea, hot and sweet, and toast with my homemade raspberry jam, your favourite."

"Thank you, Mother." June shifted in bed and tried to sit again.

This time, her mother helped. She got her daughter out of bed and settled where she laid the breakfast.

"Have you heard anything from your husband since he went overseas?"

"I've had a few letters. He was training for battle in Plymouth, England. He said in his last one he expected to be sent to the Western Front at any time. I want to write to tell him about William. How do I know where to send it?"

"Try sending it to the Canadian Expeditionary Force in England, where he trained. They'll know where he is and can forward your letter to him. It would take some time for it to reach him, though."

June nodded. She looked at the breakfast things on the table. Everything smelled delicious. Twenty-four hours with no food or drink made her stomach growl. She poured a cup of tea, and spread some of her mother's jam on a slice of buttered toast. A few mouthfuls of food and a sip of tea were all she could manage.

"Thank you, Mother, but I can't eat anymore. I'd like to write to Robert and then lie down again."

"Very well." The woman wrapped her powerful arms around June's shoulders and hugged her. She picked up the tray and left.

June pulled a small writing pad, her fountain pen, and ink well out of the drawer on the side of the table. When it was an eating table, they stored cutlery there. Now that it was in her room, she kept her writing supplies there instead. Pen readied, she began to write.

February 23, 1915

Dear Robert,

I hope this letter finds you safe. I wasn't sure where to send it, so I've addressed it to you in care of your unit. I trust your superiors will get it to you somehow.

I have to tell you some exciting news! You are now a father. That was why I insisted we move the wedding ahead. I wouldn't be showing too much, if at all. If anyone asks, we'll say he came early. Our parents would disown us if they knew we had relations before marriage.

June stood, walked to the cradle, and lifted her infant son to her chest. She held him in her left arm so she could continue writing. The baby opened his eyes. She had to sit the pen down and stroke his soft cheeks.

We're now the proud parents of a little boy who I've named William. He looks so much like you. Your blue eyes, strong, dimpled chin, and a headful of your brown hair. They tell me the hair will all fall out, and then he'll grow new. It might remain the same colour as yours, or he might end up with hair the colour of straw like mine.

Please be safe and come home to me and your son.
Love,

June
xx

She left the letter out flat so the ink would dry. While it did, she addressed the envelope to Private Robert Holbrook, c/o Canadian Expeditionary Force, Plymouth, England, and hoped they would see the letter reach the intended recipient.

Chapter Three

Nicole picked up the phone and put it down again. She was determined to find out if her father had put the battered cardboard box containing the china head doll in her car. Still, she didn't want him to think she was losing her mind. After changing her mind several times; she dialled her father's number.

"Hello. Frank Holbrook."

He always answered the phone like that, whether in the office or home. Since the spring of 2020, when the pandemic hit, he had worked from home. Her mother was undergoing chemo. Her breast cancer had returned with a vengeance in late 2019, far more aggressive the second time and metastasized and spread throughout her body.

"Hi, Dad, it's Nicole."

"What's up? You don't normally phone in the middle of a workday. Are you okay?"

"No. I'm not. When I met you at the storage locker and got the boxes of Mummy's things, was there a smaller box? One that would hold a pair of shoes or boots?"

"I really don't remember. There were bigger boxes, like cases from photocopy paper. But I can't say I recall anything smaller like what you're talking about."

"There was a note taped to the lid and it said *for Nicole*. I don't recognize the writing."

"Has to be a logical explanation. Sorry, I can't be of any help."

"Would you swing by the office and take a look? I found the box under the seat of my car on the weekend. I always lock it so no one could have gotten in and stashed it there."

"I have to go out anyway, so I'll swing by. I'm sure there's an explanation for it all. See you shortly. Love you."

"Bye, Dad. Love you, too."

Nicole hung up the phone and stared across the room. She and Mitch had seen the newspaper articles online that reported the little girl's drowning back in 1947. This doll was the same one. There weren't many china head dolls in Canada, let alone Ontario, that had the shiny glaze and moulded hair. This doll was an antique. She needed to Google it to find out what period and from what country it originated. That would have to wait until later.

She had some designs to start on for *The Cheese Board & Café*. Several ideas ran through her mind, including combinations of images she could blend to create a striking logo for their website and signage on their store. This business, filled with promise and potential, was just getting off the ground, and the clients were coming to meet with them in person the next day.

About an hour later, Mr. Holbrook walked through the front door, which scraped announcing his arrival. Nicole, who had been sketching designs, dropped her pencil, stood and rushed over to greet her father.

"Hey, Dad, what brings you here?" Connor asked.

"Nicole asked me to stop by. Said she had something I needed to see."

"She definitely does. We've seen her photos and sketches from exploring Kembleford Manor last month. It's a dead ringer for what she drew."

"This way, Dad. The box is on my desk."

Mr. Holbrook walked alongside his daughter to where she had everything set up. The box was closed, but she had the doll photo on one of her three monitors, and the sketchbook opened on the page. "Okay, see these?"

"Yes, but I don't understand why I need to see your drawings. I know how talented you are. You don't have to prove anything to me."

Nicole picked up the cardboard box and handed it to her father. Once he held it, she removed the lid. "Now look. That doll is the same one as in these," she said, pointing to her hand-drawn image and the photograph. "I need to know where it came from and who sent it to me." Her voice trembled with emotion, drawing everyone into her plight.

Her father's eyes widened in surprise, and a puzzled expression formed on his face. His brow furrowed. "Strange indeed. I'm not sure what to tell you."

"Look at this note taped to the top. Someone meant it for me. Why else would it say *for Nicole*?"

"That looks like my sister's writing."

"Aunt Janet?"

"Yes. I've not seen my sister in a long time. Not since ... oh, never mind, but she and your mother remained close until the end. Janet might have passed it on to Julie." His voice broke when he mentioned his late wife's name.

"Thanks, Dad. I'll give Aunt Janet a call. Is she still in the assisted living place?"

"I'm sure she'd love to hear from you. I have to go. Things in the car I need to get home and put away."

"Okay. Thanks for stopping by. I appreciate it." Nicole hugged her father, and he kissed her on the cheek, turned and walked out the door.

Something in his demeanour changed when he saw the doll. It was as if he knew of its existence. Perhaps her brother was right when he mentioned having to do a hard brake. The boxes slid off the backseat, and this smaller one fell out and lodged itself on the floor, out of sight.

That doll looked familiar, like one he'd seen a long time ago, but he couldn't remember where or when. Did he mistake the handwriting and it didn't belong to his sister? Did the person who wrote the cryptic note and taped it to the box not mean for Nicole to be the recipient? Perhaps someone different, just with the same first name.

Frank hadn't spoken, really spoken, to his sister Janet in years. The family home should have gone to him because he was the oldest. Why his father left it to her, he didn't know. His relationship with his parents wasn't the greatest. He was never good enough. Didn't try hard enough. The real kicker was when he brought Julie home and told his parents he was marrying her. It all kicked off then. Someone like her was the phrase they used. She wasn't good enough. She'd tie him down. Hold him back. Maybe they'd have known differently if they ever stopped and listened.

Now, the only thing he would change was to trade places with his wife. She was a kind person. A good mother who loved life and brought out the best in him. He should have been stricken with cancer. Not her. No matter how much he wanted it, Frank was unable to turn back the clock to before his wife's illness and subsequent death. His regret was a heavy burden he carried every day.

Would he phone Janet and ask her what she was playing at, sending a box containing a china head doll to his daughter? That box wasn't in the storage locker. He'd remember one that small. Unless it was inside another. Perhaps one of the bigger boxes broke open, and when Nicole tried to sweep the contents back into it, she knocked the small container under the seat. In his logical mind, that made sense. He couldn't fathom this supernatural mumbo jumbo the kids tried to get him to believe when they returned from Kembleford Manor.

He never expected his offspring to participate in urban exploration as a hobby. It was a surprise, to say the least. At least the police had never charged them with anything. Cooper cut his leg badly on one of their expeditions. That was the first time he and his wife knew what the kids were doing. By then, they had all left home and lived on their terms.

Chapter Four

Despite being in uniform, no one on the streets in Lützkampen, Germany, noticed the Canadian soldier. They carried on about their business as if the war wasn't happening. Robert supposed that was a good thing. The army deployed him to the Western Front, which wasn't near the city. From what he'd been able to find out, the Eastern Front was far away. They received one night's leave before assembling and being ready for battle. He supposed he shouldn't have crossed the border from Belgium, but he did without difficulty.

The local architecture captivated him, so much so that he didn't notice the woman until he had already collided with her. She dropped the basket, and loaves of bread scattered onto the ground.

"I'm sorry, let me help you," he said, kneeling to pick up the food. He looked up from his task into the bluest eyes he'd ever seen. They were eyes you could get lost in.

"You're foreign," the woman said, haltingly.

"Canadian."

He watched her brow furrow in concentration and could tell English wasn't her first language.

"I deliver bread from our family bakery to cousins," she said.

"I'm Robert, and you are?"

"Ute."

"It's lovely to meet you, Ute. Since it's because of me your baked goods ended up on the ground, let me help you deliver them."

"No. No, it's fine. I go now," Ute insisted.

Nervous. He understood her fear, even though he had no intention of causing her harm. After all, he was a foreign soldier in her country, a sight that would understandably instil fear.

Ute picked up the filled basket and scurried up the street. She looked over her shoulder to see if he followed her. She couldn't allow her cousins to see her in the company of a Canadian soldier. Even if they only met over spilled bread.

She arrived at the house, knocked and waited for someone to come to the door.

"Ute, you're late this evening, and you're flushed. Have you been running?"

"Yes," she said, nodding. "Late getting away from Wiesbaden."

"Come in. Come in. Have some tea," her cousin beckoned.

"No. I must go. Valter is waiting for me." Ute couldn't be more nervous if she stood before a firing squad. Something about the soldier sent feelings, long since dormant, rushing through her veins. Her husband hadn't made her feel that way in such a long time. The contrast between her feelings for the soldier and her husband was stark, and it filled her with a mixture of guilt and longing.

Ute turned and hurried back down the street. Would she find him again? Would he wait for her? When she reached the corner where they'd run into each other, he stood leaning against the wall, smoking a cigarette.

He grabbed her hand, wrapped his arms around her, backed her against the wall, and drew her in for a long, passionate kiss. Ute's knees weakened, and she could barely hold herself up.

"We shouldn't," she breathed when the kiss finally ended. Her heart raced, torn between the thrill of the soldier's touch and the guilt of betraying her husband.

"Where can we go? Someplace private where no one will see us."

Ute turned her head from left to right and raised it to look over the soldier's shoulder.

"Down there. A barn. I'll go first. People can't see us together." She suggested, her voice trembling with fear and excitement. The soldier's reaction was unreadable, his eyes hidden behind a veil of smoke.

She stepped around him and dashed down the street to the farm with the barn she mentioned. Ute hoped it would be unlocked. The loose hay would hide them and be comfortable. What was she thinking? A strange man in the hay? Unable to stop herself, she looked over her shoulder to ensure he was coming.

Her actions intrigued Robert. On the one hand, Ute seemed hesitant, as if she didn't want to do anything. On the other, there was an undeniable eagerness in her, a desire she couldn't suppress. The way she returned his kiss told him that.

She stood outside the barn door until he was almost there, then ducked inside. When he joined her, their bodies locked in another passionate embrace, a mix of desire and guilt, before they fell into the soft, loose hay.

Robert realized what he was about to do was wrong, but his physical desires made him continue. He slowly unbuttoned Ute's dress and pulled it from her shoulders, before letting it fall to the floor.

When they put their clothes back on, Robert felt no remorse. Yes, he had done something he never thought he would do. But then he didn't think he'd be going to war either.

"What will you tell your husband?" he asked.

Her jaw dropped. "How did you know?"

"Wedding ring."

"I will say nothing. Tell no one. I will leave first. Then you."

"But what if you ...?"

"Fall pregnant?"

"Yes."

"We will do it, too. Not tonight, but perhaps tomorrow."

She sneaked out the door and disappeared.

Robert followed. Ute was up the road about fifty yards ahead. He paused in front of a small general shop that was still open. In the window was a collection of china head dolls. He chose one with glossy black hair, walked in and bought it.

He had to run when he exited the shop because Ute was getting into a vehicle. From his vantage point, he couldn't tell if she was alone or if someone picked her up. He got to the car just in time. Ute was alone. She was the driver.

"Here. To remember our night together."

"But ..."

"Keep it out of sight, and when you take it out to look at it when you're alone, think of me and our time together."

"You shouldn't have," she protested.

"I know, but I wanted to."

Robert pushed the doll inside the car and gave her one last kiss before walking away and returning to the Belgian border.

Chapter Five

"You guys up for a little exploration on Saturday?" Connor asked.

"By then, we'll likely need a break so what did you have in mind?" Cooper asked.

"What do you think of a gothic mansion with towers and steep gables and not too far from here?"

Nicole joined her brothers as they looked at the house Connor had brought up on his screen. "That place gives me the creeps. And after everything that happened at Kembleford Manor, I'm not sure I want to check out a house that might have a few ghosts rattling around."

"Are you sure it's even empty? It looks like it's in reasonably decent repair for a house of that age," said Cooper.

"This street view is from a few years ago," Connor said. "No vehicles. Uncut grass. If I go back to another image, this one in the winter, no one has shovelled the snow. That says empty to me."

"Where is it?" Nicole asked.

"Just outside Brighton."

"You're right. It's not too far. Still ..."

Connor understood his sister's reluctance to explore this property. Weird things happened at Kembleford Manor, and she saw, sketched, and photographed psychic phenomena. "If I find another property, are you willing to go with us?"

"Maybe."

"We might have to go farther away, like up around Toronto. Lots of places up there lying empty because developers have bought them to be torn down and new buildings put up."

"Pike Falls was quite the drive. Yeah, Toronto isn't as far, but it's still a long day, and the traffic up there is horrendous. Just promise me, if I start to feel any weird vibes, we'll leave," Nicole said.

"Deal." Connor shook her hand. It was the least he could do. "Do you want me to ask Mitch to join us? Things worked well for you last time, with him showing up at the same place."

Cooper turned, and Connor would cease to exist if looks could kill.

"What happened between you and Mitch, anyway?" Connor asked. "The four of us used to be close." He leaned on the desk so his face was almost in his twin brother's. "Something major by the way you react every time his name is mentioned."

Connor turned towards his sister. Her cheeks were red as beets. Were she and Mitch more than just good friends? If that was the case, he was happy for Nicole. Unlike Cooper, Connor still liked Mitch.

Nicole returned to her desk and looked at the preliminary drawings she had done for *The Cheese Board & Café*. She liked them. Now, wait-and-see if the clients did too. She hoped so, her heart filled with anticipation. They had several designs to choose from, which turned out far better than the *Barnsley's Bakery* one from last month. But, if she had the same issues going from sketch to digital image, it would look flat, too.

She noticed the dirty look Cooper had given Connor at the mention of inviting Mitch to come with them. Nicole didn't need a keeper. Yes, she appreciated Mitch being at Kembleford Manor because the place was so weird. Nicole liked him, but would she want to date him? That would be akin to dating one of her brothers.

Something about this gothic mansion piqued her curiosity. Why would someone build something so elaborate in the middle of nowhere? Maybe when it was built, it wasn't? Did the house have a name?

Nicole glanced at the box still on her desk — the doll laid out on layers of tissue paper. It brought back the visions she had of the little girl who drowned. What made her go into the water? Did she drop her doll? Was she pushed? The child had no one to advocate for her. Running a hotel kept her parents occupied. Was it their fault she drowned? Poor little girl ... Grace. The name came back to her. When she had found the newspaper articles online, she showed them to Mitch. That box wasn't in her apartment then, was it? Why not ask him? She picked up her phone.

When you came to my apartment and I showed you the photograph. I still swear I didn't take it. Do you remember a shoebox mixed in with all the others? N.

Nicole's trust in Mitch was unwavering. He wouldn't lie to her. If that box was in her apartment, he'd have noticed it. As a contractor and renovation expert, he required an eye for detail. She didn't think her father would lie to her either, but once his sister's name came up, he couldn't wait to get out of the office.

If Mitch was on the job, he might not respond to her message until the evening. Nicole realized she had found the shoebox under the seat of her car, so it had never been in her apartment. He would never have seen it, so she sent him another message.

Sorry to bother you. I'm confused.

"You wanted to see me?" Mitch asked as he pulled open the sticking door at CNC IT Solutions.

Nicole's head popped up from behind her monitor. Connor turned around. Cooper glared at him before standing up and leaving the room.

"I didn't mean for you to rush over here," Nicole said.

"That's okay. Connor sent me a message, too. Something about the doll."

"Come have a look."

Mitch walked around the corner of Nicole's desk. A dusty cardboard box sat on the corner. His reaction to seeing the doll was one of complete surprise, much like when he'd read Connor's text. "What the ...? How can that be?" he exclaimed, his voice filled with astonishment.

"You tell me. This china head doll is the last thing I ever expected to see outside of the scene that manifested in front of me at Kembleford Manor. But, it gets even stranger," Nicole said, lifting the lid from the desk's surface. "Look." She pointed to the sheet of paper taped to the lid.

"For Nicole," Mitch read the note aloud.

"Yes. I found the box under the passenger seat of my car on the weekend. It has me so rattled that I texted you to see if you remembered it being in my apartment. That's impossible since I just found it."

Things became stranger by the minute. "Maybe the Nicole on the lid isn't you, but another person with the same first name?" Mitch suggested.

Nicole wasn't the only young woman to have that name. Now, she should be freaked out if both her names were on it.

"Someone put it in your car as a joke?" Connor asked.

"Not funny. And I always keep my car locked. There's no way to unlock it without the key fob."

"Hey, what's that poking out from under the tissue paper?" Mitch asked.

"Where?"

"Here." Mitch reached into the box, took hold of the small triangle of the foreign object, and pulled it out from under the paper and the doll. "It looks like a letter," he said.

Nicole snatched it from his hand.

Nicole's hands trembled as she read the address on the envelope. "Ute Birkhoefer, German Chocolate Bakery & Pastry, Rüdesheimer Str., Wiesbaden, Germany." She turned the envelope over, but there was no return address, adding to the mystery of the letter.

"Birkhoefer! That was the name of the family who ran the Kembleford Manor Hotel. It was their daughter who drowned." Nicole removed the thin paper from the envelope, feeling a connection to the past. The ink, while faded, remained legible.

15 March, 1915

My dearest Ute,

I count the days until I am back in your arms. I hope you are well and that the doll I bought for you when we first met comforts you and makes you think of me.

It was pure fate that someone as beautiful as you walked into my life in Lützkampen. I wish I could turn back the clock and relive that moment, not the hell we're living in the trenches.

Please be careful. I would die if anything should happen to you.

All my love,

Robert
xoxo

"It's a love letter from someone named Robert to Ute." Nicole's eyes glazed over with unshed tears after reading it.

"Sounds to me like it was a one-night stand before he shipped out for battle," said Mitch.

Nicole re-read the letter. No, Robert had to be her lover. He said they first met in Lützkampen. He bought her the china head doll.

She lifted the memento from the box and removed the tissue paper. More envelopes remained hidden in the bottom. After placing it on the desk and laying the opened letter beside it, Nicole picked up the pack of correspondence. The same person wrote all, and the writing was identical. That would be reading for later.

Chapter Six

Valter, Ute's husband, had stopped thinking of her romantically some years before. Their relationship had developed into a more practical one, with Ute feeling like she was only an employee of the bakery and a broodmare. She didn't qualify for that now that she had given him two sons. Still, to cover up her indiscretion, she felt the need to maintain a physical relationship with him. That way, if she fell pregnant, Valter was the father.

Despite being exhausted after a long day baking bread, cakes and other treats, she returned to their small flat, determined to make Valter want her again. She fed their sons, Walter and Friedrich, and settled them into their shared room. The boys had a few games which occupied them, their favourite being *Mensch Ärgere Dich Nicht*. Valter had bought it for them on a trip to Frankfurt the year before. Ute's love for her sons was the only thing that kept her going.

Now, to focus on her appearance. She had to look perfect. After a strip wash in front of the kitchen sink, she entered her bedroom and opened the wardrobe doors. What to wear? Ute didn't have many dresses to choose from. Most of hers were everyday ones she wore in and around the bakery, including when she delivered bread to her cousins.

The best one she had she wore on her wedding day. Did it still fit? She'd maintained her figure. At least she thought she had. Ute pulled it out from the back and laid it on the bed. It buttoned at the back, and she couldn't reach all the buttons. On her special day, her mother had looked after her. Stepping into it, she pulled it up and put her arms through the sleeves. She fastened the bottom four buttons. Her chemise under it kept her decent.

When the apartment door slammed shut, Ute entered the small lounge, dining room, and kitchen. Standing before Valter, she took a deep breath. "What does my handsome husband need after working so hard all day? Beer?" She walked to the icebox and retrieved a crock.

"Where's my supper? And what are you dressed like that for? You look like a common ..."

Ute didn't let him finish his sentence. "You didn't think so on our wedding night."

"That was eleven years ago, woman. Stop acting like that and get my meal on."

She bit down on her knuckles to hold back her tears. It didn't work. By the time she fled to their room, they flowed like a waterfall. Hot, scorching rivulets streamed down her face. At that moment, she felt a surge of hatred towards Valter. Had he somehow discovered what happened with the Canadian soldier? If he did, she wished he'd just come out and say it. Her internal conflict was tearing her apart.

The wedding dress returned to the back of the wardrobe. Ute donned the dress she'd worn all day and then returned to tend to her husband's supper. She couldn't look at him. His rejection of her advances shattered her heart into pieces. Two sausages remained in the pan. She stabbed them with a fork, much as she'd like to do to him, dumped them on his plate, and did the same with the boiled potato. Without speaking, Ute let his plate fall to the table with a clatter and strode back into the bedroom.

Valter couldn't fathom what had come over his wife. Her recent actions were a departure from the woman he had known for years, the woman he had married. They had fallen into a steady rhythm of work and home life. After a long day in the bakery, Valter was too tired when he returned home at the end of the day to bother with anything other than his supper, newspaper and sleep.

He noticed the sorry state of the meal Ute had prepared, the sausages now charred beyond recognition. The lone potato, a symbol of their modest means, shrivelled and unappetizing. Valter always made sure they had wholesome food, but this was a far cry from it.

He stabbed a sausage with his fork, raised it to his mouth and bit a chunk off the end. Before Ute cremated them, they were prime bratwurst. Now, they were inedible. Still, he couldn't bring himself to throw the food away, so he ate them. It was as tough as boot leather. Not that he'd ever tried chewing on that.

At least there was butter for his potato. That made it slightly more bearable. He washed the disgusting meal down with the beer Ute had poured for him earlier.

Ute had failed to return from the bedroom after she flounced off. He hoped that by the time she returned; she had come to her senses and had stopped acting like a silly schoolgirl.

The *Frankfurter Zeitung* sat on a side table next to Valter's chair, where he liked to sit and read. He moved from the table to the other room and picked up the newspaper. The Dardanelles Campaign remained in the news.

Now, with the war raging all around them, Valter had often found himself lost in thoughts of selling their family business and fleeing Germany. He had even broached the subject with Ute, but she adamantly refused to go along with it. She believed they belonged in their homeland, no matter the dangers. Even his arguments about the safety of their boys fell on deaf ears when it came to leaving Germany.

Chapter Seven

Although the appearance of the china head doll freaked Nicole out, the letters hidden in the box's bottom intrigued her. For her supper, she made herself a grilled cheese sandwich and a microwavable cream of tomato soup — just the right size for one person.

The stack of letters sat on the table beside her plate; the one she'd read earlier, face-down on her left. She picked up the top one and pulled the flimsy paper out of the envelope.

25 April, 1915

My Dearest Ute,

I know you are one of the good people in Germany, so please don't be angry with me for what I'm about to tell you.

I still don't know how I'm alive to write to you today. Yesterday, the German forces used chlorine gas on us for the second time. Men were dropping all around me from the yellow-green poisonous cloud. We had to cover our mouths and noses with urine-soaked cloths. It was unpleasant, but it kept us from dying. Some men dropped into the trenches, but the gas was thick and heavy, and it killed them as they tried to shelter from it.

Nicole returned to the top of the letter. Yesterday,

the Germans used chlorine gas on them. She pulled her laptop out of its bag, and when it powered up, googled April 24, 1915 gas attack in WWI.

Without revealing to his lover where he was fighting, he gave it away for future generations. The battle was called the Second Battle of Ypres. Urine-soaked cloths were bad enough, but to drown in your own bodily fluids. What a horrible way to die. Nicole's stomach clenched, and she gagged. The article put her off the rest of her meal. She rushed to the kitchen, poured the soup down the drain, and tipped the sandwich from her plate and into the garbage can. Nicole leaned over the sink praying she wouldn't be sick. Once the wave of nausea passed, she returned to the table.

My dear, it pains me so that we can't be together. I do love you so much. But, we're both spoken for by others. I cried when you included the photograph of you with your husband and young boys. I confess I have a wife back in Canada. Her name is June. I became a father to a son on 21 February of this year. His name is William. Apparently, she was with child when I shipped out.

We're both in a conundrum. We must keep our relationship a secret. I do hope we'll be able to meet again before this awful war ends. If not, then afterwards. That is if I don't become one of the many Canadian casualties.
All my love,

Robert
xoxo

Still no clues as to Ute's lover's last name. He only signed his first and never included a return address. But what would you use for one if you're in the middle of a battlefield? Both were married and parents. Nicole wanted to discover how they met. All she knew was that it was in Lützkampen, and Robert bought the doll for Ute to remember him. That would explain why the woman hid the letters under tissue paper at the bottom of the box. The poor soul had to hide the gift and her lover's correspondence from her family. Were they actually lovers? Did they have a sexual encounter? What if Ute got pregnant? Nicole knew she was jumping to conclusions, but what else could these passionate letters mean?

Even though that letter had put Nicole off her meal, she took another off the unread stack and pulled it from the envelope. June? Who was she? Robert addressed the envelope to Ute Birkhoefer. Did he have two lovers overseas?

30 June, 1915

Dear June,

Your news about me becoming a father has made me the proudest man. I can't wait to get home and see little William. I might call him Willy for short. Will that bother you?
I'm pleased things are going well for you, and you have friends and neighbours you can count on while I'm overseas. You shouldn't have to shoulder all the burden of outdoor work on top of everything you do inside the home. That is more than enough work to handle with a small baby in the house. It grieves me I'm so far away and can't be home with you and our son.
With luck, this awful war won't last too long, and I'll be back home with you soon.
Your loving husband,

Robert

The contents of the letter shocked Nicole. She hadn't expected to find a letter home amongst the ones to his lover. The passion revealed in what she'd read in his letters to Ute was absent in this one. No *xoxo* signature. Just your loving husband. This letter was about day-to-day life back home in Canada. Somehow, he'd put it in the wrong envelope and sent it to his lover instead. Did the one meant for Ute end up being sent to his wife in error? Oh, to be a fly on the wall if that happened. The contrast between the two letters was like a knife to her heart.

Chapter Eight

The past two weeks had been a test of Ute's resilience. The possibility of being pregnant from her night with Robert, followed by the failure of her attempt to seduce her husband, had left her in a state of turmoil. How would she explain her condition? She worried for naught. Her courses had started.

Ute was relieved she hadn't because she'd have to explain to Valter how she ended up that way when he no longer had any interest in lovemaking. She was saddened because she wasn't carrying Robert's child. One borne out of a deep desire for one another.

Valter had risen before dawn to prepare the bakery for the day's trade. Usually, she got up with him and ensured he ate something first. This morning, Ute was too tired. Too unmotivated. But she had two young boys to feed and send to school.

So far, the war hadn't come to Wiesbaden, although it had come close. Most of the fighting occurred on the Western Front in Belgium and in France. Economic hardships had befallen much of the country, causing shortages of basic essentials.

Because of Valter's age, Ute doubted he'd be called up to fight, but lived in constant fear he would. Her boys were too young, thankfully.

She paused outside her sons' shared bedroom door and then knocked. "Walter, Friedrich, it's time to get up. Aufstehen! Raus aus den Federn!" Despite her worries and melancholy, she remained upbeat for the

31

boys. They didn't need to know her fears.

With any luck, a letter would arrive from Robert after she got them off to school. There had been heavy fighting on the Western Front earlier in the month. She had seen it on the front page of *Frankfurter Zeitung.* The Battle of Neuve Chapelle. The Canadian military sent Robert there after his training in England.

Until she met Robert, Ute didn't read the war-related articles in the papers. They were too depressing, but now she had a vested interest in the war news. She clung to the hope that he remained safe despite the uncertainty of war. She doubted the country's newspapers would report the names of enemy soldiers killed in battles, but she hoped for a sign of his survival.

Just then, the boys spilled out of their shared room, tumbling over one another in their rush to the table. Ute smiled. They were so innocent, their laughter and playfulness a contrast to the events in the world around them. They were untouched by the war, bringing relief and envy to Ute.

Once Ute got the boys fed and out the door, she sighed with relief. She loved her boys to bits, but they were boisterous. At least it was still safe to send them to school or let them play outdoors.

Last night had been a disaster, and she wanted to make it up to Valter. The bread, from their bakery, was only a day old and still fresh. She sliced it thick and spread a layer of butter on it. She removed the bacon from the pan before the it became a burnt offering. One ruined meal was one too many. The butter ensured the grease kept the meat from drying out.

"I'm sorry I overslept. I brought you breakfast, Valter. You were away long before I got up."

He mumbled something unintelligible.

"I'll leave it here for you? I'm going to get the mail. I'll be back to help you in no time." Ute slipped out the bakery's front door before her husband said anything else. At least the post office wasn't far from their business and home.

She strode into the small store that housed the

post office in the back corner. "Good morning, Frau Krüger. Do you have anything for Valter or Ute Birkhoefer today?"

"Ah, hello, Frau Birkhoefer. Give me one moment, and I'll check for you."

Were people talking about Ute receiving letters? Robert had never disclosed his name or location on the envelope. If the gossip mongers started spreading stories, she'd pass it off as a family member who lived in another part of the country.

"Here you are, Frau Birkhoefer. That's all for today, I'm afraid."

"Thank you, Frau Krüger," Ute said, accepting the small bundle of mail.

She leafed through the envelopes once outside the shop, and away from prying eyes. One from Robert lay in the bundle. Her heart skipped a beat. Now, she needed to find a place to read it without being disturbed.

Ute started towards home but turned up a narrow side street before hers. Farther along was a park. She brought her boys here in their buggy as infants for the fresh air and tranquility. She found a bench and sat. It had been ages since she'd visited, either too busy working alongside Valter in the bakery or looking after her boys.

At first, Ute didn't open the envelope. She sat with it on her lap, her hands resting on it. Finally, she picked it up and ripped it open.

14 March, 1915

My dearest Ute,

> *We have just been through one of the heaviest battles. Four days of intense fighting. We lost members of our company, and I suffered a minor injury. Do not worry yourself about it. It's only two broken fingers and they will heal.*

> *It's hard to believe it's only been a fortnight since we were together. I miss you, my love. I'd much rather be with you, even if it's in a barn, than here on the*

battlefield. I think about you all the time. When I close my eyes, I see your beautiful face. I wish we could be together for eternity.

Please believe me when I tell you I love you and have loved you since our night together in Lützkampen. I could go on, but I fear some might find my words pornographic. I don't want you to think of me in that light. I love you.

Robert
xoxo

Ute brushed a tear away. It seemed like an eternity since they'd spent time together in the barn in the small village near the Belgian border. He had promised to continue writing to her and fulfilled his promise. It wrapped her in a warm glow and she hugged her arms around her body to prevent its escape.

Chapter Nine

NOVEMBER 8, 2022

Frank couldn't stand it any longer. He had to find out from his sister if she had put the doll, not even an attractive china head one, in a box for Nicole. A phone call wouldn't do. This required a face-to-face meeting. That way, he could read her expressions and tell if she was lying to him.

After eating two slices of toast slathered with peanut butter and drinking a black coffee, he readied himself for the trip to the assisted living home where Janet lived. The air between them was frosty even the day he helped her move in. But he was her brother, and it was the least he could do after a fall paralyzed her from the waist down.

Dressed in a black polo shirt and khaki cargo pants, he walked to the front door. His winter jacket hung on a peg. After he shrugged it on, he picked up his wallet and keys from the bowl on the table. He dreaded this meeting, his stomach churning with a mix of anxiety and anticipation. But his duty as a father meant caring about his daughter's mental well-being.

As he walked to his car, he tried to determine the best way to approach the subject. His sister wouldn't tell him anything if he entered with guns blazing. She might not anyway, but being friendly and subtle was better.

About ten minutes after Frank pulled out of his driveway, he turned onto the tree-lined avenue leading to the facility. The place looked like a mansion, but it had everything needed for people with limited to no mobility.

When did he last visit? The day he moved her in. The place made him uncomfortable. Or was it the residents and not the facility? He drove into a parking spot and exited his car. On his way towards the front door, he pressed the lock button on his key fob.

When he entered through the front door, he strode to reception.

"I'm here to see Janet Holbrook," he said.

"And you are?"

"Her brother."

"At this time of day, you'll find her in the lounge. Down this corridor, and it's the last door on the left." She pointed in the direction he needed to go. "Please sign the visitor's log before you go." The receptionist ensured a pen sat on the book.

Frank pulled his own pen out of his shirt pocket. "No, thank you," he said, "I'll use my own." He had never used another person's pen or allowed anyone to use his. He remained healthy that way, and wore a mask during COVID.

Janet's room was on the second floor. He remembered that from the day he moved her in to this place. The building had stair lifts for people who were able to walk but not climb stairs. Wheelchair lifts installed for those confined to them could get from one floor to another, and elevators, too. Everyone wore a fall alert button around their neck for emergencies.

Why was it that these places smelled funny? Adult diapers needing to be changed. Disinfectant. Old people. Death.

He'd made it this far without turning around and leaving. He'd make it the rest of the way. When he entered the room, he didn't see her at first. A motorized wheelchair faced the window at the far side of the lounge. The occupant was short and he was unable to see the person over the back of the chair. Frank walked towards it, and the chair turned to face him as he drew nearer.

"Frank, what are you doing here? You're the last

person I expected to visit me," Janet said.

"It's not a social call." He pulled a chair out from under a table, turned it to face his sister and sat.

"What is it, then?"

"Why did you send that china head doll to Nicole? You remember the one we found in the tower room as kids?"

"And why would I do that?"

"That's why I'm here. My daughter is out of her mind with worry and fright about where this thing came from." He leaned forward with his forearms resting on his thighs. "There's a note on the box says *for Nicole*. I think it looks like your handwriting."

"I know nothing about it. I've never had one to pass down to someone. Are you absolutely certain it's my handwriting?" Janet leaned forward towards her brother.

"No. Not one hundred percent." His face flushed. "I know you and Julie were close. I wondered if you had passed it to Nicole through her. I gave Nicki boxes of her mother's things I'd put in the storage locker after Julie died. I wondered if it might have ended up in one of them."

Janet exhaled with a snort. It was just like her brother to accuse her of things — like he did when he found out she inherited their father's house, not him. The tension between them was indisputable, a result of their strained relationship with their parents. That's why she got the house, not because she talked them into changing their will.

"I can assure you, Frank, I know nothing about this china head doll. I do not know how it got into Nicole's car. I didn't put it there. Directly or otherwise."

"All right, I believe you," Frank spat and stood.

"I'd love to see Nicole and her brothers sometime … that is if they want to see me."

"I'll pass your message along." He turned and walked out of the room, a sense of closure finally settling over the tense atmosphere.

If accusing her of things she didn't do wasn't bad enough, he didn't have the courtesy to even say goodbye. When Julie was first diagnosed with cancer, Janet helped by visiting her sister-in-law in the hospital after her surgery. She ensured the kids and her brother ate. She took the woman to her chemo sessions. Frank hadn't handled the diagnosis well. He retreated into himself much like he did when he was younger and had argued with their parents.

Janet recalled the china head doll her brother mentioned. Back before all the bad blood between them, they were close. When did they drift apart? Frank hadn't been to visit her since he moved her into Willow Glen Manor. He looked terrible. Cheeks sunken and thin. He wasn't taking care of himself. Not her worry. Not anymore. He'd made that perfectly clear a couple of years ago.

Nicole burst into the office. "You guys will never guess what I discovered last night."

"What?"

"Well, I was reading the letters in the box with the china head doll. One envelope in particular wasn't what it said it was."

"You're talking in riddles, sis," Connor said, folding his arms across his chest.

"The envelope addressed to Ute, the lover, but the letter inside meant for June, the wife. Can you see the potential love triangle here?" Nicole leaned against her desk.

"And you're thinking that the wife accidentally got the letter meant for the lover," said Cooper.

"I'm not sure. It's possible. So far, I only have one-sided correspondence, all from this soldier Robert, who doesn't sign his last name or use a return address."

"That's fine, but we meet with the people from *The Cheese Board & Café* in less than an hour. Let's concentrate on that, and we'll save the detective work for another day."

"Okay, Cooper. You win." Nicole set aside her excitement and began preparing her preliminary designs for the clients.

Cooper stood in front of the whiteboard, armed with an erasable marker. He was ready to create a flowchart of the point of sale/inventory software he and Connor would be designing for their latest client, *The Cheese Board & Café*.

Nicole stood on the other side of the conference room, showing the couple her designs for their logo and signage. He believed the logic part of the development should come before the graphics, but the Smiths were eager to see the artwork.

Connor hooked the projector to one computer to demonstrate the basic version they used for their customers and built on it. Each wanted or needed something different, but the core was always the same.

Once his sister finished with the artwork, the Smiths came over to the large table and sat. This was Cooper's chance to shine. This was where he was in his element. He enjoyed showing off his computer prowess and did it without confusing the people for whom he was designing the custom software.

Nicole took notes to document the proceedings. In a little over two hours, the three siblings had devised a viable plan for the custom program that would run *The Cheese Board & Café's* business. They would incorporate their custom software into a commercial, financial package, most likely NetSuite, a cloud-based program. CNC IT Solutions software would also run from the cloud.

Some clients wanted their business software to be totally in-house, with a single server and PCs connected to it. Gradually, they had moved those folks away from that.

Chapter Ten

June stared at the letter before her. The envelope had her name on it.

30 June, 1915

My dearest Ute,

Who was this Ute woman, and why had Robert written to her?

We have been under heavy attack, but things are quieter today, so I am writing to you. I'm sorry we only had one night together. You are such a beautiful woman. I try to hold your image in my mind.

He hadn't had extra-marital relations, had he?

Sometimes, you blur away, and I see my wife's face instead. Not that it's a bad thing. June is a wonderful woman, but she's not the same exciting lover as you.

He had! Why would he mention exciting lover, if he hadn't.

Perhaps, I only think of you that way because of our circumstances inside that barn in the hay mow in Lützkampen. I yearn to be with you that way again, but in a proper bed. Someplace where I can admire your beauty. Perhaps in a hotel room or a room at an inn. Hotels seem more anonymous, so there would be no danger of your husband finding out about us.

I miss you, my darling. The image of your face is burned into my brain, and the thought of your smile gives me the strength to endure another day.

Despite being drawn away from one another, I hope we'll find each other again one day, but under a kinder sky, free from the shadows of war.

I hope the china head doll gives you comfort in my absence. I bought it and gifted it to you with all my heart and soul.

The days may grow darker, but thoughts of you are my light.
All my love,

Robert
xoxo

In her anger at his infidelity, June picked up a clay statue he'd given her and hurled it at the wall, where it shattered. The shards of the shattered clay statue and the letter that had brought her world crashing down affected her deeply and she wished him dead. With any luck, he would be killed in action. That would save her the trouble and stigma of a divorce. Should she return this letter and tell him of her intentions once the war ends? The thought of his betrayal was a wound that festered, and she was unsure how to heal it.

June pulled a sheet of paper from the desk drawer and took the cap off her fountain pen. Then she stopped. She wouldn't give him the satisfaction of knowing he'd mixed up his letters. She assumed that he'd written one to her and put it into another envelope. He thought he'd been so clever, not getting caught, keeping his dutiful wife in the dark over his indiscretions. Hah! Not replying was the thing to do. Maybe go so far as to never open another letter from him.

The uncertainty of her decision weighed heavily on her shoulders, and she was unsure if she could bear it. Before William got up from his nap, she had to clean up the mess she'd made so that he didn't get cut on the broken statue. June sighed and headed to get the broom and dustpan.

Chapter Eleven

NOVEMBER 12, 2022

Nicole drove from her apartment to the one her brothers shared. It wouldn't be as late getting back as their trip to Pike Falls the previous month. Depending on the house's condition, they might even be back before it got dark, which this time of year happened around five o'clock.

After parking her hatchback alongside the curb, she climbed out, grabbed her backpack and locked her car. Anytime they went on these exploration excursions, they took Cooper's vehicle.

As Cooper maneuvered the car out of the parking lot, Nicole's heart raced with anticipation of the beginning of another adventure. Connor, as always, claimed the front seat, leaving Nicole to squeeze into the back. She settled in the middle, ready for what lay ahead.

"Do we have any more clues about this mysterious property?" Nicole asked, her curiosity piqued.

"Nope," Connor said, turning to speak to his sister.

"Well, we didn't know anything about Kembleford Manor either. If we want to know ownership, I suppose we could visit the local genealogy centre and hope they have those records for the area or, if not, the land registry office."

"As long as it's empty, that's all I need to know," said Cooper.

"It will be quite the shock if we get there and some little old lady is inside," said Connor.

Cooper pulled away from the curb, and their adventure began.

"Wouldn't it just," said Nicole.

About forty minutes later, Cooper slowed down to find a place to leave his SUV so it didn't get trapped in the driveway to the property. "Best always to go in on foot," he said.

"You say that every time," Connor said, laughing.

"Except Kembleford Manor. We drove up the driveway to it," Nicole reminded her brothers.

"Yeah, but that place was out in the middle of nowhere."

At that moment, they drove past the property they planned to explore. It looked empty, as if it were uninhabited. No one had mowed the grass all summer. It had a huge front verandah and a smaller one off the side. Whether or not it had one, it looked like there was an open porch above the front door. The windows were all tall and narrow with rounded tops. Steep gables and a tower reached towards the sky.

"Feeling any weird vibes, Nic?" Connor asked.

"Not from here. When we're closer, I might." She scrunched down to get a better look out the SUV's rear passenger window. "I don't even see a driveway. It must be on one of the other sides of the property?"

"There's a road up here off to the right. I'll park on it, and we'll walk in from there. It should be fairly straightforward," Cooper said.

The road on the GPS screen seemed insignificant compared to their current path. It turned out to be a narrow dirt road. Cooper parked the car off the track as far as possible, and they prepared to embark on their journey.

Connor opened the front passenger door of his brother's SUV. It was going to be tricky getting out because the ditch was right there. "Go out the driver's side, Nic. We're right tight to the ditch on this side."

"Okay."

Cooper had already exited the vehicle and stood in front of it.

Connor, determined to overcome the obstacle, was going to have to do the same, but it would be more awkward for him. He closed the door, maneuvered himself over the console, and gear shift into the driver's seat. Finally, he was out.

"There's a culvert up here, so we can use it to cross the ditch," Cooper said, pointing to the spot.

The three walked in single file along the narrow road to the place mentioned. Not long after they crossed, they were in tall grass and saplings with little room between them.

Connor led the way through the maze until he encountered a page-wire farm fence with a string of barbed wire on top of it. "You think the house wants to keep us out?"

Nicole and Cooper stopped on each side of him. "Only way past it is over. I don't see any posts nearby, though. It will be easier to climb at one," said Cooper.

"There has to be one, but it's hard to tell with so many trees," Connor said.

"Down here. I found one," Nicole called from about twenty feet farther along the fence line. The twins walked to their sister's location.

It was the perfect place to get over. A sturdy, Connor tested it for strength, post and a substantial tree with a branch they could grab to get over the top. To prove the ease of climbing the barrier, he scaled it first. When Connor got high enough on the wire foot holds, he reached with his left hand, keeping his right on top of the post until he gripped the branch. Then, he grabbed the tree with his other hand, swung his legs over the barbed wire and dropped to the ground.

Both Cooper and Nicole had backpacks with them, so they handed them over to him. Nicole, first, then his twin, followed Connor's lead and got over the same way.

They only had to contend with waist-high grass on this side of the fence. The ground was flat, but Nicole kept her head down, watching for groundhog holes. A wrong step into one of them could break an ankle. The other obstacles were large rocks. If a person tripped over one, the result might be the same. Not necessarily the same bone broken, but an injury nonetheless. That was the last thing she wanted in the middle of nowhere.

The house stood before her, a silent sentinel of the past. Nicole paused to document her discovery. She retrieved her Canon DSLR from her backpack. Before leaving her apartment, Nicole had formatted a new SD card and ensured she had charged the battery. Did she want to add a sketch to the collection of images? Why not?

Nicole pulled a fresh sketchbook out of her pack along with sharp, medium-soft lead pencils. It didn't take her long to have the house drawn and her pad and pencil back in her backpack.

"You ready to move on now, sis?" Connor asked.

"Yup. I'll draw the house from all four sides and take pictures with my phone and camera, too."

"We knew that," Cooper said.

"You'll thank me later when we have proof of our visit." Nicole walked ahead of her brothers, her mind buzzing with anticipation. At every location they explored, she followed the same routine. Phone. Camera. Draw. Kembleford Manor images showed much more than the naked eye, and while it freaked her out, she hoped this one might offer some ghostly goings-on, too. Just no ghosts of dead people. That made no sense. Ghosts *were* dead people. Nicole meant like Ophelia Kembleford, who had hanged herself, and little Grace Birkhoefer floating face down in the river inside the boathouse with her china head doll. The same one that Nicole found under the seat of her car.

While his sister documented the back of the house, Cooper's curiosity led him to the back porch. Three steps to get from the ground to the landing. He tested each tread before putting his full weight on it to ensure its safety. He repeated the process on the decking to verify its soundness. He didn't want any of them to fall through a rotten board and get hurt, like happened to him on a previous exploration.

The screen door creaked as he opened it, revealing a large wooden door with a window that filled almost the entire upper portion. Cooper turned the knob and the door moved. That was weird. Who went away for an extended period of time and left their house unlocked? Maybe out here in the country you could get away with it.

"It's not locked," he exclaimed to the others, surprised. "Follow me." He pushed the inner door open and it protested even louder than the outer one.

Cooper led the way into the kitchen. Pale green wainscotting covered the walls to about the four-foot mark. Above that, embossed tin, like what you would see on a ceiling in a house of this era. He tipped his head back. The same finish as on the upper part of the walls adorned the ceiling, too.

An enormous wooden cook stove stood next to the back door. A table, covered with a flowered vinyl cloth, and four chairs stood along the wall. Along the opposite wall stood a small cupboard with a sink. Dishes were stacked in a built-in cabinet next to that. For all the world, it appeared like the occupant had stepped out to the store and would return any time.

The strangest thing about this room was the lack of a refrigerator and stove, electric or gas — just one more modern than the wood stove.

Two doors led off this room. One was open and led to the front of the house. Cooper tried the other. It led to a utility-type room that housed the fridge and stove, some counter space between them for meal preparation, and a washer and dryer on the other side. The washing machine wasn't automatic like the ones in the laundry room at his apartment building, but an old wringer one.

Back between the cookstove and the table, an archway led into a dining room. The doors, trim, window mouldings, and baseboards were stained — not painted.

A vintage tablecloth covered the table, likely crocheted by the woman of the house. Salt and pepper shakers, a sugar bowl, and small tongs sat in the middle.

Given a choice, Cooper always gravitated towards exploring older houses. Their character, and the echoes of history in their walls drew him to them.

He didn't believe in ghosts, but after Kembleford Manor, he began to have doubts. The things he noticed in this house so far were things his sister was more apt to take in, not him.

Nicole wandered through the downstairs rooms with her Canon slung around her neck and her phone and sketchbook in her hands. The air was thick with the musty smell of old books and the faint scent of lavender, indicating the house's neglect and its former owner's attempt to preserve it. So far, nothing untoward inside. A fine layer of dust covered everything, but not so much as she expected. Did someone come around once a month, or more often, to dust and vacuum? If so, she hoped it wasn't today. The last thing they needed was to get caught by the owners or someone acting on their behalf.

She walked out the front door and down the steps. Nicole wanted to capture the front and east side of the house while the light was in the right spot. Even a short span of five minutes affected it. Indoors wasn't as dependent on light levels as outdoors. Nicole hoped for a vantage point from where no one would see her from the road. A stand of tall cedars at the corner of the property gave her the desired cover. First, her phone, followed by her camera, and finally, the sketchbook.

As she sketched the front of the house, Nicole noticed something peculiar. Images that resembled handprints appeared to be pressed against the glass of the narrow windows on the second floor. She blinked, hoping they would disappear, but they remained. And to her surprise, more handprints had appeared on the small, rounded tops of the upper windows.

Had children lived here at one point? Was it an orphanage that housed many boys and girls? It was large enough for that.

"Connor, Cooper, can you guys come out front, please?" she asked.

"In the windows up there, do you see hand prints on the glass?" Nicole pointed to the location she had seen them in. "Like someone had cupped their hands on the window to look out?"

After a few moments of silence, Connor said, "I see nothing. Are you sure you're okay, Nicole?"

"Nor me," Cooper said. "I think your imagination is getting the better of you — again."

Nicole brushed off Cooper's comment and hurried up the steps into the house, determined to uncover the truth behind the handprints.

Nicole walked towards the massive staircase in the front hall, fully intending to investigate the marks on the upstairs windows. A light was fixed to the top of the newel post. She'd heard of them but had never seen any. This one appeared to be a Greek goddess holding an orb in the air. While the handprints upstairs were important, this fixture took precedence for the moment. The crystal globe had an intricate design etched into it and its many facets would reflect the luminance. She wished the power functioned in the house. Seeing this lit and the way the beams would refract and illuminate the walls would be something she could only wish for. The hydro couldn't be connected. There was no sign of a stack or a meter on any of the outer walls she'd seen.

Someone wired the place at some point because there were outlets, light switches and ceiling fixtures. Nicole hadn't seen appliances when she passed through the kitchen, but that meant nothing. The wiring was so old that the switches, at least this one in the hall, comprised two round push buttons, one over the other. On a whim, she pushed one. Impossible, no. The light came on. Nicole got her wish. She stopped sketching and snapped photos of the effects of the light on the surrounding walls and ceiling with her phone and her DSLR camera. Next, she incorporated the dazzling effects into another sketch of the great hall and staircase.

Now, she would resume her search for the handprints she'd seen in the upstairs windows. The steps were solid, proving the house's enduring strength. The occasional creak under her foot reminded her of the countless feet that had trodden these stairs. Most of the treads showed worn patches that spoke of the passage of time. Before she left, she'd draw this, too, capturing the history etched into the staircase.

In the upstairs room where Nicole had seen the cupped handprints on the window, there were no signs of anyone having been there. She walked to the windows, and the marks remained. Someone had been in the room. She took photos with her phone and camera and sketched the greasy marks.

Engrossed in her task, the unexpected sound of children's laughter echoed from another part of the house. The giggles persisted even after Nicole had finished her sketch, piquing her curiosity. She followed the sound, finding that all the doors in the rooms open except for one. She pressed her ear against it; the laughter emanating from within.

With a twist of the knob and a push, the door remained shut. Nicole tried again, this time pulling. To her surprise, the door swung open onto the landing. It was unusual, as most doors opened into the individual rooms.

It was once a playroom or nursery. A giant rocking horse stood in front of the fireplace, its creaking filling the room. It was still moving, its gliding mechanism echoing in the space. Nicole set her phone on video to capture the movement. A cradle sat under the window, and a rocking chair was next to it, the chair's fabric cushions worn and faded.

"Cooper, Connor, can you guys come up here, like now," Nicole yelled. She didn't know what part of the house they were in, so she had to be loud in hopes they would hear her.

A few minutes later, they both stood in the doorway.

"What's up?" Connor asked.

"Is this rocking horse moving?"

"No, why?"

"Then it just stopped." Nicole turned her phone so her brothers could see and played back the video. The riderless horse rocked back and forth like a child pushing it for all it was worth — not the subtle rocking expected after a little girl or boy dismounted.

"What the?" Cooper said, his eyes wide with disbelief.

Connor was speechless, his mouth opening and closing like a fish out of water.

Chapter Twelve

AUGUST 13, 1915

It had been a long day of fighting, but things had quieted down somewhat. Robert took advantage of the moment. He sat down with his back against the trench wall and pulled out paper, and a pencil. As he settled to write, an enormous rat ran over his foot. A soldier nearby, pulled out his knife and stabbed the creature.

13 August, 1915

My dearest Ute,

Life in the trenches is brutal. The random shelling and snipers are terrifying. We never know when we'll be killed. I've seen men die from this trench warfare. It's not a pleasant life. If that's not bad enough, we're tormented by rats and lice. A few men have succumbed to this persistent dampness are suffering from trench foot. One fellow had to have a leg amputated because of it. I'm sorry if the opening of my letter upset you.

We may have only had a few fleeting hours together, but I can't stop thinking of you. You're in my thoughts constantly. I'm madly in love with you. If I survive this war, which I pray I will, I promise I'll find a way for us to be together. Every time I close my eyes, I see us together in the village of Lützkampen.

I'll never forget our hunger for each other and the sparks that ignited between us. You are a passionate *woman and deserve to be treated well, which I suspect is untrue. Maybe that's jealousy speaking. Your husband has you all of the time and I'm longing to be with you again.*

My dearest Ute, my love for you is unwavering. I long for the day when we can be together again, if only for a fleeting moment. Let's relive the passion and desire that bound us together. I promise to cherish and protect you, always.

All my love,

Robert
xoxo

How thoroughly did the Germans scrutinize the mail? With boring letters home or to loved ones, it wouldn't be too much. There were no secrets in them. The letters home were mundane and talked about family. The ones to his lover, the heat, whether stated explicitly or implied, spoke of passion and desire for another human being.

He was always careful to keep his location confidential within the body of the letter or on the envelope.

Chapter Thirteen

NOVEMBER 12, 2022

"If I didn't see it with my own eyes, I'd never believe it," Connor mumbled.

"Tell me about it," said Nicole.

"Do you want to leave?" Cooper asked.

"No. This isn't scaring me like Kembleford Manor did. I think this was a happy family home. Follow me." Nicole led the way to the room where she'd first seen the hands in the windows. "Residue from someone cupping their hands against the glass. The oils from their skin marked the panes."

Connor looked at the windows more closely. His sister was right. Someone had been looking through them. How tall were they? There were even handprints on the round-topped ones. Their bottoms had to be close to seven feet off the floor. He and his identical twin, Cooper, both stood at six feet, three inches. He stood against the wall to get an idea of where the top of his head came in relation to the frame. He was wrong. More like eight feet. The ceiling in the room had to be at least twelve feet high, if not higher.

He wished Mitch had come with them. If he had, he could have told them more about the house. Their friend specialized in restoring old homes and would have been interested in seeing this one.

An icy chill passed through the room, and Connor shivered. It was as if someone or something walked from one side of the room to the other. "Did you guys feel that?"

Nicole was standing near the dresser along the end wall, but between where he stood and the door. "What?"

"A chill like someone walked through here."

"Not me," she said.

"Me neither," Cooper said from where he stood in front of an open closet door. "Wonder if there are any secret passages in this place. It's the style of house where you'd expect to find them."

"Push an andiron, and the back of a fireplace moves, revealing a set of secret stairs," Connor said, laughing. "Bro, I think you've watched *The Ghost and Mr. Chicken* too many times."

"I don't think he's far off the mark with secret passages. A lot of old houses had more than one set of stairs. The family used the main staircase like the fancy one at the front of this place. The servants used the back ones to do their daily chores without being seen. They may have been hidden or closed in at some point," Nicole said.

Nicole left her brothers in that room and entered the one next to it. One floorboard moved when she stepped on it. At first, she didn't think much about it. After all, they were in a house well over one hundred years old. Over time, nails did work their way loose, but were hammered back down so people didn't hurt themselves.

She dropped to her knees and inspected the loose board. Not a single nail in it. The ones around it had two at each end and in the middle. Curiosity got the better of her, and she started playing *what if* scenarios in her mind. Not enough of a gap to get her fingers into it. One of her pencils? She took the one she'd been using and tried it. It was too big around, as well. She needed something flat. Nicole turned on the flashlight on her phone and shone the beam around the plank. If she pressed on one end of the board, it might raise up the other end. Even if it was only enough to get her fingers into the gap.

Nicole pushed, but nothing happened. She stood

and used her foot to exert pressure. Still not enough. She walked to the opposite end and tried there. This time, she succeeded and lifted the board away from the cavity between the floor and the ceiling below. Why would one end of a floorboard not have a beam at one end to support it? Shining the beam of her phone's light, Nicole found what looked to be an old blanket or sheet. When she picked it up, it was heavier than expected. What was in it?

"Guys, can you come here, please?" she asked.

"Where's here?" Connor asked.

"Front bedroom next to the hand-printed windows."

Both her brothers stopped in the doorway. "What's that?" Cooper asked.

"Not sure, but it's heavy."

"How did you find it?" Connor asked, walking towards his sister.

"The floorboard was loose. I pulled it up and found this under it. I need you to video me unwrapping it."

Connor pulled out his phone and started to record.

"I've found this bundle under the floorboards of the front bedroom on the left side of the house if you're outside facing the building. I don't know what it is, just it's heavy." Nicole peeled a corner of the blanket back. "Nothing yet." She pulled more of the covering back. "It looks like whatever is in here is rusty."

"Unless it's dried blood," Cooper said, and laughed.

"Stop. I don't need that vision in my head as I'm unwrapping." Nicole continued unfolding the woollen bundle. "It's a dagger — its blade is rusty, or as Cooper suggested, it's covered with dried blood. The handle looks like it's bone or maybe antler? Ornate carvings on it. Definitely old and worn. I don't want to pick it up without something on my hands."

"Don't want to leave fingerprints," Connor said, laughing.

"More like DNA," Cooper said.

"Not funny, guys. What if this knife was used to kill someone and hidden under the floorboards?"

Nicole rummaged through her backpack and found a pair of blue nitrile gloves.

"I'm not even going to ask why you have those," Connor said, shaking his head.

Once she donned the gloves, Nicole picked up the knife and inspected it. "I've seen these symbols somewhere before. This one," Nicole pointed to one near the end of the handle, "looks like a pentagram, but the surrounding carving looks like a goat's head. And these are the horns." She pointed to them.

"Aren't pentagrams associated with witchcraft?" Connor asked.

"Not necessarily. Definitely occult. Same with the goat. I'm going to take pictures of the handle." Nicole placed the dagger on the floor and used her Canon to photograph the handle from various angles. "The blade might be carved, too, but I can't tell."

"Wrap it up and put it back where you found it. I vote to get out of here, well, this room anyway," said Connor.

After Nicole painstakingly photographed the dagger handle from all angles, she sketched it, then reverently wrapped it back in the blanket and returned it to its resting place. The mystery of the dagger lingered in the air as she joined her brothers in the corridor.

"I wonder what that symbol is," she said, opening the browser on her phone and typing in what she'd seen on the dagger's handle. Within seconds, the results were on the screen. "It's a Baphomet. A symbol of the occult and secret societies."

"What kind of secret societies?" Cooper asked.

"If we knew that, they wouldn't be secret." Connor laughed.

"The article mentions Knights Templar," Nicole said.

"That's going back quite a way," Cooper said.

"What's left to explore here? I don't think we're going to find anything else."

"There's one more room on this level and then the tower," Cooper said. "You're not scared, are you, bro?"

"N-no."

"You hesitated there. I think finding the dagger spooked you."

"Okay, Cooper, let's drop it. If we're going to finish exploring this place, let's get on with it," Nicole said.

The siblings found no other strange things or heard any on this level of the house, so they climbed to the next. They had to duck often because of the steepness of the gables. The rooms on this level had no furniture in them. With the dust and cobwebs, no one had been up here in years.

The access to the tower was through the room above the one where the handprints appeared on the window. A spiral staircase led up to a door. Nicole let her brothers go first. Something in this room beckoned her, but she couldn't identify it. She lingered, waiting for a more straightforward message, but none came.

By now, Connor and Cooper had reached the top of the stairs and opened the tower room door. Even though they all wore running or track shoes, their footsteps echoed off the metal steps. Partway up, Nicole got into a sneezing fit. It had to be all the dust. Something else lingered in the air. She sniffed. Perfume. She and her brothers didn't wear scents when they explored. They believed in taking nothing, leaving only footprints. Scented products would give them away.

She continued up the steps, her heart pounding with anticipation, and entered the small tower room, a place shrouded in mystery.

"You okay? That was quite the sneeze fest," Cooper said.

"Yeah, I'm fine. I got a whiff of perfume. I know none of us are wearing any."

"Never smelled a thing," Connor said.

The tower room wasn't huge. Tall, definitely. But not so much width-wise, and crowded with two other people. A mirror hung on one wall, but too high for anyone to use. Did someone hang it there because a nail was already in that spot? Cobwebs stretched from it to the peak of the roof.

Nicole brushed aside cobwebs to move from one place to another. They stuck to her fingers, and despite shaking her hand, they remained firmly in place. Disgusting. She needed something to wipe her hand on so that the sticky webbing stuck to it and no longer to her. With her other hand, Nicole rooted around in her backpack and found a microfibre cloth. It was one she used to clean her camera equipment with, but it would do. Back home, she'd put a clean one in and launder this one.

One she had her hand cleaned and the dirty cloth shoved in a side pocket of her rucksack, she took pictures with her phone and camera and sketched the room, too. Something was stuck in the mirror's frame. She reached for it but couldn't quite get it. "Cooper, can you come here for a minute?"

Her brother arrived at her side.

"There's something in the frame of the mirror. I can't quite reach it."

Cooper, who had about six inches on her, plucked the object from the frame. "Here you go," he said, a small smile on his lips.

The photograph was dusty, so Nicole wiped it off to see it. It appeared to be sepia-toned. She turned on her phone's flashlight to get a better look. Even then, it was unclear. "I know I can't take this with me, but I need to get pictures of it. I might be able to enhance it on my computer and see who or what it's a photo of." Nicole turned off the flash on her phone's camera and snapped the front of the picture. She then turned it over and did the same with the back. Repeated the process with her Canon. "You can stick it back in there now." Nicole handed the old photograph to her brother, who returned it to where it had been.

Nicole crept towards the lone window high in the narrow wall. The only things in the room were the mirror with the small photograph in the frame and three people — nothing and no one else.

A small doorway off the far side of the room

attracted Nicole's attention. She approached it and tried to open it, but the lock held. A rusty key hung from a nail. Was that the key to this door? Nicole removed it and tried it in the lock. It worked.

"Guys, I may have stumbled upon a secret passage," she announced, her voice tinged with excitement.

Cooper kicked himself mentally for not bringing one of his headlamps. They were invaluable for going through dark places, leaving your hands free for other things. Instead, he had to depend on his phone, which made things more cumbersome.

He peered into the opening and shone his light around. A steep, narrow staircase led down into the unknown. How far? Where did it lead? Most important of all, was it safe? The uncertainty of the staircase's destination added to the suspense.

This wasn't a set of servants' stairs. This could be a death trap. Did he take the risk and climb down or err on the side of caution and go back down the same way they came up to the tower room? That was the safe thing to do, but an unknown force compelled him to continue.

"I'll go first. And you'll have to go sideways or backward like you're on a ladder. It's going to be dicey," Cooper said, his voice tinged with fear at the thought of the dangerous descent.

He started down sideways but ended up turning around. He held his phone in one hand to shine the beam of light around which complicated things. The last thing he wanted was to break through a stair tread or fall to the bottom. His phone's flashlight dimmed, and the battery was dying. He silently prayed to the light gods it stayed lit until he reached the floor.

Nicole was above him, creeping down the ladder.

"Slow down, please," Cooper called up to his siblings. "I don't fancy getting my hand stepped on." His sister wouldn't do it on purpose, but if he stopped and she didn't, it wouldn't bode well for his fingers.

After what seemed to be an eternity, he found the

base of this narrow room. The air was musty, and the walls were damp to the touch. If there was a door, it was disguised. The walls were stone and lath and plaster.

"Stay where you are. I can't find a door down here. At least if you're still on the ladder, you won't have as far to go to get back to the top," Cooper called up to Nicole, his voice echoing in the narrow space.

A range of terrifying scenarios raced through his mind. What if the door at the top closed, locking them in, and he couldn't find a way out at the other end? They'd be trapped. If they suffocated in here before he could get them out, it would be on his conscience for eternity.

Cooper poked here and pressed there, but nothing happened. He pushed against the walls with the same result. When he was about to give up, he found what looked to be an old light switch. Not a push button like on the main level and throughout the rest of the house, but one that turned. He turned it to the right, and nothing happened, so he turned it in the other direction.

The room shook, but a panel moved. Light beamed in from the room this door opened into. It took a long time before the passage opened wide enough for him to escape.

"It's safe guys. You can come down now," he shouted to his siblings, the urgency of their escape clear in his voice.

What room was this? He didn't recall being in it before. Cooper shoved a brick into the gap to ensure the passage didn't close up before Connor and Nicole joined him on the same side of the wall.

Connor exited the secret passage last. He didn't recognize this room either, so he walked to the window and looked out. They were on the side of the house, behind and below the room where the handprints covered the upper windows.

They hadn't been in here. The question now was, how to get out? There was a porch but no door leading to it. Just the window. Dark mahogany panelling covered the walls. Were there pocket doors in the wall? If so, they, too, were camouflaged.

Connor approached the wall to his right. It appeared solid. They could open the window and climb onto the porch if they needed to get out. There had to be a way from here into the rest of the house. Why would you have a room with no access? It made no sense to him. So far, the only door he'd seen was the one they came through after descending from the tower.

"See anything that looks like it might be a door to another room?" he asked.

Both Cooper and Nicole shook their heads. She was involved in her usual routine — photos and sketches — while he stared at the ceiling.

The room was reasonably well kept, not nearly as dusty as the tower and passage rooms. Connor knew little about furniture; the furnishings in this room looked antiques. His sister was a better judge of that kind of thing than he. But the mystery of the room truly piqued his interest. Why would you have a room you could only access from a narrow, steep, vertical corridor?

Connor stopped and looked where Cooper held his gaze at an enormous ceiling medallion. But not just any medallion. It had the Freemason's symbol of the square and compass. An enormous crystal chandelier hung on a chain through centre of the G in the middle of the emblem.

"Looks like we're in a Freemason's house," Connor said.

"Did you see this, Nicole?" Cooper asked.

She joined her brothers and began to photograph and sketch the object.

"At least the crystals aren't jangling like they did at Kembleford," Connor said.

As if on cue, a delicate tinkling began. Connor raised his head towards the ceiling. He should have kept that thought to himself. The chandelier vibrated. It started out slow, then built up to a fever pitch, startling them all. Afraid it would drop to the floor, he grabbed his brother and sister and pushed them out of the way.

The three siblings looked at each other, their expressions a mix of fear and confusion. They backed away until they were against the wall, well out of range if the light fixture should fall. The jingling stopped, but the tension in the room remained.

After seeing the dagger handle, the ceiling medallion made a shiver run up Connor's spine. He knew little about the Freemasons other than their existence. His interests lay in urban exploration and creating computer software. Since he hadn't found a way from this room into the rest of the house, he continued his search now that they were out of danger.

Pocket doors seemed the most likely solution, so he returned to that wall. He ran his hands over the surface that he could reach. The ceilings in this house might be closer to twenty feet. With his siblings occupied, he pulled out his phone. He'd text Mitch, who was knowledgeable about historic properties, to see if he knew anything about this one.

Do you know the old gothic-style house outside Brighton?

Connor continued to look for a door leading to the rest of the house.

If it's the one, I think, the old Graham house? Don't know of any others.

To Connor's disappointment, the reply didn't offer any clues about the property. When he searched Google Maps for a place to explore, he didn't come across any other gothic houses. The only way to determine if they were discussing the same property was to send the man a picture.

"You have pictures of the front façade on your phone, right?"

"Yes."

"Text it to Mitch. We'll know for sure then if it's the same house."

Nicole showed her brother the pictures on her device. He chose the best one and had her send it. Now they waited for a reply which could come to either of them or both.

Nicole was uncomfortable going behind Cooper's back like this, but it was the only way, given how her brother felt about Mitch. She tucked her phone in her back pocket and continued sketching. If she received a reply, her device would vibrate.

She worked her way around the room. Something occupied Cooper in front of the fireplace.

"Think an andiron will open another secret passage?" she teased.

"If it's like the last one, I hope not. That was one long, steep staircase, and the room wasn't much wider than it. If there are any creepy crawlies or other things in this place, then it's in there."

The handprints on the windows. Nicole was confident there were people in that window before she went upstairs. Children's laughter, toys, a cradle, a crib, rocking chair, and that rocking horse filled the nursery. It wasn't on rockers like any she had seen but on a frame. It had to be old — possibly as old as the house.

Nicole pulled her phone out of her pocket, opened the browser, and searched for antique rocking horses. She chose a website based on the photo on the screen. The one upstairs in this place sure looked like those on the *Classic Rocking Horses* site. So, made between 1890 and 1915 or thereabouts. She would recheck the steed if they found a way out of this room. Maybe she'd luck out and find the manufacturer's name and date of construction.

She wandered around the room some more, alternating between taking pictures and sketching. A portrait of a man in a military uniform hung over the fireplace mantlepiece. Who was he? And when did he serve? Was he a casualty? Did he die in battle, and his widow had this room sealed off because the picture reminded her of him? Wouldn't it have been as easy to take it down and put it in the attic? Up in the tower? Burn it even, although that was going to the extreme.

Nicole noticed that the soldier's eyes seemed to follow her movements. That was just the trick of the camera used at the time? When she looked closer, it wasn't a photograph, but an oil painting. The brush strokes were so precise, it fooled her. Back then, cameras weren't as sophisticated as today, so blowing a photo up to this size would have resulted in terrible results. The artist must have painted it from a small picture — 4"x6" at the most. Whoever the soldier was, he was handsome. She spent some time sketching and capturing the image with her Canon camera.

Satisfied, she walked to Connor's side, where he struggled to find a way out.

Chapter Fourteen

OCTOBER 12, 1915

U te picked up the mail that morning as usual. Most of those letters related to the business and came addressed to Wilhelm. Why he insisted on using his middle name was beyond her. She always used his forename — Valter. Her mundane daily routine contrasted with the war's chaos and uncertainty.

One letter was addressed specifically to her. She tucked it into her pocket to read later when she was alone. Despite being on the same continent, the mail moved slowly, each day adding to the anticipation. This letter was from Robert. She recognized his handwriting. He might have mailed it two months ago, yet he wasn't that far away, being stationed on the Western Front.

She finally got the solitude she needed and tore open the envelope.

14 September, 1915

My dearest Ute,

I pray this letter reaches you swiftly, though I write it with a heavy heart. These days are long, and the nights bring little rest. The fighting is relentless, a complete contrast to the peace and love we shared. The memories of our time together sustain me, though they now feel like a dream slipping further from my grasp.

I miss the smell of your hair, of you, of the sweet hay where we spent a night of passion. You have given me the strength to endure this chaos, but in doing so, you have also awakened a longing that feels impossible to fulfil.

In you, I found something that feels truer than anything I have ever known.
All my love,

Robert
xoxo

The opening tone of Robert's letter frightened Ute. His words sounded as if he was finishing with her. She read on and discovered it wasn't the case. Heat rose up Ute's cheeks, and her heart beat faster with each word of his letter. His love for her, despite the rigours of the battlefield, filled her with a mix of joy and sorrow. She prayed for his safety and for his return to her when the war ended. Sadly, no signs of the war drawing to a close existed.

Ute shoved the letter back into its envelope and into her apron pocket. She would put it in the box with the doll and the others the first moment she had to spare. And had their apartment over the bakery to herself.

Chapter Fifteen

NOVEMBER 12, 2022

Connor's determination showed as he ran his hands over the wall once more. There had to be a hidden button or something to release a panel. But where? He hadn't found it yet and had been over the barrier many times. What if it wasn't there? What if it was on the floor instead? With the intricate design, the door could be in plain sight, but the decorative mouldings kept it hidden.

"No luck?" Nicole asked when she reached her brother.

"Not yet. I'm thinking the only way out is through the window," Connor said, his mind already working on an alternate plan.

"Don't give up yet. Hear anything from Mitch?" Nicole asked, her voice a reassuring anchor amid uncertainty.

"Yes," Connor said, handing his phone to his sister.

That's the place I thought.

"That doesn't help us get out of this room, though," Nicole said.

"No."

"Did you try pushing on these mouldings? There *has* to be a way out. And it's not through a passage in the back of the fireplace." Nicole pushed on an upright length of trim. Nothing happened.

"I've tried just about everything I can think of." In frustration, Connor hit the wall with the side of his fist.

Creaking and groaning. Scraping. The hidden door released from its closed position and retreated into the wall. Connor was right about pocket doors. He'd never seen any mechanized, though. This door's mate also disappeared into a cavity.

Nicole photographed the openings. The edges of the doors. "You did it," she said.

"The button was hidden behind the millwork."

Together, they stepped through the opening into the room at the front of the house. Cooper joined them.

Rich panelling lined the wall of this room that butted against the one behind it. Delicate flowered wallpaper, which had yellowed with age, covered the others. The furniture suited the age of the house. Likely Victorian, like the rocking horse. A fireplace dominated the inside wall that would have backed against the hallway. Cast iron radiators stood under the windows on the other two sides.

An enormous desk acted as a sofa table, pushed tight to the back of the couch facing the fireplace. With windows on two sides, the gigantic fire, and the pocket doors, there wasn't much space to have it along a wall.

Nicole opened the drawers one at a time and leafed through the contents. When she tried the top centre drawer, it refused to open. What was in here that was important enough to lock the desk? The mystery of the locked drawer piqued her curiosity. Did she have anything in her backpack that might be useful in getting the drawer open? She sat on the chair and rummaged through her bag. All she came up with was a nail file. It would have to do.

She glanced around the room to see what her brothers were doing and shoved the pointed end into the lock. After some wiggling, she found the mechanism. Turned the pick, and it unlocked. Nicole pulled the drawer towards her slowly so not to damage anything that might be within. Look at what's inside. Photograph it and sketch it. Put it back and close the desk up again.

The first thing Nicole pulled out was a sympathy card. Not elaborate. A simple front with white lilies cascading towards the centre from the upper left corner. The message read *With Deepest Sympathy.* Nicole opened the card. The typical printed message printed on the inside, but someone had written a note below it. *He was a man of great courage and heart. Everyone who knew him will cherish his memory.*

No signature and no date. Obviously, the sender knew something about the man considering the handwritten message mentioned *he.* Who was he? And better yet, who was she? Nicole assumed it was a woman because of the delicate hand. She readied her camera and photographed the front, the inside, and back. There were no clues anywhere on it that identified the sender.

Nicole set the card aside and reached into the drawer again. She pulled out a picture frame. Inside was an elaborate marriage certificate. Angels, bells, doves and white roses adorned the surface. Beneath that, a scroll with the bride and groom's names and their witnesses.

"Guys, come look at this," Nicole said.

Her brothers joined her at the desk.

"Where did you find that?" Cooper asked.

"In the top centre drawer. But look at the names."

"Charles Graham and Myrtle Crowe," Connor read aloud. "On June 1, 1886."

"I wonder if the portrait in the other room is him?" Nicole mused.

"Might be."

"This sympathy card was in the desk as well." She showed the card to her brothers, handling it with caution. "I need to photograph this certificate, but I might have to take it out of the frame so there's no glare from the glass."

"No. We'll figure something out. It might stick, and you'd damage it," Cooper said.

"Okay, I'll do my best leaving it as is."

Nicole placed the framed certificate on the floor and stood over it. It was dark, so she moved it around until she found the best place for it and took pictures of it with her Canon and her phone. As much as she wanted to keep it and the sympathy card, she put them back in the desk drawer but didn't lock it.

"You two ready to leave? I've seen just about everything there is to see here."

"I'm not. I want to go back and see if I can find more information on the rocking horse. A brass plaque or something from the manufacturer. It's definitely an antique from what I saw when I searched online. Sometime between 1890 and roughly 1915."

"Don't be too long."

"Come up with me," Nicole said.

"Afraid there's a ghost up there?" Cooper teased, his skepticism clear in his tone.

"No." Nicole led the way up the grand staircase in the front hall. The wood creaked under their weight, and a musty smell filled the air. The same musty smell from the secret passage. When she reached the landing outside the nursery, she stopped dead in her tracks. Cooper almost ran into her.

"What's up?"

"Don't you see it?"

"What?"

"A child. A little boy, I think. He's riding on the rocking horse."

Cooper didn't see a thing, but he knew not to dispel any of his sister's findings when they explored old properties. He watched over her shoulder as she sketched the rocking horse and the little boy. When she finished, she took pictures of the scene and attempted a video with her Canon.

"I hope your camera agrees with what you sketched," Cooper said.

"Hard to say. Sometimes, the camera picks things up. Sometimes it doesn't. There's an aura around the little boy."

"Not that again."

"Yes."

At that moment, children's laughter filled the air, stunning Cooper. He'd not experienced anything supernatural before. And if he did, he'd passed it off as his imagination or devised a logical explanation.

Not much more than two years of age, this small boy pumped the rocking horse harder and harder. It went back and forth faster. If he didn't hold on tight, he'd fall off and hurt himself. The actions mesmerized Nicole and she couldn't take her eyes off the rocking horse and the ghostly image of the child at play.

Then, a gut-wrenching sob yanked her out of her reverie. A woman in her late twenties ran through Nicole and bundled the child into her arms. The weight of her sobs seemed to press down on the entire room. What had happened? Had she received bad news? The mother and child now sat in the rocking chair, rocking gently as the woman sobbed into her son's hair.

So far, this house hadn't yielded many echoes through time, but now they were on fast forward. Nicole flipped to a clean page in her sketchbook and drew the uncertain scene before her. The two wore early 1900s fashion. Was this woman the bride on the marriage certificate she'd found? Was the soldier in the portrait her husband? Did she receive bad news? Or were the two unrelated? The uncertainty of the situation kept Nicole on edge.

Once she had sketched the scene, she photographed it but doubted the pictures would reveal anything more than an empty rocking chair. A chair that seemed to hold the echoes of a bygone era. A chair that had witnessed the joy of a child's play and the sorrow of a mother's tears.

"Shall we get out of here?" Cooper asked. "We've already stayed longer than I intended. I don't want to walk across the field in the dark."

Nicole reluctantly picked up her supplies and stowed them in her backpack. The house had opened up to her and revealed some of its secrets — the connection between the woman and the child. What caused the woman's distress? Who were she and the child? But now she had to leave, her mind buzzing with unanswered questions.

Nicole handed Cooper one of her portable batteries so he could plug his phone in to charge while they made their way back across the field where they entered the property. She needed to come back to this house. Mitch might go with her. He had a logical mind regarding the supernatural and tried to dismiss any phenomena with a rational explanation. He and Cooper were too much alike. Maybe that's what rubbed her brother the wrong way about him?

On the return trip to her brothers' shared apartment, they relegated her to the back seat again. After some deliberation, she texted Mitch.

On our way home now. Still more to see. Do you want to come with me tomorrow?

Nicole was excited, wondering if Mitch would accompany her the following day. She knew he might be busy with work, but she hoped he'd find time for her request. As she waited for his response, Nicole couldn't help but feel a twinge of excitement. However, the incoming message notification would also alert her brothers, Cooper especially, to a conversation she wanted to keep private.

When they pulled up at her brothers' apartment, Nicole jumped out of the backseat and dashed to her car.

"What about the charger?"

"I'll get it from you on Monday. I'm anxious to see what I can find out about the family and how my pictures turned out. See you!"

Nicole had no sooner pulled away from the curb than her phone pinged. Since she was driving, she couldn't respond. It would have to wait until she reached her place. Depending on the traffic, her flat was about a ten-minute drive from Connor and Cooper's. Today, it was light, and she arrived home in less than that.

As soon as Nicole parked in her allotted space and turned the car off, she was eager to check her phone. It was the first thing she reached for, and her curiosity about Mitch's response was almost overwhelming.

Gothic revival house. Sure. What time?

Good question. Early? That would give them more time to explore the house and see if it would give up any more secrets.

Why don't you come over now? We can order pizza and look at my pics and sketches.

Nicole's heart skipped a beat as she hoped Mitch would accept her invitation. While she waited for his next message, she unloaded her things from the car and walked to her building, her mind filled with thoughts of their potential meeting.

Chapter Sixteen

APRIL 30, 1916

Robert recognized the handwriting on the envelope as Ute's. He tore it open anxious to read her words, written in her delicate script.

15 April, 1916

> *Meine Liebe, My love, the days are long without you. Although I must keep the doll hidden, it's a precious reminder of our time together. I pray for your safety every night.*
> *The future is uncertain, Robert. I don't know if Valter somehow suspects what happened that night or if he merely wants to escape Germany. He has us leaving for Canada on 8 May on the SS Nieuw Amsterdam. We must travel by rail through Belgium and then into Holland and Rotterdam, where we'll sail from.*

Robert stared at the letter, his heart heavy with the news it carried. He would never see his beloved Ute again. Her husband's decision to take the family to Canada to escape the war dealt him a bitter blow. Or had Valter discovered the truth about the night he had met Ute in Lützkampen and what had transpired?

> *Walter and Friedrich think of it as an adventure. I've told Valter I would follow him anywhere but across the ocean. Yet, what am I doing? I am bound out of loyalty to my family to make this trip, but my heart*

remains with you.

This will be my last letter to you, my love, but please know this. I will never forget you or the short time we had together. My love for you is unwavering.

Please, stay safe for me. I cling to the hope that when this awful war is over, we may find each other again.
Until then,
I love you with all my heart.

Ute
xoxo

Young boys would think of an ocean voyage an adventure. He did when he sailed from Canada to England to train for battle. There was no time to write to his German lover, because with how slow the mail moved, his letter would never reach her in time. The ship sailed nine days from today. Add the extra time to travel by rail from their home in Wiesbaden to Rotterdam. He couldn't risk trying to intercept their train along its way. That would be a dead giveaway that he and Ute were involved. He was utterly helpless in this situation.

Robert crumpled the letter into a small ball and tossed it away. Once he realized what he'd done, he searched for it. He couldn't destroy it because it came with bad news. The worst news. It was written by his beloved Ute. When he found it, he carefully, pulled it out of the wad and flattened it as best he could.

Chapter Seventeen

NOVEMBER 12, 2022

Mitch enjoyed spending time with Nicole, a close friend who felt like the sister he had never had. Her artwork was fabulous, a talent he had admired since they were kids. The sketches she drew at Kembleford Manor were as good as black and white photos, a confirmation of her skill and dedication.

Be there soon. Need to shower first.

Even though it was Saturday, he had started the job at the Anderson house — at least the demolition portion. He'd rented a dumpster as soon as she accepted his quote so he could begin removing debris and pulling down the ceiling when he arrived at the house.

Mitch was exhausted, but the prospect of pizza and Nicole's company gave him his second wind. He'd have to make it an early night, though. Nicki wanted to return to the Graham house and asked him to accompany her the next day. Of course, he accepted. He didn't want her going alone. Anything could happen. And he wanted to see the inside of the old place himself.

About half an hour later, he arrived at her apartment.

"The pizza's ordered. It should be here anytime. I got us a large all dressed. That okay with you?"

"Fine. And hello to you, too."

"Sorry, Mitch. I've got so much on my mind right now." Nicole related the events from earlier to him, her voice filled with excitement and concern. She took plates and cutlery out of the cupboards as she spoke. "You want a beer? I think I've still got a couple Corona in the fridge."

"Nah, you're fine, shouldn't, since I'll be driving later."

After she put the dishes on the dining room table, she removed her sketchbook from her backpack and placed it on the coffee table. "Have a look at those from today. We can look at the photos after we eat."

Mitch, seated on the sofa, leaned forward and opened the pad. The drawings, a collection of intricate details, captured the essence of the Graham property in a way that only Nicole could. The lamp on the newel post. He'd seen some before, but none as ornate as this one. He flipped through the pages, skimming over the drawings. When he got to the dagger, he stopped.

"Isn't that cool?" Nicole said when she sat on the sofa beside him.

"Not the first word I'd use to describe it."

"Look at the handle. A goat's head with a pentagram on its forehead."

"I'm going to say that's creepy. And you found this knife where?"

"Under the floorboards of one room upstairs. And before you ask, it's back there."

The pizza delivery interrupted their conversation. Mitch left the book on the coffee table when he headed to the dining room to eat. He was glad she had decided to have their pizza in there. That way, neither of them would get grease on Nicole's sketches. He had noticed in her books that she only used one side of the page. Never anything on the back.

"I like milk sometimes when I'm eating pizza. I know I have plenty in the fridge. Want some?"

"Okay, sure." When was the last time he'd drank milk? He rarely bought it unless he was making something that required it.

Nicole returned from the kitchen with two large glasses filled almost to the top.

Over supper, Mitch told her the story of Mrs. Anderson and her bathtub. "So, I get to this house and everything looks in excellent repair. Okay, the hinges on the front door squeaked, but that's nothing that a little WD-40 wouldn't fix. I still can't get over what I saw sitting in a downstairs room in a pile of rubble. Remember the scene in *The Money Pit* when Tom Hanks is pouring buckets of water into the bathtub?"

"Yes, that scene cracked me up," Nicole said before taking another bite of her pizza.

"Well, you don't know how hard it was for me to keep a straight face when I walked into the same scenario. Her cast iron clawfoot tub sitting in a pile of rubble and a gaping hole in the ceiling above."

"For her sake, I hope you didn't laugh. Poor woman."

"I managed to hold it together."

After their meal and Nicole cleared the table, she took the SD card from her camera and inserted it into her laptop. She ran the cable over to her TV and plugged it in. "I've not previewed these yet, so I don't know if the camera picked up anything," she said.

The first images showed the house from the side they entered from. The house, a grand Victorian structure, stood imposingly against the overcast sky. Nothing strange about these. Nicole had walked from the back of the home through and out the front door to capture images from the front — sketches and photographs.

Flanking the steps stood two large cement urns with enormous jade plants growing in them. Nicole had forgotten about those, but how? She couldn't grow a plant of any variety without killing it within weeks.

Her sketches showed the prints from hands pressed against the windows, but from the outside, the camera hadn't picked them up. Yet, when she entered the room where they appeared and took pictures, the oily residue was visible on the glass.

"Back that up," Mitch said.

Nicole clicked back until she had the image from outside on the screen. No handprints or residue.

"I don't get it," he said. "From one side of the window, they're visible, but from the other, they're not."

"May have been how the light reflected off the glass," Nicole offered.

"Might."

She carried on through the rest of the photos. In some, the camera had picked up light she hadn't with her eyes. In others, it was the opposite.

She had taken stills and a video in the room she referred to as the nursery. The latter showed the horse gliding back and forth without a rider. Something had to have caused it to move like that. With the windows closed, a draft wasn't the cause.

When she got to the pictures she'd taken in the tower, she paused at one photograph. She saved it to her laptop's hard drive, opened Photoshop, and loaded the picture. Using noise reduction and other filters, an image appeared.

"That's the soldier in the painting over the fireplace in the room where we got trapped," she said. The soldier, a stern-faced man, seemed to stare right at her. She tried using the same process on the back, but the faded handwriting made it difficult to determine the name.

"I've got to go, Nicki. It's been a long day. Thanks for the pizza. Pick you up at eight tomorrow morning?" Mitch said, stretching.

"That sounds good. I'll be ready."

Nicole walked him to the apartment door. Before he left, Mitch kissed her on the cheek. After she tidied up from their pizza, she put the card back into her camera. When she closed her sketchbook, she wondered what other secrets the house would reveal when her brothers weren't there the next day.

Chapter Eighteen

MAY 8, 1916

U te continued looking over her shoulder, scanning the crowd for Robert. She knew he wouldn't be there but couldn't help herself. She meant what she had said about following Valter anywhere but across the ocean, but she was duty-bound by virtue of her marriage. Ute wanted leave now and get lost in the throng of passengers, well-wishers, and others who had gathered to see off the ship.

The thought of sailing across the vast, unpredictable ocean sent shivers down Ute's spine. The unknown terrified her. What if their ship was torpedoed? Hit an iceberg? It had happened before. *RMS Titanic* had and sank. *RMS Lusitania* ran afoul of the German military and was torpedoed. She had read about both of those incidents in the *Frankfurter Zeitung*. If the Germans thought this ship transported people, it shouldn't; they wouldn't think twice about sinking it.

Valter snapped her out of her reverie when he nudged her to move up the gangplank.

"Come, my dear. We must get on the ship."

Ute's feet felt like lead, resisting every step toward the looming ship. That was the last place she wanted to be.

"Come on, Mutter," Walter, her oldest son, said.

"Ja," added Friedrich.

Her two sons tried to encourage her to board the ship. Not only did she fear travelling across the ocean, she worried about the doll and Robert's love letters. Had she hidden them well enough? She hoped so. Ute had stashed them in the bottom of enormous steamer trunk, riding in the ship's cargo area, then covered them with a layer of blankets. She had also packed precious mementoes from her parents and grandparents. Some of those were more delicate than others so she had wrapped them in blankets and placed them in different part of the trunk. Ute packed their few dishes and cutlery, a reminder of their meagre income despite Valter owning and operating a bakery. Practical things she would need when setting up a new home. Pictures, some drawn by her sons, and others that were actual small paintings of Wiesbaden and the area. She could keep the past a secret if she collected the trunk's contents first. If either of her boys married and had a daughter, Ute would pass the doll down to her, and tell her the family passed it down from generation to generation.

They had only left the port a short time before the German forces boarded the SS Nieuw Amsterdam and searched it and everyone's papers. They hadn't departed the Nieuwe Waterweg and not yet reached the North Sea.

When the knock came on their cabin door, and the demand was uttered to see their papers, Valter made Ute shelter the boys behind her in the farthest corner of the room. The looming threat of the military's potential actions against his family reminded him of their vulnerability in the face of the war.

Valter picked up their documentation and tickets and opened the door. He extended his arm, holding the paperwork.

The man grunted a few times as he perused the documents and checked against the copy of the passenger manifest. His intense scrutiny added to the tension. "Checked baggage?"

"A large steamer trunk. We have a few items of clothing and personal items here in our cabin."

Ute's heart pounded in her chest at the mention

of the steamer trunk in the ship's hold. Would the German navy men search it? If they did, they would find Robert's letters and her worst fears would be realized.

"Please, it is only filled with household items to start anew," she pleaded, her voice trembling with desperation.

"Frau Birkhoefer, I did not ask to speak with you. Go back to your boys. Do it now, or I will arrest you for interfering with our investigation."

She wanted to slap the smug expression off the man's face but did as he ordered. Ute wrapped her arms around her sons. Periodically, she turned and looked over her shoulder to see if the member of the German navy had gone.

He hadn't left yet, but he and Valter were still in deep conversation. They spoke so low she couldn't make out what they said.

The door slammed shut. Ute turned around. It was just her, Valter, and the boys now. The uncertainty of how much longer they would be held up hung in the air, a heavy shroud over their heads. Other passengers aboard the vessel could bring on spies or contraband, adding to the tension.

Valter's expression was a storm of anger, a clear sign of his fury towards her. He might have lashed out if Walter and Friedrich hadn't been there. Thankfully, he restrained himself.

What in blazes was his wife trying to do? Get them thrown off the ship and straight into a German prison? He fought to control his rising anger, taking deep breaths and flexing his fingers. He supposed she didn't want strange men pawing through her personal things.

The ship vibrated as the engines powered back up, and they were soon underway. But how many more times would this happen before they reached the port of Halifax, Nova Scotia, in Canada? He clung to the hope that this was just a onetime occurrence, praying for a smooth journey ahead.

Now, he was more puzzled by his wife's reaction to

the search than angry. At least they were moving once again. Valter had heard that previous crossings from neutral countries had been stopped several times, including in the middle of the ocean.

Chapter Nineteen

NOVEMBER 13, 2022

Nicole was up early, showered and dressed, her heart racing with anticipation of Mitch's arrival. She had a view of the street from her apartment, so she would see him pull up outside. She didn't want to keep him waiting since he'd given up his Sunday to explore an old house with her.

The two had worked well together at Kembleford Manor, despite Mitch's unwavering skepticism about auras and some of the things she saw. What surprised her was that he didn't pick up on the room being closed off. He who renovates old homes. How did he miss that?

She'd packed her backpack the night before, after Mitch left. All she had left to put in it was her camera, which she'd left out to charge the battery. A fully charged battery was a must on these adventures.

Mitch's truck arrived. Nicole shoved her camera, battery, and phone in her backpack, snatched up her keys, and dashed out of the apartment to meet him.

"You're keen," he said when she opened the truck door and climbed in.

His vehicle was higher off the road than her brother's SUV, making getting in and ensconced in the seat more difficult. Thankfully, he had a grab handle in the door frame.

On their way to the Graham house, Nicole told him where they parked and how they got across the property.

Mitch turned off the road before the house and took another road parallel to the first one they took behind the property. A narrow lane, two tire ruts, and grass in between led into the house, which was shrouded in mystery. But they would walk up it, ready to uncover its secrets.

"Here we are. You ready?" Mitch asked.

"Yes. I can't wait," Nicole said as she slid off the seat and out the open door. "I've never heard of the Grahams, but there's something familiar about this place. I've never been here before yesterday, so it's hard to explain."

"I think I know what you mean. It's happened to me at some houses I've fixed up. I can only say that it's because I've worked on that house style before."

He waited at the front of the truck for her, and they began their trek up the narrow, overgrown lane. The sense of adventure hung in the air. Because of his height, Mitch had to duck a few times because of the low-hanging branches. "This track hasn't been used in years," he said.

Nicole had stopped and was taking photos of the approach to the house. He waited, knowing she'd also want to sketch the view.

Something made the hairs on his neck prickle and a chill came over him. It was chilly that morning, and he wore a heavy fall jacket, so he shouldn't be cold. He shook it off and wrapped a protective arm around Nicole's shoulders. If anything happened to her when they were here together, neither one of her brothers would forgive him. He'd keep her safe.

"We found the back door unlocked yesterday. That's how we got in," Nicole said.

"Providing no one has been here since then, it should still be. We'll plan on using that entrance."

The trees cleared, and what once was a massive manicured lawn was waist-high grass. "Except it's too late in the year; some farmer should come and cut this for hay," Mitch said. The gothic revival house loomed ahead of them.

"Watch out for groundhog holes," Nicole warned. "When we came in from the side, there were quite a few. Woody and his family have been busy."

He laughed at her last sentence. Leave it to Nicole to name the woodchucks.

She stopped again and sketched the back side of the house. He didn't recall seeing that angle in her sketches from yesterday.

Watching for holes in the ground made it impossible to drape his arm around her shoulder, so he held her hand instead. If she needed to draw or take pictures, he let go.

The back of the house appeared plain compared to the front and sides. A wooden screen door hung at an angle, the top hinge broken. Nicole hadn't noticed that the previous day. Perhaps it wasn't. It might have happened after she and her brothers left the property.

Because of this, it made the door more difficult to open. Mitch moved it into position long enough for Nicole to try the inside door. It remained unlocked, so hopefully no one had gained entry and destroyed things.

Again, today, the house looked like the occupants had gone out and expected to be back. Since it was Sunday, they were likely at church and would return home for a lunch feast.

Nicole wandered around the kitchen. "Nothing seems out of place since yesterday," she said.

Mitch watched in awe as she took in every detail in the kitchen and sketched it. She did the same in the dining room. A huge sideboard stood against the back wall. Nicole opened the door and discovered delicate china dishes in this end. Before leaving the room, she opened every door in the piece. In his eyes, nothing was untoward so far in the house.

On this side's front of the house was a small living room, separated from the dining room by pocket doors. There was no television, but a huge cabinet radio instead. A stuffed barn owl perched on a branch mounted on the wall.

The stuffed bird was another thing Nicole found creepy about the house. A shiver ran down her spine.

"Wonder if it still works," said Mitch, reaching for the radio's on-off button. He turned it on, but nothing happened. "Can't blame a guy for trying."

A huge grate took up a good section of the floor space in the hall between the front door and the staircase.

"Floor furnace," Mitch said. "I've seen a few of them renovating old houses. The wood stove in the kitchen would have heated the back of the house."

"This is where I found the sympathy card and marriage certificate," Nicole said, walking to the desk and opening the drawer. "That's funny. They're not in here. I put them back after I finished with them." She dropped onto the chair. At least she had documented them the previous day. Still, their disappearance upset and frightened her.

"Maybe someone came in after you guys left. They might have taken them,"Mitch said, walking into the back half of this space separated by an archway. That was the only logical conclusion he could come up with. He hoped Nicole believed him. "This the room you guys got trapped in for a while?"

"Yes. Connor finally figured out how to trip the button to open the pocket doors. Button was behind the trim. And over here is where the secret passage came out. Not that you can see a lot."

He knelt down and examined the floor where Nicole had pointed. "The hardwood is scratched, which aligns with your discovery. But it's odd that there's a porch outside this room with no visible access." Mitch drew the curtain aside. "No steps leading up to it, either."

"That's bizarre, unless one window was a door at one time. They renovated and made it a window, so they had a place for a radiator. At one point yesterday, Connor thought we might have to climb out one of those windows to get out of the room."

"Possible." Mitch wandered through the room, taking in the details from the woodwork to the wallpaper to the high ceilings. This was the kind of house he could get stuck into. The period details like the enormous fireplace, the bay windows that led onto the porch, and the millwork on the wall where the pocket doors were located.

"Look at that medallion. Have you ever come across one like that?" Nicole asked.

He tipped his head back and gazed towards the decorative fixture the chandelier hung from. "Freemason symbol. They might have met for their secret meetings, which is why the room can be closed off like you found it." Mitch hoped he didn't scare Nicole with mention of secret meetings.

"You've got to see this," Nicole said, her voice filled with anticipation as she led the way upstairs.

When they reached the bedroom where she said she'd found the dagger, Mitch found the loose board and pried it out of place. The cavity was empty.

"That's impossible. It was here yesterday. It didn't get up and walk away under its own power. Things are getting weird. First, the marriage certificate and the sympathy card from the desk have vanished, and now the dagger," Nicole lamented, a shiver of unease creeping up her spine. If these were gone, did that mean the handprints on the windows in the next room had vanished, too?

"You believe me, don't you, Mitch?"

"Yes. I've seen the pictures and your sketches. You had to see the objects to get them," he reassured her, his voice a steady anchor in the swirling uncertainty.

"The handprints. They *have* to be there, still." Nicole stood and rushed into the other front bedroom. They remained on the glass.

"A person would have to be a giant to put marks up on those windows," Mitch said when he followed her into the room.

"Or standing on a ladder."

"That, too," he conceded.

Nicole left this room feeling somewhat better about what she'd seen the previous day and entered the nursery. It appeared to remain unchanged. Still, she took pictures and sketched the room again. A creaking sound came from the spot by the window where the rocking chair stood. It swayed back and forth in a rhythmic motion like someone was rocking. Every forward tilt brought a faint groan of wood, as if protesting under the shifting weight. "Do you see that?" she asked.

"What?"

"The chair is moving."

"Wind."

"There isn't any. Yesterday, it was the rocking horse moving." Someone or something was in the house besides them. Nicole shivered, but stood transfixed on the moving rocking chair.

Since sketching movement was difficult, she used the video function on both her phone and her camera. One of them should pick up the motion, as well as the groans and squeaks from both the floor and the runners. It wasn't subtle, either. Whoever or whatever sat in that chair rocked with purpose.

"The tower room, and then we'll leave. I don't want to go near that secret passage again."

Nicole led the way to the stairs leading to the tower, each step echoing with the weight of their impending discovery.

Determined to uncover the truth, Mitch followed Nicole up the narrow flight of stairs, which creaked under their weight. Still, they seemed sturdy enough. He had to duck more often than she did because of his height. The spiral staircase that led to the tower was in the far corner. He used the flashlight on his phone to illuminate the dark corners under the gables. He didn't expect to find anything except mice or rats.

Their cautious footsteps on the iron treads of the spiral stairs echoed with a metallic clang throughout the room. Mitch's work boots made far more noise than Nicole's running shoes. In his eyes, her runners weren't appropriate footwear in a house of this age and lack of occupancy. Anything could penetrate the sole and cut her. The last thing they needed was for Nicole to step on a rusty nail and make a trip to the nearest hospital for a tetanus shot.

She had to shoulder open the door leading to the tower room so they could enter.

"It wasn't stuck like that yesterday."

"Were you the one who opened it, or one of your brothers?"

"Connor or Cooper, I don't remember now; it just didn't seem stuck."

The floor showed the arc pattern of the door scraping against it. Some scratches were deep.

Nicole pulled a proper flashlight out of her backpack, turned it on and aimed the beam around the room.

"That the mirror you mentioned? The picture stuck in the frame?" Mitch walked towards the wall where the looking glass hung. Even it had a rounded top like the upper portion of the windows.

"Yes."

"Shine it over here. I think I see something." It was hard to distinguish anything in the room. The windows in the space were high in the tower, dirty and cobweb-infested.

The beam of light caught something shoved back in a corner. Mitch moved towards it. It was a trunk. When he lifted the lid, the missing dagger wrapped in the blanket, the marriage certificate and the sympathy card lay inside.

"I don't get it. Those things weren't in that trunk yesterday. They were where I told you I found them." The disbelief in Nicole's voice was clear as she struggled to comprehend the situation.

"I believe you, Nicki. I think someone has been in the house since and moved them. I don't know what their motivation was."

"That trunk wasn't up here either, I swear."

"You're okay." Mitch drew her close to him and put his arms around her. He believed her, didn't he? She had no reason to lie about where she found those things. And the pictures she'd taken and sketched of them weren't in this room. Ghosts? No. Ghosts didn't exist. "Seen enough for one day?"

"Yes."

As Nicole turned to leave the tower room, the beam of the flashlight picked up something. "What's that?" she whispered. "It looks like a person," she said, ducking behind Mitch.

He took the light from her and walked towards it. "A dress form. Nothing spooky."

She crept towards it. It was a wedding dress, wasn't it? The colour, once white, was now obscured by a thick layer of dust. A veil added to the illusion of a person. Nicole's fingers trembled as she snapped pictures, the flash momentarily illuminating the eerie room. When she finished, she sketched it, trying to capture the uncanny feeling it evoked.

"I've seen this before. But where? Maybe a photograph in one room downstairs? On a dresser, a mantle, nightstand." Her voice trailed off, uncertainty creeping in.

"We'll check on our way out of the house. You okay now?"

"Yeah. Sorry, I was such a wuss."

"You weren't. I don't blame you for being spooked when things you saw in one place yesterday were in a different place today. Let's go."

Mitch shone the light towards the door, and Nicole left the tower room to go ahead of him. The rubber soles of her shoes squeaked occasionally on the treads. The hollow ring of each step grew louder as the two descended.

On the second floor, they inspected the bedrooms and nursery to see if that was where Nicole had seen a picture of a woman wearing the wedding dress in it. There was nothing there.

Downstairs, in the room where the painting of the soldier hung above the fireplace, was a smaller photograph on the mantle of the military man and his wife, most likely taken on their wedding day. Nicole's breath caught in her throat as she realized they had found what they were looking for.

Not wanting to leave without getting images of this committed to paper and her devices, Nicole photographed the small image in its ornate frame and sketched the couple. The man was tall and stern, his military uniform crisp and his eyes piercing. The woman was petite and demure, her wedding gown elegant, and her smile shy but genuine.

"Now we can go," Nicole said, her voice tense. But as they turned to leave, a sudden gust of wind slammed a door shut. The sound of footsteps echoed in the silence, growing louder and closer. They were not alone. Someone else was in the house. She sidled closer to Mitch for protection. This house was beginning to rival Kembleford Manor for weirdness.

Later that night, Nicole settled in with more letters from the soldier to his German lover. This next one was out of sequence. Dear June? He had addressed the envelope to Ute Birkhoefer. So what was a letter to this woman doing in it? It filled her mind with confusion.

Then, like a bolt from the blue, the realization hit her. This was Robert's wife. She had read this letter the other night and must have put it back in the wrong stack.

There was no *xoxo* at the end, contrasting how he ended his letters to the other woman. It seemed that his feelings for his wife didn't run as deep as they did for his lover. That revelation added a layer of emotional complexity to the situation.

Chapter Twenty

After the weekend's events, Nicole did not want to be in the office. She had everything she needed to work from her apartment.

It had been a week since Nicole stumbled upon the china head doll under the seat of her car. Little did she know that discovery would unexpectedly lead her on a journey of self-discovery. She had stopped reading the letters when she stumbled onto the one for his wife mixed in with the others to his lover. More of the stack would be reading material for today.

After the weekend's events, Nicole found herself drained and not in the right frame of mind to be in the office. She decided to work from home, not feeling well, both physically and emotionally. She tapped out a message to her brothers.

Not feeling well, so working from home.

Her phone pinged. A reply from Connor.

Take care, sis. Hope you feel better soon.

Cooper's message came in.

Okay. See you tomorrow?

Typical Cooper. Short, sweet, and to the point.

Where to start? Nicole had the image of the marriage certificate on her devices. Why not search their names online and see what came up? Charles Graham or Myrtle Crowe might not factor into her family, but seeing where they came from would be interesting.

Once her laptop powered up, she opened her browser and typed *Charles Graham Myrtle Crowe marriage 1886.* Few results came back from her search, but Ancestry.ca was where she needed to concentrate.

Since she found their marriage certificate in the desk drawer, she first searched for the couple in the marriage records. Why would someone hide something that beautiful away in a desk. If it was hers, she'd have it displayed in a prominent location for all to see. At one time it might have been, but whoever lived in the house after their deaths took it down and put it away.

So far, she had the who and the when, but most of the other information on the elaborate certificate was illegible because of fading and being behind glass.

Nicole considered the 14-day free trial but registered for a full-fledged account. There was no guarantee she'd have the time to find everything she needed within that short time frame. Nicole was eager to discover more with how gnarled her family tree was from what little she'd found on her mother's side.

First, Nicole needed to create an account. So, she returned to the main screen and opted for all records. That way, she could find her ancestors who weren't born in Canada. Before exploring the Kembleford Manor Hotel, Nicole had no interest in genealogy. Not so much the exploration that did it, but the pedigree chart she found in the boxes of her mother's things. The chart that linked her and her brothers to the Kembleford family.

Nicole entered the groom's name, and the year and hit enter. The website listed more Charles Grahams than she thought possible, but only one married Myrtle Crowe, so she selected it. The sense of accomplishment in finding the marriage records filled Nicole with satisfaction.

There, they were in black and white. It listed Charles's name, age, where he lived, where he was born, his marital status, occupation, and his parents. What? His parents? Nicole looked closer at the document and noted their names — George and Bertha. Something else she could check later. Beneath them, the information for the bride was listed. It contained the same data list, but with the witnesses recorded under her parents' names, followed by the place and date, church, denomination and the minister who married them.

Nicole now had concrete evidence of the couple's marriage and parents for both of them. The only thing missing was how it tied to her family; perhaps that was only a dream on her part. This search was mainly to see how the website worked — it was pretty slick. She returned to the previous screen and found Charles and Myrtle in the 1891 census, living in the same area where they were married. The mystery of their connection to her family deepened, leaving Nicole intrigued and eager to uncover more.

By now, they had a daughter, June, who was only a year old. However, the most interesting nugget of information she found was that both Charles and Myrtle's parents were born in Scotland. So, that meant they emigrated to Canada before their children were born. The census clearly listed their place of birth as being Ontario. Might she find a birth record for June?

Nicole returned to the main page and changed the search for birth records with June's name and year. This might all be for naught, but she was hooked. Finding June's birth record took longer than everything she'd already seen. The first searches were giveaways. This one proved more difficult, but she eventually found what she wanted. Could she find the family in the 1901 census? Ten years later, June would be around eleven, depending on when the census was done.

She searched the census records for the family, which lived in the exact location as before. The way the page was laid out, the first columns related to the home's location. It appeared the Graham family still lived in the same location as they had ten years previously, but still had no other children. But what? It couldn't be. Nicole did a double-take at the screen. A Holbrook family was living next door. Claude, Elizabeth, and a son, Robert. It couldn't be her Holbrooks, could it? She printed that page and returned to the previous census sheet on her table. The family must have moved to that area after the 1891 census. Curiouser and curiouser. The potential discovery of a family connection left Nicole feeling hopeful and excited.

When she looked up at the clock, she discovered three hours had elapsed since she sat down and started into researching the couple whose marriage certificate she found. Genealogy was addictive.

Despite her curiosity, Nicole knew she had to focus on her work at CNC IT Solutions. She had wasted enough time already on non-work related tasks. She signed out of Ancestry, reminding herself of the additional graphics she needed to create for *The Cheese Board & Café* website, menus, flyers, and other tasks that awaited her.

Nicole's images attested to her skill and dedication. They turned out vibrant and lively, a stark contrast to the *Barnsley's Bakery* design, which looked like deflated dough after the first transfer.

Nicole was eager to share her findings with her brothers the next day, but couldn't bring herself to admit she had spent part of the day on it. The images she had printed from the Ancestry website weren't time and date-stamped, so she could tell them she had tackled that in the evening. But the guilt of visiting the Graham mansion with Mitch the previous day weighed heavily on her. She didn't enjoy lying to them, especially Cooper. Connor would be more forgiving, as he still got along well with Mitch.

Now after five o'clock, Nicole's stomach growled. She gathered her work-related materials and put them in her backpack so they'd be ready to take in the morning. The documents printed from Ancestry remained on the table. Maybe while she ate, she'd look up more information on the Graham and Holbrook families.

Nicole opened her fridge door and peered inside. She pulled fresh romaine lettuce out first, followed by a red onion. Real bacon bits and Feta cheese came out next. Then she opened her spice cupboard and took out her bottle of Garlic Expressions dressing. The bottle's label said to refrigerate after opening, but there was enough vinegar in it to keep it fresh without refrigeration.

Salad bowl in one hand, and dressing in the other, she returned to the table to eat and research. The first bite sent her tastebuds into overdrive. Lettuce, onion and Feta in that delicious dressing. Black olives were missing, because she had none. She'd have to buy a small jar the next time she bought groceries.

Inspired, Nicole logged back into Ancestry and delved into the Graham family history again. The Holbrook family, including Robert, still lived next door in the 1911 census. Undeterred, she tried the 1921 census. Now, June Graham was listed as June Holbrook with a six-year-old son, William. This discovery piqued her interest. She printed both censuses, eager to share her findings with her brothers the next day.

Back to the marriage records, Nicole typed in June's first and last name and only the surname Holbrook. The marriage took place after the 1911 census and before 1915. Once she entered that information, she chose a plus or minus five-year range. While the computer chewed the information she'd provided, Nicole finished her salad and took her dishes to the kitchen.

When she returned to the computer, the results had come back. She clicked on the thumbnail image. To her surprise, Robert Holbrook was the groom. His parents were also listed. This was getting better and better. June and Robert married on June 21, 1914. That was the year the First World War broke out. Did they have a whirlwind romance before he went overseas? Did he go overseas? Military records. But first, the birth of their son, William. She included a range of plus or minus a year since he could have been born in either 1914 or 1915. With the area being narrowed down as much as it was, there weren't many results to search through. She found his birth registration and printed it, too.

Nicole's excitement grew as she opened a new tab in her browser and searched for World War I military records. Canadian Expeditionary Force records were searchable. She entered Robert's first and last name and hit the search button, eager to uncover more about his past.

The database search yielded a name of profound significance: Holbrook. A mere click led Nicole to a treasure trove of information. His entire service record from enlistment to his fateful day on October 29, 1917, in the Battle of Passchendaele. Among the records were an image of the man and a paragraph that revealed his valour — awarded the Victoria Cross for his unwavering courage during the battle.

As Nicole delved deeper, she stumbled upon two columns from the London Gazette detailing his heroic deeds. The thought that Robert Holbrook could be a part of her family filled her with hope and anticipation. Imagine a war hero in the family!

Nicole chose not to print the file but transferred it onto a USB stick. The arrangement of the documents made printing them tricky, and would not do justice to their integrity. If this man was indeed her ancestor, Nicole was determined to preserve his legacy with the utmost respect. With the file on a stick, she was ready to share with her brothers.

She ejected the stick and placed it on top of the documents she would take to work the next day, shut down her computer and got ready for bed.

Chapter Twenty-One

MAY 17, 1916

The ocean crossing had been fraught with problems, the first being boarded by the German navy. The seas were rough, and huge swells broke over the ship's bow. Valter's sons found it fun to be rocked violently and sprayed with the frigid seawater.

Ute had taken to her bed with illness. Her normal complexion turned a greenish-gray, and her skin was clammy to the touch. He had tried cool cloths applied to her forehead, but they were useless against the seasickness.

Neither Valter nor his sons, Walter and Friedrich, had succumbed to the illness that their mother had. For that he was thankful. Their cabin was small and not well-equipped for four sick people.

When Valter went in search of the ship's doctor for medicine to help Ute, walking in the corridor was hazardous. He was bounced off the walls. Right then left repeated over the distance. His wife wasn't the only one suffering, he discovered. The moans of other passengers emanating from the cabins reached his ears, and the sour stench of vomit assailed his nostrils.

Along the way, he met other passengers who had gone to find food or drink to help their loved ones through the ordeal.

"Spirits," a gentleman about his age said.

Valter wondered what spirits had to do with seasickness.

"Brandy, whisky. Get her drinking those."

Ah, that kind of spirit. He didn't see how that would help. It would most likely compound the problem.

"No, you've got it wrong. Ginger. Ginger tea. It will calm her stomach. Peppermint oil will work, too. Or, if you like, I can whip up a batch of my herbs," a female passenger suggested.

Valter opted for ginger and headed off to find it, rather than the herbal concoction.

After a thorough search, he found a small stash of ginger in the ship's pantry. He never did find the ship's doctor. Valter assumed the man must have been busy looking after passengers in the classes above theirs. He secured enough ginger to last the entire voyage, relieved that he had found a solution to Ute's illness.

By the eighth day, the sea had calmed. Ute sat up and nibbled on some dry toast, although she still looked as if she would relapse at any moment.

The crossing was to take about ten days. The ship left Rotterdam on May 8, and today was May 17, and they still hadn't made it to the port of Halifax. Thanks to the German navy, they had been delayed before they even hit the open water.

When they finally docked in Halifax Harbour on May 24, Valter gathered Ute and his sons and their personal possessions, which they kept in their cabin. The next leg of their journey was by train. They had sailed in third-class, so they had to wait for the first — and second-class passengers to disembark before it was their turn.

"Other than some heavy seas, we made it across safely, Ute," he said.

"Yes, we did. I was being silly. I knew you wouldn't let anything happen to us," Ute replied.

Chapter Twenty-Two

Nicole was up, showered and dressed long before she had to think about leaving for work. She made herself some toast and a second coffee and sat down with the stack of papers from the day before. It seemed a stretch that these Grahams and Holbrooks were related to her family. From what little her father ever talked about growing up, he never mentioned them living anywhere other than Belleville. She might be spending all her efforts for nothing. The families she discovered who lived in the gothic mansion might not have anything to do with her family.

When Nicole looked at the clock again, it was time for her to leave. How had that much time elapsed since she sat down? The sudden realization surprised Nicole and she dashed to the bathroom to brush her teeth. Then she took her hair out of the towel and combed it out. She had no time to dry it, so she'd have to go with wet hair. Before retiring the previous night, she packed her laptop case with all the documents she'd found, her work sketchbook, the USB stick and her computer.

"What time do you call this?" Connor asked when she breezed into the office ten minutes late.

"Sorry, got distracted with something else," Nicole answered.

"I'm only teasing," he said, nudging her shoulder.

"Where's Cooper?"

"Gone to check out the building *The Coffee Bean*

& *Café* is moving into. See what has to be done for LAN wiring."

"All my artwork is complete for them. I just hope they like it. Working from home without interruptions helped tremendously. I poured my heart into this project," Nicole shared, her eyes shining with pride.

"Glad it worked out for you. Are you feeling better?"

"Much. I did some research during and after supper related to some things we discovered when we explored the house on Saturday."

Her statement piqued Connor's curiosity. What did Nicole find? His sister wasn't one to leave a stone unturned in the name of research. Whether it was for a work-related project or personal. She was like a dog with a bone when she put her mind to doing something. There were a few things that still made him feel uncomfortable about the place. The Freemason's symbol on the ceiling medallion. The dagger with the occult symbols, but most of all, those damn pocket doors that didn't want to give up their secret to open them. What had Nicole discovered about these mysterious elements?

"Care to share?"

"Definitely, but can we wait for Cooper to get back? I'd just as soon only have to go through it once."

Although disappointed, Connor agreed. Why explain a story multiple times? "Can I see your artwork at least? I'm interested in what you've created."

"Sure." Nicole connected her laptop to her work terminal and transferred *The Coffee Bean & Café* files from her computer.

The smaller screen on her computer wouldn't do the images justice. They all had three 21-inch monitors in the office. At home, Nicole often connected her PC to her TV, which was larger still. Connor had been there when she'd done it. He thought Cooper and he had a techie apartment, but his sister's might have been more so.

Eager for his twin to return, Connor wanted to find out what his sister had discovered. He thought about shooting off a text but decided against it. When, on a job, Cooper didn't like distractions. Connor respected that about him.

As it turned out, he didn't have to. The wandering brother returned, surprising them all with his sudden appearance.

"Why are you two looking guilty? Or better yet, like the cat that swallowed the canary?" Cooper asked when he entered the office.

"Nicole's showing me her artwork. It's fantastic. Come see," Connor said.

Cooper rounded the desk and looked at the images on his sister's screen. "They're gonna love them. I know they will. When do you meet with them again to show off your results?"

"We've not set a date yet. This entire project has them running scared, I think. You know, what have we gotten ourselves into? I'm sure we all felt the same when we started this business. It was a long time before we could afford to have an office. Our start-up was in your apartment," Nicole said.

"Ah, those days. I'm glad they're behind us. Being a start-up business is a scary place to be. You will notify them that the finished images are ready for them to review?"

"Yes, Cooper. I will do that."

"Nicki says she did some research last night based on what we found at the house on the weekend," Connor said. "Go on, tell us, sis."

"Okay. Remember, I found the elaborate marriage certificate in the desk drawer? Well, the handwriting was faded, making it hard to read."

"Okay, go on," Cooper urged.

"I ended up signing up for a full account at Ancestry.ca. With what information I got from the marriage certificate, I found the registration for the event." Nicole pulled that sheet of paper off the stack. "Now, I have Charles and Myrtle's parents. I checked the census for Charles and Myrtle and found them in 1891 with a daughter, June. Ten years later, in the 1901 census, a family named Holbrook moved next door.

Parents and son Robert. But when we visited, there was no house next door. The mansion was the only place on that side of the road for miles."

"Fire, maybe? It happened more than you might think back then," Connor said.

"An old map of the area would be helpful. Google Earth might pick up an anomaly where the house might have stood. And Charles Graham was a farmer. No barn or other outbuildings stood on the property," Nicole said.

"Barn fires were common, too. Hay being put away when it was too green. Poof, up in smoke," Cooper said.

Firefighting techniques weren't nearly as advanced back then as today. The Holbrook house could have burnt. Not necessarily to the ground, but enough that over the years, it fell in on itself. She'd seen some when she and her brothers were travelling from home to an exploration location.

"Okay, but now, if I move ahead to the 1911 census, there's still no change. It's the same as 1901." Nicole pulled out the next page. "But when I searched the 1921 census, June Graham was now June Holbrook. Head of the family with a six-year-old son, William."

"Wow," Cooper said. "You found all that last night?" His baby sister was quite the detective, besides being a talented artist.

"Believe it or not, it gets better. I searched for William's birth and discovered that his father was Robert Holbrook. I searched for Robert and June's marriage and discovered they married in 1914. I now have his parents' names, too."

"Where are you going with this, sis?" Connor asked.

"They married before the war. I think Robert enlisted and headed overseas sometime in 1914. So I searched the Canadian Military records, and I found him! I didn't print the documents I found on file, but he was a war hero and awarded the Victoria Cross. He died in the Battle of Passchendaele."

"So, this Robert Holbrook might be an ancestor?" Cooper asked. Finding a war hero in their family tree wasn't something he expected.

"I need to dig deeper. The more recent the events, the less information there is online. I downloaded Robert's military records. If, and I emphasize *if*, I can prove that he's related to us, then I'll print everything I found online."

"What about the painting on the mantle? Do you think it was him?" Connor asked.

"I forgot about that. There was a rudimentary line drawing of Robert in the records I downloaded. Perhaps they are the same person?"

Cooper stood beside his brother, behind Nicole. She opened up the documents on her USB stick and scrolled through to the line art image. Then, she opened her sketchbook, which she had with her the day they explored the Graham mansion, to the drawing of the painting over the mantle.

"It's the same person. I'd stake my reputation on it," said Cooper.

"I think you're right," Connor agreed.

"It's unanimous. But we still can't prove if this Robert Holbrook is a relative. It will take much more time and searching to find out," Nicole said with a sigh.

When Nicole got home from work, she phoned her father. His reluctance to talk about his family, other than his sister, had always intrigued her. Perhaps this time, with come gentle coaxing, he'd open up.

"Hello, Frank Holbrook."

"Hi, Dad, it's me," she said.

"Nicole. I didn't expect to hear anything from you. Is everything okay? You're okay? Your brothers?"

"Yes, we're all fine. I'm calling because the three of us explored the old Graham mansion near Brighton on the weekend. I found the marriage certificate for Charles Graham and Myrtle Crowe in a desk drawer. It was beautiful. I've never seen anything so fancy. I wondered if those names meant anything to you."

"No. Can't say as they do."

"Well, they had a daughter, June, and she married a Robert Holbrook just before World War One broke out. She must have been pregnant when he went overseas because her son William was born early the following year."

Nicole's father made a garbled noise.

"Are you okay, Dad?"

"I'm fine. Nothing to worry about."

"You sure?"

"Yes. I need to go. I've got some work to catch up on. I'll talk to you again soon. Bye."

"Bye, Dad."

Why did her father act the way he did at the mention of the Holbrook name? The mystery deepened, leaving Nicole with more questions than answers. Were those people related to him?

What on earth was Nicole doing digging up the past? A past Frank wanted to stay buried. He needed to think of a way to quash this family history kick she was on, and fast. But how?

He picked up the phone and dialled the number of the assisted living facility his sister lived in. Since he called at mealtime, the receptionist told him she'd pass the message on to Janet.

About an hour later, Frank's phone rang.

"Hello. Frank Holbrook."

"Frank. It's Janet. You called?"

He detected something in her tone but couldn't put his finger on it.

"Has Nicole phoned you or been to see you?" he asked.

"No. Should she have?"

"I thought she might after that china head doll turned up."

"You're the only person who's been to visit. What do you want?"

"If Nicole calls or visits and asks about certain members of the Holbrook and Graham families, don't tell her a thing."

"It's all water under the bridge now, Frank. Get

over it."

"Easy for you to say when you got everything, and I got nothing," he spat, his voice filled with bitterness.

"I don't want to discuss this right now. If you want to rant and rave about what happened between you and our parents, go do it in front of someone else. I've heard it all before. Too many times."

Janet slammed the phone down in his ear.

That didn't go as well as he hoped. He needed to dissuade Nicole from researching his side of the family. Too many skeletons rattled around in the Holbrook closets. The ones he knew about, like the truth about his father's death, were bad enough. Who knew how many others there were?

Janet found herself trapped in a whirlwind of conflicting emotions as she replayed the conversation with her brother. His adamant stance of keeping Nicole in the dark about the family's past had left her in a state of unease. The boxes of family secrets, now languishing in her storage locker, constantly reminded her of her internal conflict. If she passed those on to her niece, she didn't tell her the things Frank wanted to remain secret. The young woman would find them out for herself. After all, no family is perfect.

She was tempted to phone Nicole right then and tell her to come get those cartons of family memorabilia, Janet picked up the phone, but never punched in the number. The weight of her brother's words and the burden of the family secrets held her back. Instead, she returned the handset to the cradle and powered over to the window.

It got dark so early this time of year. Janet couldn't see anything beyond the bit of lawn illuminated by the lights on the building. A stand of trees wasn't far from the facility, and she sometimes saw wild animals making their way out from the trees' protection. They might be there tonight, but it was pitch black, exaggerated by the lighting, so she could not tell. Janet should have done this before supper since dusk was the usual time for plenty of animal activity.

Here in her room, Janet felt alone, unsure what type of company she'd be if she returned to the lounge. Instead, she picked up the remote and turned on her television, seeking comfort in the flickering images on the screen.

Nicole's father's reaction to what she told him on the phone ignited a fire of determination in her. There had to be a reason he coughed and got defensive at the mention of those names. She resolved to pay an overdue visit to her aunt. With working during the week, Saturday would be the earliest Nicole had the time available for a visit, but she would call now to make the arrangements.

Nicole pulled out her wallet and found the business card from Willow Glen. On the back was the direct line through to her aunt's suite. She punched the numbers into her cell phone and waited.

"Hello," said the woman on the other end of the line.

"Hi, Aunt Janet. It's Nicole. It's been a long time. How are you?" She twirled her finger through a lock of hair as she spoke and waited for the answer. Nicole and her aunt had always been close, but their relationship had strained over the years after the woman moved into the assisted living facility.

"About the same. Your father called me. Came to see me, too. Something about a china head doll you think came from me?"

At least her aunt was aware of the situation. Nicole felt a wave of relief wash over her.

"I'd like to come and see you on Saturday if that's all right with you. I realize it's been too long."

"I'd love to see you. Shall we say morning? Ten-thirty, eleven?"

"Brilliant. I'll see you then. I'll bring the doll with me." Nicole hung up before her aunt said anything else.

Now, she had to wait until the weekend to visit the woman and find out what she knew.

Chapter Twenty-Three

MAY 24, 1916

Ute meant what she had said. Her heart, torn between two lands, remained in Germany. It yearned for a Canadian soldier fighting on the Western Front. If she had stayed behind, there were no guarantees she would see him again. There had been no word of the war out on the open sea, at least none she'd heard. Her Robert might be dead by now, and she wouldn't know.

When she finally reached the pier, Ute dropped to her hands and knees and kissed the planks. She stood on land, off that dreaded ocean.

Her sons ran around chasing one another. They had been cooped up for too long. Their father may have let them venture onto the ship's deck. She never left the cabin, her heart filled with love for her boys.

"Walter, Friedrich, Komm, setz dich, jetzt," she scolded.

"But, Mutter," her youngest son whined.

"Jetzt." Ute raised her voice.

"Ja, Mutter." Friedrich dropped his chin against his chest, but obeyed his mother's wishes.

"We must stay here. This is where your father will look for us after he finds our trunk. Then we'll be on our way to the train."

"Mutter, wo werden wir in Kanada leben?" Walter asked.

"St. Jacobs in Ontario. Your father has cousins there. You must learn to speak English, both of you.

That is the language here," Ute said, hoping for a better life for her children.

"Who, Mutter?" asked Friedrich.

"Heinrich and his wife. He is a cousin on your Großmutter Glück's side."

"Have we met them before?"

"No."

While not keen on losing her mother tongue, Ute hoped she would retain enough of the language that, in the privacy of their home, they could still speak it among themselves and Valter's cousins.

About an hour later, a horse-drawn coach approached, signalling the start of their long-awaited journey. Valter walked alongside. Their enormous trunk secured to the rear, packed with the anticipation of the unknown. The driver climbed down from his seat and opened the door for Ute and the boys. She made them go in ahead of her, their excitement clear. With Valter's help, she put one foot onto the small step and climbed aboard, ready to embark on their family adventure. Her husband stowed the remaining luggage inside and boarded.

The carriage lurched when the driver returned to his seat, and the wooden wheels against the cobblestone road echoed in the air. While comfortable, the interior was cramped with the four of them and their smaller bags and trunks. The smell of leather and the faint sound of the horses' hooves filled the space. It wasn't long before they stopped, and their coachman stood at the door to help them alight. The man motioned towards the train station, and a stocky man in overalls approached, pulling a substantial cart with metal-rimmed wheels.

The driver and the other man manhandled the Birkhoefer's massive steamer trunk off the back of the carriage and onto the wagon. Ute followed the man and her husband as they approached the awaiting train. She felt a mix of excitement and apprehension about the journey ahead. How long of a wait they had before the train departed, she didn't know, but it was a relief to travel on dry land.

Valter showed their train tickets to a conductor on the platform, who directed them to the carriage they needed. Ute was thankful that her husband had taken charge of all their travel arrangements. She didn't have a head for it. Put her behind the wheel of a vehicle, and she could deliver their bakery's products anywhere.

They stopped at the carriage where they were directed. It looked unaffordable. Heavy drapes adorned the windows, adding to the appearance of opulence. Another person checked their tickets, opened the door, and directed them to board.

The railway employees here acted more professional than the ones back home when they travelled by train to Rotterdam. On that train, there were two seats on either side of a centre aisle. Once the family was on the train, this employee joined them and led them to the compartment that would be theirs. And a compartment? How luxurious. Ute had never experienced train travel like this. Only the wealthy back in Germany could afford to travel in this fashion.

"You have storage for your luggage here," he said, opening a narrow door. "And above the seats are two upper berths. A porter will come along while you're at dinner to set them up."

"I want to sleep on the top," Friedrich shouted.

"Me, too," said Walter.

"We'll be stopping in Montreal for an overnight layover. You'll change trains there. When you board your next train, you will have a different crew with you for the balance of your journey to Toronto."

"But we're not going to Toronto," Ute protested. "We're going to Saint Jacobs."

"Ah, my dear woman. You'll have to change trains there to continue your journey into southwestern Ontario."

"Thank you for explaining. We've only just arrived, and I know little of this country," Ute admitted, her lack of knowledge about the journey making her feel vulnerable in this new land.

"You're forgiven for your lack of knowledge.

Perhaps it is I who should apologize to you. I should have explained it better knowing your final destination."

Ute sat on what she hoped was a forward facing seat. She wanted to be able to look and see where they were going. What was going on back in Germany with the war? Her thoughts drifted to Robert.

Valter stowed the bags in the small cupboard the porter had pointed out. He sat next to it and patted the seat beside him, closest to the window, for his wife to join him. He nodded, directing the boys to the seats across from them.

"Ich möchte am Fenster sitzen," Friedrich pouted.

"You can both sit by the window. You take my seat. I'll sit opposite your father."

Ute spoiled their youngest son, giving in to him often.

"Danke, Mutter."

People passed by their window on their way to other carriages. Some passed in the train's corridor towards other compartments. Valter had ensured they wouldn't have to share with anyone else. The family would have one to themselves. Unless Ute objected, he had no qualms about the boys sleeping in the upper bunks as long as there was a rail or something to keep them from falling out.

It had been several years since he last saw his cousins. They had written him, stating how wonderful it was here and that the people in the community where they settled had made them feel welcome. With the war raging, it was the perfect opportunity to take his cousin up on his invitation to come to Canada.

Their family baking tradition would continue. Heinrich, a cousin on his mother's side, and his wife Mathilde started a small bakery specializing in German goods. They had offered to employ him and Ute and to help them find a home. Until that happened, Valter's family would stay with them. It was an extremely generous offer. His cousins didn't have children, so they did not know how boisterous two young boys could be. Walter showed signs of maturing, no longer given to the more juvenile antics of his younger brother, Friedrich.

Chapter Twenty-Four

NOVEMBER 19, 2022

The days dragged on, each hour feeling like an eternity as Nicole's mind raced with anticipation of the meeting that might unravel the mystery of her family's past. Finally, the day arrived. Shortly after ten-thirty, Nicole pulled her compact car into the visitors' parking area of Willow Glen Manor. The exterior impressed her. But would the inside? She strode to the entrance and to the reception desk.

"I'm here to visit my aunt, Janet Holbrook," she told the young girl.

"Let me buzz her room and see if she's there."

A pause.

"No answer, so she must be in the residents' lounge at the end of the corridor. Down to your right, and it's the last door on the left. You're the second person to visit her in the past couple of weeks. Her last visitor was a man. But you must sign the visitors' register before I let you go further." The woman pointed to the book on the counter.

"My father," Nicole said as she signed in. What business would it be for the receptionist if her aunt had more than one visitor recently?

The assisted living home was bright and airy, which gave it a pleasant appeal. Inside the lounge, various seating areas, allowed for watching television, playing board or card games, or working on jigsaw puzzles. Most of the people here were white-haired folks over retirement age. Aunt Janet was younger than

Nicole's father so not even sixty yet, much younger than the other residents.

Her aunt sat on the far side of the room engaged in a lively game of euchre. Nicole walked to the table, clutching the box containing the china head doll. She had left the letters from the German woman's lover back at her apartment.

"Hi, Aunt Janet. It's been a long time." Nicole's voice trembled with emotion.

"Nicole, it's wonderful to see you. And it has been a long time. Your mother's funeral, I believe."

"Yes." Nicole wasn't proud to mention that. Her aunt was still able-bodied then, not confined to an electric wheelchair.

"Come, we'll go up to my room. More private, so we can have a good chat. Bella, want to take over for me?" Janet Holbrook asked a woman who might have been in her early seventies.

"Sit down, Nicole. I won't because I already am," Janet said, laughing. "So, what brings you here today?"

"I need answers, Aunt Janet."

"I'll try to answer your questions."

"What happened between you and Dad? When Mummy first got sick, you came around all the time, and after she died, you didn't."

Janet sighed. This would not be a simple discussion. "To make a long story short, your father was angry with me because I inherited the house, not him. He thought our parents should have bequeathed it to him because he was the oldest."

"I didn't realize."

"I don't imagine you did. Your father and grandfather were always at loggerheads. They were too much like the other. Then, when he quit university to marry your mother, that was the final straw. It's a tangled web, isn't it?"

"Oh."

"Well, it looks like karma got me. Life has a way of throwing unexpected twists, doesn't it?"

"What happened, if you don't mind talking about

it?"

"Since I inherited the house, I moved out of my small apartment and into it. I was upstairs dusting or something. That part doesn't matter now. I stood at the top of the stairs, and Bruiser, my big yellow Maine Coon tom, you remember him. Well, he started weaving himself around my legs, and the next thing, I came tumbling down the steps. The fall broke my back, and I'm paralyzed from the waist down."

"I didn't know. I'm sorry."

Janet patted Nicole's knee. "Don't be."

Nicole's father and grandfather didn't get along. That was the first she'd heard of it, but it explained her father's silence when it came to discussing his childhood. So they fought? Who didn't argue with their parents at some point? She had and so had her brothers.

Nicole had brought the china head doll with her to show her aunt since the writing on the label looked like the woman's, according to her father. "Do you recognize this?" Nicole asked, removing the china head doll from the box.

Janet's face paled.

"So you do. I first saw it in a vision at Kembleford Manor up in Pike Falls last month. It belonged to a little girl, Grace Birkhoefer, who drowned in the manor's boathouse in 1947. I found newspaper articles online about the drowning. This box with the doll inside turned up under the passenger seat of my car." Nicole stood and walked to the window. "My friend, Mitch, he spotted a letter sticking out from under the tissue paper. It was love letter to a Mrs. Ute Birkhoefer from a soldier named Robert. He bought the doll for her as a memento of their night together. I have no idea what his last name is; he never used it." The mystery of the doll's origin hung in the air.

"I see."

"You know more than you're telling me, don't you," Nicole said, her voice sharp with suspicion.

Janet closed her eyes and shook her head.

Why all the pretence and denial? What was it with the generation of Holbrook's before her? Nothing was straightforward. The colour draining from her aunt's face told her the woman knew. Nicole scrolled through the pictures on her phone. She stopped when she reached one of the front of the house where she and her brothers had explored the previous Saturday.

"Do you know this house?" Nicole turned her phone to show her aunt.

Janet turned away.

"You do. Mitch told us it was the old Graham house. Were the Grahams part of our family?"

"Yes. That's the house where I had my accident. What were you doing in there?"

"My brothers and I, and Mitch, are urban explorers. We investigate abandoned houses, and prefer older properties because they have more character."

"That's trespassing."

"I'm aware of that."

Janet sighed. Urban explorers. What next? She'd let it slip that that was where she had her accident that broke her back. And that the Grahams who once lived there were part of the family. Well, her brother could go to hell. She was tired of the secrets.

Nicole deserved the truth, no matter how ugly. She powered her chair to the nightstand and opened the drawer. She wasn't telling her niece the story if she gave her the documents. The girl could figure it out on her own. "Here, take this key. It's to my storage locker in the basement. Tell the receptionist I told you there was something in it for you. She'll show you where to go."

"How will I know I've found the right box or boxes?"

"They're the only things down there."

"Do you want me to bring them back here?"

Janet shook her head. The memories were too painful. If Nicole found closure from the items in them, then she was welcome to them. In Janet's eyes, it was good riddance. She had been through them before her accident and sorted the items: letters, newspaper articles, and other documents.

She never had the letters from Robert to Ute, but the ones she wrote to him were there. As were the ones that Robert and his wife exchanged. The army had gathered all of Robert's personal effects after his death at Passchendaele. Unopened letters from Robert to June were stored in the house. Janet had never opened them. The last one she read was the last one Robert's wife opened, written to his lover, Ute. Somehow, he had mixed up the letters and sent them to the wrong recipients.

"I found a marriage certificate in a desk drawer. Also, a sympathy card with no signature."

"No doubt I missed some things when I packed it all up. I want you to go back to the house and retrieve anything like that that's left behind. I'll worry about the dishes and furniture."

"What about photographs and paintings?"

"You take them."

"The wedding dress?"

"That, too."

"What about the rocking horse? I fell in love with it. I've never seen one that style before."

Janet considered Nicole's request. She had no need for it. Janet had never married and now lived in Willow Glen Manor. She likely never would, being beyond her child-bearing years. Nicole might still marry and have children. Women nowadays, established their careers first and had children later.

"Everything in the nursery is yours. I have no use for it."

"Thank you."

Nicole hugged her aunt, picked up the box containing the china head doll. Now, she had to find her way to the basement to collect the boxes down there. Janet was adamant she didn't want the contents or some of the personal things in the house. She would need help to get the stuff out of the house and back to her place. Her car or Cooper's SUV wasn't big enough. She might have to enlist Mitch's help since he had a truck.

How much of the family history did her father know? All? None? Her aunt's explanation of her father's relationship with his parents explained why they had never visited. Nicole would have remembered that house. So would her brothers. Being there on the weekend was a first for the three of them.

"My aunt has some things in her storage locker she wants me to take away," she said at the reception desk.

"I'll call her and confirm that."

"I have the key."

"I still need her confirmation."

"All right then." Nicole leaned on the counter while she waited for the confirmation to come through. When it did, the receptionist led the way to the elevator that went to the basement.

"It goes right into the storage area. You need the unit number, and that's on the key tag."

Nicole sighed as she stepped into the lift. Her aunt's unit was number thirty. With any luck, it would be close to the elevator, and she could load up and head back to her apartment.

The numbers were on the ends of the units with the lockers in that row. Nicole located the one her aunt's storage was in and strode down the aisle. Two boxes sat side by side in the cage, bearing the proper number. She unlocked the door and entered. The containers weren't huge, but as she found out when she got the ones from her parents' storage, paper was heavy. She struggled to lift the first box, feeling the weight in her arms and back, and carried it to the elevator, then returned for the second.

It was about the same size, but heavier than the first. How much did secrets weigh? Judging by the weight of these two boxes, quite a bit. She hefted it up and out, then returned and locked the door. With both boxes in the lift with her, and the box containing the china head doll, she rode back to the main floor, unloaded them into the lobby, and handed over the key. A sense of relief washed over her. She had completed the task.

"You'll see that my aunt gets that back?" She asked as she handed it over the counter.

"Yes."

"I'm leaving those there while I bring my car to the front door."

Back at her apartment building, Nicole struggled to get the two heavy boxes up into her apartment. When she stacked them on the floor in the hallway next to the ones her father had given her, she sighed. She still had those to finish going through. The doll might not have come from her aunt, but it was part of the Graham family's belongings. Nicole made herself comfortable and opened the first of the enormous boxes she brought home from the assisted living facility. She pulled out a yellowed, brittle newspaper first. With the utmost care, so she didn't damage it, Nicole unfolded it and laid it flat on her dining room table.

Brighton Ensign
November 15, 1917
LOCAL HERO KILLED IN ACTION AT PASSCHENDAELE
Private Robert Holbrook's Bravery Shines in the Face of Adversity

Brighton, Ontario — *It is with deep sorrow and profound respect that we report the death of Private Robert Holbrook, a beloved son of Brighton, killed in action during the brutal Battle of Passchendaele on October 29, 1917.*

Private Holbrook, aged 29, a 4th Canadian Infantry Battalion member, served with distinction on the Western Front. His family, friends, and the entire community, including each one of us, mourn his loss and celebrate his extraordinary courage and sacrifice.

In the heat of battle, Private Holbrook distinguished himself through acts of valour that are the hallmark of true heroism. Eyewitnesses report he demonstrated exceptional bravery while leading his comrades through intense enemy fire, providing critical support and saving the lives of several fellow soldiers. His leadership and selflessness were instrumental in a key engagement, making a significant impact despite the overwhelming odds. His bravery is a source of inspiration and pride for us all.

The Canadian government has announced they will posthumously award Private Holbrook the Victoria Cross, the highest military honour, for his gallantry and unwavering dedication to duty. The medal will be presented to his widow, Mrs. June Holbrook, in a ceremony to be held in Brighton at a later date.

Private Holbrook is survived by his widow, June Holbrook, and their young son. The family appreciates the support and condolences offered by the community during this difficult time.

A memorial service will be held on November 17 at the Presbyterian Church, Main Street, Brighton. We invite family, friends, and citizens to pay their respects and honour the memory of this fallen hero.

All who knew him will remember with pride and gratitude private Holbrook's sacrifice and by the nation he served with such honour.

In Memoriam: *Private Robert Holbrook, a genuine hero whose bravery and sacrifice will never be forgotten.*

Nicole read and re-read the article. The man was a war hero and received the Victoria Cross. But how did this Robert Holbrook fit into their family? Or did he?

Chapter Twenty-Five

MAY 27, 1916

As promised, Heinrich and Mathilde waited at the small station in St. Jacobs to meet them off the train. It had been years since Valter had seen his cousin and had never met his wife. She was plump and ample bosomed with dark brown hair, which we wore in braids and wrapped over her head. Heinrich's hair had thinned and greyed, but he still sported a trimmed, albeit grey, moustache. These unique physical traits made them instantly recognizable to Valter.

"Valter, excellent to see you again," Heinrich exclaimed as he embraced his cousin.

"Please, I go by Wilhelm now. It's too confusing with a son named Walter. Getting Ute to call me that is proving problematic. She still insists on Valter."

"It will take time, cousin. It will take time." He drew Val ... Wilhelm into another hug. "Mathilde, you remember my cousin from Wiesbaden? He also ran a bakery in Germany."

"Ja. Welcome to our village," she said.

"Ute, come my dear and meet my cousin Heinrich, and his wife, Mathilde."

Valter's wife stepped forward and was instantly hugged by Heinrich's wife.

He introduced his two sons last. "It's been ten years since this one was born, and I still haven't gotten Ute to call me Wilhelm. She pronounces our names slightly differently, and that's the only way we know which of us she wants — for good or bad." He chuckled.

"Come, you must be weary from all your travels. We'll take you home and get you settled," Mathilde said.

Chapter Twenty-Six

NOVEMBER 25, 2022

When Nicole arrived home, she debated how to tell her brothers what she had discovered since her visit with their aunt. As far as Nicole knew, only her father, her aunt, and now she were the only ones who knew. After all, it was part of their family history, too, and she felt a deep sense of responsibility to share this with them. After all, Connor and Cooper had a right to know that they were the line of that family the house belonged to.

It wasn't something you could send in a text message. It needed to be said in person with the facts in front of you. This weekend? It would be possible depending on how long it took to clear the things out of the house. If not, then next week.

Nicole decided to send a text to Mitch and ask him for his help. She hadn't spoken to him since they had gone to the Graham mansion together. He was busy during the day working on the repairs at the house where the bathtub fell through the floor.

Saw my aunt this past Saturday. She wants me to go clean out pictures, letters, anything but dishes and furniture. Can you help me? My car isn't big enough.

If Mitch agreed, it might take them the entire weekend to remove the contents, depending on how much stuff was there. Her aunt never mentioned the dagger. It wasn't furniture or dishes, so it would be hers to remove if she found it again. Her mind raced with the mystery of the dagger, its potential significance, and the fear of what it might represent. What if the rust on the blade wasn't rust at all, but blood and someone had committed a murder? Now she was letting her imagination run wild.

Her phone pinged, pulling her out of her ruminations.

Tomorrow? Sunday? Both?

Not knowing how much was in the house, Nicole didn't know what to tell Mitch. It wasn't like she had opened all the closets and dresser drawers. If they got away early in the morning, they might get it done in one day. And if not, then it would have to be both.

Start tomorrow and see where we are at the end of it?

Nicole didn't want Mitch to think she was taking advantage of him. She'd have to make it up to him somehow. Dinner and a movie? She'd have to go one better than ordering pizza. She'd have to cook, a gesture of her sincerity and goodwill towards Mitch.

Removing the things from the mansion would take most of the weekend. Where did Nicole plan to store them? She lived in a cozy, one-bedroom apartment, with small rooms. The living room, dining room, and hallway surrounded the galley kitchen. He had never seen the bedroom, so he had did not know its size. Was there a storage room in her building? If so, some of the things could be stored there. She still had boxes in her hall that came from her parents' storage locker.

Mitch would offer to store some of the things at his apartment, but with blueprints and a huge drafting table and models of houses he'd like to build, he didn't have the room.

His stomach growled. He'd worked hard all week, and hadn't eaten properly. Just what he could grab on the go. He walked to his fridge and stood in front of the open door. This weekend should be spent getting groceries. The cupboards resembled Mother Hubbard's. Mitch opened the freezer door. A couple of large frozen dinners languished inside. Fettuccini Alfredo or Mac and

Cheese. Which did he have the taste for tonight?

Mitch decided on the Alfredo dish. As he put it in the microwave, his house guest joined him and wound herself around Mitch's legs. The black cat let out a chirp, a cross between a meow and a bird's peep, telling him an empty food dish needed to be filled.

Once Mitch started his dinner, he took out one of the fancy pouches of cat food provided by Mrs. Anderson and filled the demanding feline's bowl.

Chapter Twenty-Seven

NOVEMBER 15, 1917

Frantic knocking on the front door sent June running. Her first thought was to reach the door before the racket woke William. He had just gone down for his nap, and she hoped the noise didn't disturb him.

"What's wrong?" she asked, holding the screen door open.

"Mrs. Holbrook. I'm sorry. You need to see this," Stanley Buell, the general store owner, said as he handed her the latest edition of the Brighton Ensign.

"Local Hero Killed in Action at Passchendaele," she read the headline aloud. The news hit her like a physical blow, her thoughts immediately going to Robert.

The subheading confirmed her fears.

June's knees buckled under the weight of the news. If Stanley had not grabbed her, she would have fallen. He helped her from the door to the sofa in the living room.

Why had she wished Robert dead? She didn't mean it. Did she? She was angry and hurt. Perhaps, they might have worked things out if he'd come home to her? Now, she'd have to live with the knowledge she had wanted her husband to be killed in action. The weight of her own conflicting emotions was crushing her.

Chapter Twenty-Eight

Although the Graham mansion trip was a retrieval day, Nicole still packed her cameras and sketchbooks. There was always the chance that something or someone would manifest themselves.

She climbed into her small hatchback. The anticipation of visiting Mitch's apartment gave her goosebumps. Nicole had never been to his place and was anxious to see it. Anytime they did anything together, he always came to her flat. When they were younger and still living at home, she'd been to Kane's house several times — on her own and with her brothers.

After she pulled up to the curb, she exited the car, grabbed her backpack from the hatch, and locked the vehicle. The building Mitch lived in was at least ten stories. Her brothers' building a baby by comparison, being only three floors, the same as hers, but hers was a one down, two up.

Nicole entered the lobby, found the button for Mitch's apartment, and pressed it. A few minutes later, he buzzed her past the security doors. Because of the number of floors, two elevators were in line with the entrance. She pressed the up button, and the doors to the one on the right opened.

Mitch lived on the top floor. When Nicole stepped off the elevator, she looked left and right, trying to determine where she needed to go. The decision was made for her when Mitch stuck his head into the hall. To her surprise, a fluffy, black cat darted into the corridor from inside Mitch's home and trotted to meet her.

Without appearing too eager, Nicole took a deep breath and strode towards the flat. She bent down and picked up the cat as she walked down the corridor. Once inside, she noticed the contrast between her cozy apartment and Mitch's spacious living-dining room kitchen area. Her entire flat would fit inside this one room.

"When did you get a cat?" she asked.

"Looking after it for someone," he said, closing the door behind her. "It's a she, and her name is Raven."

"That's a perfect name." Nicole placed the animal on the floor and took in her surroundings.

The dining room table was the only place in this part of Mitch's home that looked unkempt. A laptop sat open, surrounded by rolls of paper. Plans?

"Sorry about the mess," Mitch said, scooping a bundle of the rolled blueprints off the table and onto a sideboard.

"You're fine. You don't need to move them for me."

"I'll give you the fifty-cent tour if you're interested," Mitch replied. "This is ..." He didn't get a chance to say anymore.

"Oh my God, the view!" Nicole stood at the sliding doors, which led to a small balcony.

"Do you want to go out?" He unlocked the door, pushed it aside, and did the same with the screen. "After you." He stamped his foot to deter the cat from following them outside.

Nicole stepped through the opening first. Mitch pulled the sliding door shut. The waterfront was close by. Boats bobbed up and down on the waves in the harbour.

"You must love waking up to this every day," she gushed. "All I see is the house across the street and the junk car in the driveway."

She could wake up to this daily if he and Nicole became an item. He didn't dare say it out loud. They had a wonderful friendship and an excellent rapport. The worst thing he could do was suggest that the two get together and that she move in. That would end their friendship. And not just with her, but with her brothers, too. But where Cooper was involved, that ship already sailed.

"I hate to break this up, but if we're going to the Graham house to retrieve the stuff your aunt said you can take, we should get moving. Besides, it looks like it might rain."

"You're right. The sooner we're done, the sooner we're home, and I can go through everything. I already have two boxes from my aunt's storage at her assisted living place. I've just gotten started, but Robert Holbrook, who received the Victoria Cross, might be the Robert who had an affair with the German woman."

The expression on Mitch's face told Nicole she hadn't brought him up to speed. He only knew about the first letter. The one that languished in the box containing the china head doll.

"One letter with the doll, he'd actually written to his wife," she said.

Mitch furrowed his brow.

"Yes. The soldier put it in an envelope addressed to the German woman, Ute, but the letter was to June, his wife. I'm hoping that Aunt Janet has the letter that he sent home by mistake. Can you imagine the shock of opening a letter in an envelope addressed to you and finding one written to someone else?"

"Sounds like Robert bit off more than he could chew." Mitch put his arm around Nicole's shoulders, and they left his apartment.

"I've never seen either woman's handwriting, but I wonder if the sympathy card I found came to June from the other woman? It is possible. No signature and no envelope to offer any clues."

"Probably burned. Back then, people had burn barrels on their property and incinerated their garbage, or a wood stove in the kitchen."

"I suppose you've come across these things when

you work on old houses."

"I've seen a few rusty 45-gallon drums in back yards. One place, someone was burning something when I arrived."

What if the documents she hoped to find had been burned? The potential loss of important papers added to her concern. She had proof the house belonged to her ancestors and had been passed down to her aunt rather than her father. But, she still hadn't proven that the Robert in the letters was a Holbrook. If those papers were destroyed, she might never know.

"Did your aunt give you anything in writing stating you have permission to remove things from the house?"

"No. Should she have?"

"Just thinking that if anyone sees us taking things, they might call the police."

"Never thought of that."

The elevator doors opened, and they stepped in. Mitch pushed the button to take them to the underground parking. Soon, they arrived in the garage. Despite the overhead lights, it stayed dark and full of shadows. It didn't bother Mitch. He'd become used to it. Nicole had never been in his building. She sidled towards him as they walked towards his truck.

When they reached it, Mitch pressed the unlock button on his key fob. "Any idea how much stuff is in the place your aunt said you could take?"

"No. Just anything other than dishes or furniture. I asked Aunt Janet if she would let me have the rocking horse, and she told me I could have everything in the nursery," Nicole said, climbing into the passenger seat. "I have no idea where I'm going to put it. I'll have to rent a storage space with everything from my father and mother's locker. You saw all those boxes stacked up in my apartment. And with what we could be taking out today?"

"I remember the stacks of boxes you had lined up along the wall in your hallway."

"I still haven't gone through all of them. I stopped

when I found the pedigree chart and discovered that my mother descended from the Kemblefords who owned the manor house and lumber mill."

Mitch pulled away, and the tires squealed on the cement floor. It didn't matter how he sped up; they made a noise.

"When we get there, where do you want to start? Top and work down, or bottom and work up. It's up to you. I'll park closer than last weekend, so we don't have to cart the stuff as far."

"Thanks, Mitch. I don't fancy walking any great distance carrying heavy boxes."

"No problem, Nicole. I wouldn't want you to hurt yourself."

Chapter Twenty-Nine

Ute checked the newspapers every day since their arrival in Canada for fallen Canadian soldiers. It had been her hope Robert wasn't one of them. But today, her heart was shattered when she read through the list of soldiers killed in action. Robert Holbrook. There was no mistaking him since a picture of him accompanied the article. The article went on to say that at a later date, he was to be presented with the Victoria Cross for his heroic actions, a public recognition that blatantly contrasted with Ute's personal loss.

She dropped onto the chair at the kitchen table, placed her head on her folded arms, and wept. Her Robert. The man who swept her off her feet that night in Lützkampen, a memory now overshadowed by the war's cruelty. Too many good men died. So far, she'd kept the china head doll he'd given her after their night of passion in the hay mow hidden. His letters to her were tucked away in the papers under the doll, a constant reminder of the life she once had and the one she was now forced to live.

Her sons rushed into the room for breakfast, so she hastily folded the newspaper, dried her eyes, and greeted them with a forced smile. She hoped they didn't notice she'd been crying. Once she had them fed and on their way to school, Ute planned to hide away in the loft and re-read the letters from Robert. The ones filled with so much passion. The promise of a life other than drudgery, her current fate.

Chapter Thirty

A little over half an hour later, Mitch pulled into the driveway at the rear of the property. Nicole stared at the back of the house. Something looked different. Like something had changed since her last visit. But what?

Despite Mitch's driving with care over the rough terrain, working his way towards the house at a snail's pace, she got jostled in her seat; making her happy, she had fastened her seatbelt. When he approached the back door, he turned the truck around and backed the rest of the way toward it.

Whatever was off here today, Nicole was glad she'd brought her camera and sketchbook.

Mitch had already exited the truck and stood, holding the passenger door open for her. He held out his hand for her to make it easier to get out.

"We'll be able to walk straight from the top step onto the truck bed. No extra climbing," Mitch said. "I've got a rope in the toolbox to tie the stuff down."

Nicole started up the steps. Suddenly, a faint rustle from inside the house caught her attention. Her heart skipped a beat, and a startled squeak escaped from her lips.

"What's wrong?" Mitch asked.

"I thought I saw someone or something inside."

Mitch stepped ahead of her and opened the screen door. Someone had fixed it since their last visit. Had Janet called someone to secure the house since

Nicole had told her about exploring it?

The inside door opened, its hinges creaking in a way that sent shivers down Nicole's spine.

"Hello? Is anyone here?" Mitch's voice echoed through the empty house, a comforting sound amid her unease.

"Stay here. I'm going to take a quick look around. Make sure it's safe." He entered the kitchen. No one inside. He checked the dining room and the living room on his right. The same result. Even the utility room and the two large adjoining rooms on the left. The pocket doors remained open.

If anyone lurked in here, they had to have gone upstairs. They'd be trapped if they did with Mitch and Nicole downstairs. "It's safe. You can come in," he shouted.

Nicole was at his side in minutes.

"Do you remember where Connor hit the wall by the pocket doors to open them?"

"No, why?"

"Just thinking if it somehow closes when we're in that room, it would be nice to know where the switch is to open it."

"Are you trying to spook me, Mitchell Kane?"

"No. Sorry. Just thinking of all contingencies."

"Let's do that room first. Get it over with. I want the painting over the fireplace."

Mitch walked into the grand room and tried to remove the imposing portrait that hung over the fireplace. It wouldn't budge. Someone or something fastened the painting in place with super glue. While he thought of how to remove the piece without damaging it, he cast his eyes downward. An old photograph lay on the grate, curled like it had been burned, but with no trace of fire damage on it.

"Nicki, was there a picture in the fireplace when we were here the last time?"

"No, why?"

Mitch handed the image to her.

"This is the picture in the mirror's frame in the

tower room. I'm sure of it. It's identical to the portrait."

Mitch, a staunch disbeliever in the supernatural, struggled to find a rational explanation for the photograph's inexplicable relocation. With his skepticism tested, he found himself on the edge of belief.

"Put it back, please. I want to capture it where you found it. I have the images from when we found it in the mirror frame in the tower room."

She was determined to document the scene and capture every detail. Mitch returned the photograph to its original place, and Nicole recorded the area with her phone's camera and DSLR, pencil, and paper.

A chill ran up Nicole's spine. Something was going on in the house. A former occupant who didn't want to see things removed so shifted them around to scare them? Other than Aunt Janet, her father, and her grandfather, the soldier and his wife, no one else lived here. At least no one connected to her family that she was aware of.

The rustling sound she'd heard before they came into the house was louder now. Nicole froze. What was in here? Her heart pounded in her chest so hard she thought it might explode. The noise stopped. One of the curtains on the windows at the porch twitched. Something big and brown flew towards them. She ducked.

"That was your rustling sound. Nothing to be afraid of, just a bat," Mitch said.

"How did it get in? And has it been inside all along?" Nicole ran her fingers through her hair. Tales of bats swooping and getting tangled in people's hair came to mind and she shivered.

"It's an old house. It could have come down a chimney, up from the cellar. They don't need a big opening," Mitch said.

His explanation of how the bat entered the house did nothing to soothe Nicole's frazzled state. If things weren't bad enough, the chandelier hanging from the Freemason ceiling medallion began to shake, the crystals tapping against the neighbouring ones. It started like someone had opened a window, and the breeze blew inside. From where Nicole stood, the windows were all closed. The vibrating became more violent.

"Look out, Mitch," she yelled.

He raised his head towards the ceiling and stepped back into the opening between the rooms. As soon as he did, the shaking stopped, bringing a sudden sense of relief to the tense atmosphere.

"That was weird," he said. "I can't get that portrait to budge. I tried."

Nicole walked over to the fireplace and reached for the painting. It moved, but she was too short, and it was too heavy for her to remove. "I need help," she said

Mitch took the sides of the frame in his hands, and it lifted off the hook with ease. "I swear, Nicki, it wouldn't budge when I tried before. I'll take it out and put it in the truck's backseat right now." As he carried the painting out, Nicole couldn't shake off the feeling that somebody or something watched them, something that didn't want the painting to be removed.

Nicole followed him to the hallway and watched him go out the backdoor. The lock beeped and Mitch returned.

They walked back into the room and searched the drawers in the side tables, but they were empty. There was nothing else in that room other than the small photograph. The framed wedding photo that had been on the mantle had vanished since Nicole's last visit here. It was as if it had been there one moment and gone the next, leaving no trace of its disappearance. Where would it turn up?

Nicole opened every desk drawer in the room where she first found the framed marriage certificate and the unsigned sympathy card. Most were empty, but some contained papers. "We need a box. You haven't seen one, have you, Mitch?"

"No. I didn't bring any either. Might be some in the room off the kitchen. I'll go check."

Once again, Nicole stood alone in the room. A chill came over her. In front of the fireplace, a translucent shape of a woman with blonde hair formed, startling Nicole. First, the bat and now a ghost. What else could happen on this visit? Was this June? The mother of the little boy in the nursery? The bride of Robert Holbrook, from the marriage certificate she found online?

Nicole stood transfixed on the apparition that materialized in front of her. She needed to document it, before it vanished, but she was still on edge from the bat flying towards her. She backed away, her eyes still focussed on the ghost and slowly pulled her sketchbook and pencils out of her backpack. Mitch would be back shortly with boxes and she wanted to finish before he returned.

She had just finished drawing when he returned with a wooden crate that once held apples, according to its lettering. As he did, the ghost in front of the fireplace dissolved, leaving Nicole bewildered and with a growing need for answers.

"This is all I found," he said, walking around the desk. "What's this?" He pointed to her sketch.

"She stood in front of the fireplace. I think she's the one in the wedding photograph that has mysteriously disappeared. When you came back with the box, she vanished."

Mitch wanted to believe Nicole. He had seen nothing weird at Kembleford Manor, yet Nicole had encountered many experiences with ghosts on that trip. And now this. Yet, the sketch was right in front of him. She had seen something.

He sat the box on the desk beside Nicole's sketchbook. She placed the papers she'd taken from the drawers inside.

"That's weird," she said. "When I came here with my brothers, I unlocked the centre drawer of this desk, but it's locked again. It doesn't make sense."

"Are you sure you didn't lock it again afterwards?"

"No. It was hard enough to get it opened with a nail file. I wasn't going to attempt to secure it again."

"Move over and let me have a go at it." Mitch fiddled with it without success. Then he took a zippered leather bag from his pocket and opened it.

"Lock-picking tools? You brought lock-picking tools?"

"In my line of work, sometimes you need to get into locked rooms and the owners don't know where they put the keys. This is the best way to gain access."

"But if you got caught with them while exploring, the police would charge you with more than just trespassing. You would end up going to jail."

Nicole had a point. He rarely carried them with him on explorations. Mitch rarely carried them at all unless a homeowner couldn't gain access to a room. Then he'd bring them the next time he worked at their house.

The drawer opened. A silver fountain pen with an ornate design engraved on it, a short, square bottle of ink, some more miscellaneous papers sat inside, along with something jammed way at the back. Mitch reached in as far as he could, but his arm was too big to fit through the narrow opening.

"Here, Nicki, you give it a go. There's something back there, but I can't reach it. I can see it, but that's it."

Nicole reached in and had her arm inside the drawer, almost up to her shoulder. "It feels like paper. I don't want to pull on it in case I rip it." She pulled her arm out and rubbed it where the front edge had cut into her. "Try wiggling the drawer in and out. If we're lucky, what's stuck will fall out the back and land on the floor or inside."

Mitch opened and closed the desk several times, but nothing fell to the floor or into the drawer. "Dammit, why won't you fall out," he cursed the object and moved the drawer more violently, trying to dislodge whatever was stuck over the back.

Chapter Thirty-One

NOVEMBER 29, 1917

Within days of being notified of her husband's death, someone from the military arrived at June's house with Robert's personal effects. Included were his shaving kit, socks, pens and pencils, writing paper, envelopes, and letters from both her and someone else. Were these from the woman he'd had the affair with in Germany?

The ones not written by her all had the same handwriting, and none had a return address. With a resolute stride, June carried the letter packet to the kitchen and fed it to the hungry flames of the wood stove. The accidental revelation of Robert's letter to his lover was distressing enough if it was indeed an accident. June had no intention of subjecting herself to the other woman's words.

June stood with the lid held up by the lifter in her hand and watched the flames consume the paper until it was reduced to ash, an irrevocable act of closure.

Chapter Thirty-Two

NOVEMBER 26, 2022

Nicole thrust her arm into the desk once more, determined to retrieve the object lodged in the back of the drawer. She wiggled it back and forth, refusing to give up until it finally came loose.

When she had her arm out of the drawer, she looked at the object in her hand. "That's the wedding picture from the frame on the mantle. But where's the frame?"

"Don't worry, Nicole. It's got to be around here somewhere," Mitch said, his voice steady and reassuring.

"I'm getting a bad feeling about today. I need you to ditch your lock-picking tools. Don't have them on you. Put them in the bottom of your toolbox. Anywhere. I think we're going to have a visit before we're done."

"What?"

"Just do it, please," Nicole said, her voice firmer than expected.

Mitch disappeared out the door and around the corner.

Nicole hoped the feeling she had was a false alarm, that the police wouldn't visit and perhaps arrest them. If that happened, it would destroy Mitch's business. Who would hire a contractor busted for breaking and entering? She should have come by herself and left him out of it. But even her arrest would affect the business her brothers and she ran. What a mess.

"Nicole? Can you come through to the kitchen?"

Mitch called.

Still gripping the unframed photo, she headed toward his voice.

Nicole's heart dropped when she entered the kitchen to see two police officers standing on either side of Mitch. At least they hadn't handcuffed him — yet. That was a positive, wasn't it?

She took a deep breath and asked, "What can I do for you?" Her voice was steady, despite trembling with fear on the inside.

"You realize you're trespassing on private property," the one said. This cop, a towering figure with a stern expression, was taller than Mitch and heavier. His hair was a reddish shade that looked more light orange, and his eyes bore into Nicole with an unsettling intensity.

"N-no. My aunt asked me to come and clear out anything that wasn't furniture or dishes. Oh, and everything in the nursery." She told the truth. Now did the officer standing in front her believe her. Somehow, she didn't believe he did.

"Hmm, really," the other cop said. He was shorter than the first one, but his demeanour bordered on threatening. He stood with his arms folded across his chest. His dark hair and eyes spooked her. "And you aunt is?"

"Janet Holbrook." Maybe she should have had her aunt give her written permission to be in the house and removing things. The police would still want to get it from Janet, anyway, so it didn't make much difference.

"And if we contacted this alleged aunt, would she back you up?" the taller cop inquired, his tone laced with suspicion.

"Yes, of course she would."

"And do you have a number for her?"

"Sh-she lives in Willow Glen Manor in Belleville," Nicole said, her palms sweating and her heart pounding in her chest. She had the phone number and address of the assisted living home on her phone, if the cops let her access her backpack.

"Come with us. Both of you. We'll wait outside until we can corroborate your stories."

"Mitch, I'm sorry I got you into this mess," Nicole whispered, her voice filled with guilt, as she passed him.

"Don't worry about it. We're here acting on your aunt's instructions. It will turn out okay." He put his arm around her shoulders, and they walked out the back door ahead of the police.

"Willow Glen Manor, you said? We'll get a unit from that detachment to pay a visit now. Ensure there is a resident named Janet Holbrook and she has granted you permission to remove certain items from the house," the darker man said, in a stern tone. "Can we see some identification?"

Mitch removed his wallet and opened it to show his driver's licence.

"And yours?"

"It's in my backpack, but it's in the house," Nicole said. "I can get it for you."

"No. You stay here. Whereabouts in the house?"

"Straight through to the front door, then turn left. It's in one of the two rooms on that side of the house. My wallet and ID are in it."

The taller of the two returned to the house, leaving Mitch and Nicole outside with the snarkier officer.

The red-headed cop returned holding Nicole's backpack at arm's length in front of him like it had something offensive in it. It was all Mitch could do not to laugh at the sight.

"Where is it?"

"Small pocket on the front."

He unzipped the pouch, pulled out her wallet, and opened it. Now that he had returned, the short, dark one walked to the cruiser and spent a few minutes on the radio.

So far, the cops hadn't identified themselves. The insignia on their uniforms looked like legitimate OPP, as did the decals on the car. They wore name tags over the left pocket of their protective vests. Mitch tried to memorize their badge numbers so that if he wanted to make a complaint later, he at least had that information.

"The man we sent to Willow Glen spoke to Janet Holbrook. She said she granted permission for her niece, Nicole Holbrook, to remove everything but furniture and dishes from the house."

"That jives with this one's ID. Doesn't explain the guy, though."

"I needed help and a vehicle larger than my dinky hatchback, so I asked my friend to help me."

Nicole had found her voice, and Mitch hoped she wouldn't find too much of it and land them in deeper trouble.

The two cops turned their backs to them, still possessing their wallets. He and Nicole would be even more FUBAR'd if the police didn't return those things to them.

Dark clouds formed on the horizon. A storm approached from the southwest. If they were to get anything else out of the house today, the police had to return their effects and leave them to it. A streak of lightning flashed across the sky.

As if an omen, the taller two turned around and handed back their things; a wave of relief washed over Mitch.

"Carry on. Sorry about that, but you can never be too sure."

Mitch nodded.

Nicole buzzed with nervous energy. The police had finally departed, allowing them to resume their work.

Neither she nor Mitch dared to move until the police were safely back in their cruiser, and the driveway was empty. The close call had sent shivers down her spine. She'd faced police on properties before but never after gaining entry to the building.

"I'm glad that's over," she said, sighing.

"You okay?"

"I'll be fine. The OPP sent the least personable

cops from the local detachment to check us out. I wonder who called them on us?"

"Hard to say. There aren't a lot of houses along the back road so there had to be someone along the main road in front of the house," Mitch said.

He placed his hand on the small of Nicole's back, and they returned to the rooms they'd been clearing before the interruption.

Nicole was relieved to have Mitch by her side. His calm presence helped her maintain her composure despite the fear that gnawed at her. But when she returned to the room, the photograph she had seen jammed in the back of the desk drawer was nowhere to be found. She searched the floor, the sofa, the desk, but it had vanished. Where did it go?

They still had an entire house to go through, so she couldn't waste much time searching for one photograph. It was bound to turn up somewhere it shouldn't be — like back in the frame where she first saw it

Nicole scanned the mantles in both rooms, table surfaces, and window sills, but found nothing resembling the pewter frame containing the wedding photo on any of them.

The approaching storm cast a shadow over their task, and the threat of rain added urgency to their efforts. They needed to load everything into the truck and cover it with tarps before the storm hit.

Chapter Thirty-Three

NOVEMBER 26, 2022

Nicole started up the main staircase when laughter drifted from above. She stopped where she stood.

"Do you hear that?" she asked when Mitch bumped into her.

"What?"

"Someone is laughing." Nicole took out her phone and started the audio recorder app. From her vantage point, she couldn't see anything other than stairs and walls. She crept forward, not wanting the sound to stop, certain it was the little boy she'd seen on the rocking horse in the nursery.

By the time she reached the top of the stairs, the laughing had stopped, so she paused the recording. That way, if it started again, she could restart the device. Now, a scraping sound reached her ears. Nicole turned the recorder on again, but could not detect where the noise originated. She reached out for Mitch's hand.

When they reached the second level of the house, the grating seemed to emanate behind the door that led to the tower. Nicole tiptoed towards it and put her ear next to it. Nothing. Not even a peep. She turned the knob and pushed, but it wouldn't open.

"Mitch, can you open the door, please? I think it's stuck," she said, stepping aside to give the man access.

"Stand back." He shouldered the door open, and Nicole stepped into the opening. The scraping sound remained audible.

Before she came to the mansion for the first time with her brothers, she swore she would leave if anything untoward happened. Now, Nicole's determination to uncover the source of these strange occurrences was unwavering, no matter how unsettling they were.

With her phone still recording sound, she crept up the spiral stairs, her heart pounding with each step. When she reached the room at the top, the trunk, previously tucked away under the window, now sat in the middle of the room. Drag marks on the dusty floor marked its trail from where it started.

Nicole turned around to call Mitch. She let out a startled yelp when she found herself face-to-face with him.

"Sorry. Didn't mean to scare you," he said.

Nicole patted her chest with her hand. "I'm okay."

Mitch brushed her arms. To him, she was cold, and that was through a couple of layers of thick clothing. He pulled a small but powerful flashlight from his pocket, turned it on, and concentrated the beam on and behind the chest. The drag marks from the wall to where the trunk sat were noticeable.

Nicole pulled her sketchbook out of her backpack and began drawing the room. It was quiet now. Was that because the two of them were in there? While she drew and took pictures, he walked over to the trunk, his curiosity piqued. The catches and latch released, and he lifted the lid, eager to uncover its secrets.

Tucked away inside lay the framed wedding certificate Nicole said she found in the desk downstairs, and the anonymous sympathy card. Something heavy, wrapped in a blanket, lay in there, too. Mitch picked it up and unwrapped the bundle. The dagger. The discovery of these items only deepened the mystery of this place.

The mirror hung on the wall where it had been previously. The small picture of the soldier presumably used to paint the portrait over the fireplace was tucked inside the frame. Mitch took them off the wall and laid them inside the trunk. Nicole's Aunt Janet had said everything but furniture and dishes, except for the nursery.

Getting the thing downstairs from here would not be easy. The first obstacle was the spiral staircase. But Mitch was determined. Between the two of them, they could do it. He'd seen bigger ones — the one at Kembleford Manor was enormous compared to this one.

Mitch closed the lid and secured it. He then picked it up by the handles on each end. It wasn't too heavy, not light by any means, but manageable.

"How do you want to get the dress form downstairs and into the truck?" Mitch asked, his voice echoing in the silent room.

Nicole walked to where the dress form clad in an antique gown, and veil stood. "I think it might be easier to get downstairs if it isn't wearing these," she said. "I'm afraid if we try to take it down the way it is now, we'll trip over the fabric and break our necks when we fall down the stairs."

"Agreed." Mitch re-opened the trunk.

The veil came off first. It was easy to remove, revealing a delicate lace pattern. Nicole folded it and laid it on the trunk's contents. The dress proved to be more difficult. It was a voluminous gown, with intricate beadwork and a long train.

"Can you shine your light on this so I can figure out how it's fastened?"

A beam of light illuminated the dummy. Nicole found the buttons on the back, feeling the smooth texture of the fabric under her fingertips. By the time she got them all undone, her fingers cramped. If she ever got married, her dress wouldn't fasten this way. She flexed her fingers and let the dress slide off the figure's shoulders. Once it pooled on the floor, Nicole lifted the mannequin out of the way. She then picked up the gown, folded it, placed it in the trunk with the headpiece, and closed the lid. For now, she didn't latch it. With how dark and dreary this room was, there might be other things up here.

Nicole walked around the perimeter of the tower

room, ducking under the low eaves. Once she satisfied herself that nothing else remained in the room, she latched the trunk.

"Do you think this wedding dress belonged to Robert's bride?" she asked.

"Might be. You found the picture shoved in a desk drawer."

"It doesn't explain where the frame disappeared to, though," she mused, her voice tinged with curiosity.

"Let's get this stuff down to the level below. The spiral staircase is going to be hard to navigate with the trunk. It will take both of us. I'll take the dummy down first, then come back up, and we'll shift the trunk together."

"Okay."

Mitch picked up the mannequin and tucked it under his arm. The base clunked against the railing on the steps with a regular rhythm until he reached the bottom. While he made his way back up the stairs, Nicole pulled her backpack over both shoulders so it was secure for moving the trunk.

"I think I should be the one to go down backwards," Mitch said when he returned to the tower room. "I'll just need you to steady your end, and it should slide down easily."

He dragged it to the head of the spiral staircase, then stepped around it and onto the first step. Mitch tugged on the handle to get the chest moving. The pair moved slowly, but they got it down from the tower between them.

"Anything you want to check out in here? We didn't look that closely," he said.

"Sure. It seemed empty every time I've been through on my way up, but that doesn't mean a thing. I mean, we've found things that I first saw in one place in totally different places today. But first, rest." Nicole dropped onto the trunk's lid.

Mitch didn't think it was strong enough to support both of them, so he squatted with his back against the wall. Chewing and scratching noises sounded behind him. He jumped and turned to face the wall, startled by the sounds.

"What is it?"

"Mice, rats, or squirrels, likely. Maybe even bats. The rooflines on this place are crazy, so they could be having a grand old time in the eaves."

"Right now, I'd prefer them to the unknown."

"You'll have to mention it to your aunt. She'll want to get the pest control people in to trap them and then figure out how they're getting in and get it closed before the snow flies. They don't need a large space to get through, but if they can, so can the rain and snow."

"I'm going to go visit her again, anyway. See if she can make sense of some of the things I've found here and what she'd already boxed up and had in storage at the care home."

"Let's get this stuff down to the truck and we can sweep of the rest of the house before we call it a day."

"Sounds good."

Mitch was ready to leave then, but knew Nicole would want to check for other objects that might or might not relate to her and her family. At least, the next set of stairs was wide and straight. They'd still guide it down the same way they did on the spiral staircase. Once they reached the bottom, he'd pick it up and carry it to the truck. They'd collect the dress form on their pass-through.

"I told you that Robert Holbrook was a war hero, didn't I?" she asked before taking hold of one end of the trunk.

"Sounds familiar." Mitch picked up the other end of the chest, and they started going to the main staircase.

"Anyway, he died in the Battle at Passchendaele and was posthumously awarded the Victoria Cross."

"And how did you find this out?"

"The first thing I found in one box from Aunt Janet was a newspaper clipping. I'm eager to delve back into those boxes and see what else I can uncover." Nicole's mind wandered. "I had searched on Ancestry.ca for the names of the couple on the wedding certificate, and that led me down a fascinating rabbit hole of research. I found Robert's military records online — complete with a line drawing of the man. It's a match for the man in the portrait over the fireplace downstairs which is now in your truck."

"With it only being a line drawing, how can you tell? They're not usually that detailed."

"I showed it to my brothers and they agree it's the same man in each."

"It could be. I haven't seen his military records," Mitch replied.

Nicole detected the doubt in his voice. While she was convinced this Robert Holbrook was an ancestor, he was also the one who had the affair during the Great War. "He spent a night with a woman in Germany. I looked up the name of the village he mentioned. Remember the top letter tucked under the doll. I hope to find more, but I'm unsure how or what I'll find. Better yet, do I want to find?"

"That sounds interesting. His military career, I mean." Mitch repeated the process he used to get down the spiral staircase, and they got the trunk to the main level. "You wait here. I'll be right back."

Mitch grabbed the chest by the end handles and headed for the back door.

A chill came over the room — not unearthly, but the weather outside must have changed. Nicole sat on the bottom step and gazed at the lamp on the newel post. Some things about this house she loved, and others, not so much.

There weren't a lot of pictures on the walls, which she found unusual. A few large mirrors and the portrait over the mantle. Had her aunt removed them when she moved into the house? If so, where had she put them? It would be nice to have a visual to add to the written history Nicole planned to put together. That was another thing to mention to her aunt. Come to think of it, the woman didn't have many pictures in her room at Willow Glen Manor either.

Nicole's mind raced with excitement about what

she might achieve with the lineage on this side of her family tree. And she still hadn't uncovered everything on the Kembleford branch.

Not that the Birkhoefers tied into her family. Or did they? Was there a connection between the two? Did Robert's German lover have a child fathered by him? That thought sent a shiver of excitement down Nicole's spine.

Mitch returned, interrupting her ruminations.

"Final sweep? It's starting to get dark out, so I'd rather get out of here before it's pitch black. We can come back tomorrow," he said. "The storm isn't far off."

"Sure."

Nicole climbed the steps. Inside each room, she scanned the surfaces of dressers, nightstands, and chests of drawers. Nothing in the room where she originally found the dagger. In the room next to it, the handprints remained visible on the windows. There were a few small pictures and statuettes. She opened a wardrobe door, hoping to find a box to put these in, and framed pictures leaned against the back. At least a dozen, if not more. Right before them lay the empty frame that once held the wedding picture.

Not wanting to leave anything to chance, Nicole removed the pictures and laid them on the bed. They were going with her and Mitch today. Same with the compact frame.

"Mitch, can you come here, please?" she called out into the corridor.

When he appeared, she showed him the stack of pictures. "In there," she said, pointing to the open wardrobe.

He didn't say a word, but walked to the bed, picked them up, and headed downstairs with them.

Nicole returned to the nursery, her curiosity piqued. She might get lucky and find a baby book or books that would fill in some blanks for her. There were pictures here on the surfaces and the walls, but not of family. These were prints of the characters from Beatrix Potter's children's books. They could wait for another time.

Nicole opened the drawers and ran her hands through the contents, one by one. They contained bedding, baby clothes, and cloth diapers. She turned to the rocking horse. "I wish you could speak," she said. "I bet you've got a lot of stories to tell."

"Who are you talking to, Nicki?" Mitch asked when he reached the doorway.

"The rocking horse. Do you not agree it would have much to tell if it could speak?"

"I suppose, but it can't. It's wood, metal, and maybe real horse hair."

"Inanimate object. That reminds me. When I explored here with my brothers, I came back upstairs to find a manufacturer's plaque or something on it. I never made it into this room. Something distracted me."

Nicole got on her knees and felt along the underside of the frame. Nothing there. On the sides behind the legs? She rocked it one way and then the other. Still nothing. The front? No. The back? Yes. There it was, on the upper side of the frame behind the horse. The tail obscured it. She took out her camera and photographed it.

"Okay, let's go." She started for the door, but stopped when she spotted something wedged behind the chest of drawers beside the window where the rocking chair sat. Nicole moved the dresser, and a large manilla envelope dropped to the floor. She stooped and picked it up. "Now we can leave."

Mitch secured the tarp over his truck's box to protect larger items that didn't fit in the back seat.

"Nursery tomorrow?" Nicole asked, climbing into the front seat.

He eased in behind the wheel. "Good thing we're doing it over two days. It might take even longer. We'll have to bring boxes. Tomorrow morning, on our way to your aunt's house, we'll swing by my yard. Pretty sure there are boxes there. If not, we'll have to swing by the Anderson house. I'm sure there are boxes there from the new fixtures. We can use them if we need to."

Before they had made it off the property, the rain started. A few fat, random drops splatted against the windshield before it came down steadier. The rain hitting the truck roof was a soothing backdrop to their conversation. It wouldn't be much fun unloading this stuff at Nicole's house in the rain. Still, it could be worse. It could be snowing.

"My car is at your place," Nicole said. "We'll have to get it at some point."

"Stop there first? You drive home and I meet you there to unload this lot?"

"Sure."

The conversation died after they agreed to collect Nicole's car before they unloaded the truck. Mitch let it ride for about five minutes, until he couldn't stand the silence any longer.

"You're awfully quiet. What's up?"

"Thinking," she answered.

"Care to share?"

"Thinking about something my aunt said when I visited her. My father being mad at her because she inherited the house, not him, even though he was older. Apparently, my father and grandfather fought like alley cats. She didn't go into a lot of detail on that topic. But she said the proverbial hit the fan when Dad quit university to marry my mother. She wasn't good enough. It's a mess." Nicole's family history was a tangled web of secrets and resentments, and she was just beginning to unravel it.

Mitch reached over and squeezed her hand. There was one advantage to being an orphan. He didn't have the same dilemma as Nicole. He empathized with her predicament.

"I get the distinct impression that my father doesn't want me looking into this side of the family. When I first mentioned the names Charles Graham and Myrtle Crow, he went funny. I mean, he made some kind of noise and suddenly had to get off the phone. What else am I going to find?"

"Can't help you with that one. Sorry. Do you want to stop at East Side Mario's or Montana's for supper before we pick up your car, go to your place, and we unload this lot?"

"I should be feeding you. Not taking advantage of your friendship. I'll even cook. I just need to know if there's something you don't particularly like."

He hadn't helped Nicole to get a free meal out of the deal. He did it because he wanted to. Because he liked her and they were friends. And that's what friends do for one another. "Either place, I'll park the truck close so we can keep an eye on it."

"I'd rather just go home and get this stuff unloaded and into my apartment. We'll have another full day tomorrow."

That hadn't gone down the way he intended. He only wanted to spend more time with Nicole over food, perhaps drinks. She shot him down big time, leaving him feeling disappointed.

Chapter Thirty-Four

The *Kitchener Daily Record*, the same paper where Ute had found Robert's death reported, had also mentioned his Victoria Cross presentation in a recent article.

Ute had checked and re-checked the train schedules. If she took the afternoon train, she could be in Robert's hometown and in attendance for the ceremony. She had mentioned nothing to the boys or Valter but left a hastily scribbled note and propped it up in the middle of the table where her husband would see it.

She threw a few random items into an overnight bag, along with a black mourning dress and hat. Ute hoped the town of Brighton had hotels where she could stay. With a heavy heart and one last look over her shoulder, she slipped out the back door, her mind torn between her desire to attend the presentation and her guilt about leaving.

The station, a small structure close to their new home, stood like a beacon of hope and uncertainty. Ute walked briskly, her steps echoing her determination, and was at the ticket office in less than ten minutes, ready to face the challenges of her journey.

"Ticket to Brighton, please."

"Which class?"

Ute placed her money on the counter. "How much will this get me?"

"You want one way or return?"

"Wie bitte?"

"Are you coming back to St. Jacobs?"

"Yes."

"Well, this will only get you a third-class ticket." The man took her money and stamped her tickets. "Don't forget, you must change trains in Toronto to reach your destination. Next train leaves in an hour."

Ute's heart sank at that news. The weight of her decision to leave her family behind for a moment was almost unbearable. She had to wait here for that length of time. Valter could find her and stop her by then. She sighed and made her way to a bench on the women's area of the platform, her mind a whirlwind of conflicting emotions.

After a long day in the bakery, Valter returned home exhausted. He looked forward to having his meal ready, so all he'd have to do was come in the house, sit at the table and eat.

Valter and Ute had been married for fourteen years, and their relationship had its ups and downs. But today, something felt off. Valter called into the empty room, expecting to hear Ute's cheerful voice. But he received no response and no aroma cooking food reached his nostrils.

He wandered through the house. "Ute, are you in there?" Valter opened the bedroom door. The room was empty. He checked the boys' shared room as well. No one in there either. The bathroom door was open. The kitchen and living room were one big space and their front and back doors opened into it. He was the only one there. The boys weren't even home. They were at Heinrich and Mathilde's.

Valter slumped at the table, his exhaustion turning into a gnawing worry. Where was Ute? It wasn't like her not being home at this time of day. Had something happened to her? Then he saw the envelope addressed to him in her writing. He snatched it up and tore it open, his heart pounding in his chest.

Dear Valter,

Valter, I'm sorry. I've had to leave. There's something I must do, and it requires me to leave town. I'll be home the day after tomorrow. Kiss the boys goodnight for me. I hope you can forgive me for this sudden departure.

Ute

What sort of nonsense was she talking about? He picked up the newspaper. A Canadian soldier was posthumously being awarded the Victoria Cross in a ceremony tomorrow. Why would that interest her? Then he recalled her strange behaviour after a trip to Lützkampen.

Valter tore their bedroom apart and found a box containing a china head doll in the bottom of the blanket box. He didn't buy it for her. Someone else had. He removed the doll from the box and found letters hidden beneath the tissue paper in the bottom.

He pulled the top letter out and opened the envelope. She'd taken a lover, and he did! That was why she insisted they made love that night. If she fell pregnant, she could make him believe he was the father of the child.

The idea of smashing the doll to pieces was appealing but not satisfying. It would be better to wait for Ute's return and do it in front her.

Chapter Thirty-Five

Darkness had fallen when Mitch pulled the truck into Nicole's apartment building's parking lot. At least the rain had stopped. She arrived in her car a few minutes before him. She showed him where to park, so they didn't have to lug things too far. The trunk was the heaviest and most awkward, followed by the dress form.

Between them, they got the trunk out of the truck's box and to the vestibule in the building. They would unload everything there, where it would stay dry if the rain started up again. Then, it was just a matter of carting the items to Nicole's third-floor apartment.

"You need a hand with her?" Mitch asked, referring to the mannequin.

"I'm fine, but I think her clothing should be dry-cleaned."

"We can stop by one tomorrow and drop it off."

"I don't think they're open on Sundays. No wonder she's so heavy. The entire thing is this metal cage," Nicole said.

"A naked wire woman. I can't look," Mitch said, a chuckle escaping his lips.

"Whatever will the neighbours think? I thought I'd already noticed a curtain or two twitching."

It took a little less than an hour to unload everything from the truck and into the building. Nicole first took some of the smaller items to her apartment and grabbed a garbage bag. Down in the lobby, she removed the dusty wedding attire from the trunk and put it into the bag.

The paintings found in the wardrobe upstairs were stacked on one another, so Nicole carried them upstairs in one trip. Mitch carried the large portrait of the soldier that hung over the fireplace in the Freemason's room. Soon, only the trunk and the metal mannequin remained. The trunk took precedence, since it required two people — one on each end.

"Ready, Nicki? I'll go first and you can bring up the rear?"

"Sure." Nicole grabbed the handle on one end of the trunk while Mitch took the other.

They paused at each landing. It was much easier to take it downstairs than up. Once it was in her apartment, only the dress form remained in the lobby.

Mitch disappeared and reappeared a few minutes later with it tucked under his arm. "Where do you want her?"

"Not sure. Just stick her in the corner for now. I'll figure out where to put her after."

He sat the mannequin down and started for the door.

"Thanks for all your help, Mitch. You've been a star. It's not that I don't want to have a meal with you. But I foisted myself and all this work on you, I think the least I can do is make you a meal."

"Same time tomorrow?" he asked, ignoring her food comment. "I'll pick you up here to save you driving over to my place."

"Okay. Thanks again." Nicole stood on her tiptoes and planted a gentle kiss on Mitch's cheek.

What was it with Nicole? He hadn't planned on wining and dining with her and taking her back to his to see his etchings. If that happened, it would be because she initiated it. Not him.

He debated blowing the horn when he drove away, but decided against it since it was getting late. He didn't draw any unnecessary attention. She stood inside the main door of her building and waved as he drove by.

Mitch didn't fancy a meal for just one person at the two restaurants he had suggested on their return to Belleville. He'd go through a drive-thru at one of the fast-food places and grab something.

When he got home, Raven ran to meet him. She rubbed around his legs and didn't hiss, although he returned well past her dinner time. He put his Tim Horton's bag on the counter and tended to the cat.

Being an animal owner was never something Mitch gave any thought to. With the long hours he put in at some job sites, it didn't seem fair. But when things didn't go as smoothly as he hoped at the Anderson house, and she had to move out, he offered to home the cat. Mrs. Anderson had gone to stay with her sister over in Trenton and couldn't take Raven with her. He never pried as to the reason. Allergies? Already had animals in the home? It wasn't any of his business. But he couldn't leave Raven behind. He now had a cat and, with it, a growing sense of responsibility.

At this time of night, Mitch hadn't bothered getting coffee. He'd be up all night if he drank one. He opened the fridge and pulled out a beer but returned it without opening it. Instead, grabbed a bottle of water to wash down his two Ham and Cheddar sandwiches.

He walked to the living room, turned on the television, and ate supper.

Nicole surveyed the stack of things she and Mitch had brought upstairs to her apartment. She should start sorting it out. No, that would have to wait. She still had some things of her mother's and the boxes she retrieved from her aunt's storage locker at the assisted living facility. She had already looked at the one box from there. She found the newspaper article about Robert Holbrook being a war hero.

There had to be a secret in her father's past that he didn't want her to find. His sister hadn't told her much, beyond the dynamics between her father and grandfather. And it might be, as a young boy, he asked too many questions, and the secrets went back a long way.

Reading the letters in the box with the china head doll, Nicole discovered Robert had an affair with a German woman. Did she have a child and go after the Holbrook family for support for her and the offspring.

The envelope. The one wedged behind the dresser. Would she be lucky and find a clue in it? Where did she put it? She opened the trunk. Not there. The wooden apple crate. Not there, either. Nicole checked her backpack. There lay the package she wanted.

She turned on the lamp at the end of the sofa and sat. The flap was securely glued in place. Nicole would have to slice the end to get into it. She headed to the kitchen and returned with a paring knife. The blade's point allowed her to get under a small gap. Easing it a bit more, she sliced it across with the sharp edge against the end of the envelope.

Before she dumped the contents onto her coffee table, she wondered what treasures she would find. With what little fell out, she was disappointed. One object was a box, like one for a piece of jewellery, similar to a watch or bracelet. It was a dark colour — deep purple. Nicole lifted the lid and gasped. It was Robert's Victoria Cross. A certificate from its presentation to his widow was also in the envelope. Other medals, too. All together on ribbons on what appeared like a long, thin safety pin.

Not knowing much about them, she picked up her phone and searched for them. She discovered the Victory Medal, the British War Medal, and the 1914-1915 Star. Nicole wondered about the presentation to the widow of the Victoria Cross, but assumed the other medals would have been handed over simultaneously. Or possibly the army gave them to her when they notified June of his death? Or did his widow stash these things away because she couldn't look at them? The answer to that might never be known. The important fact was she had them in her possession.

Chapter Thirty-Six

NOVEMBER 27, 2022

Mitch woke to a heavy weight on his chest. When he opened one eye, a bright green one returned his stare. Raven sat on his chest and kneaded her paws in the blanket. Crazy cat. He glanced towards the alarm clock. He hadn't bothered to set it the night before because he always rose early, especially since he brought Mrs. Anderson's cat home.

"Come on then, Raven. Let's get you some breakfast," Mitch said, moving the feline from his chest and sitting up. Talking to a cat. What next?

Once he had Raven fed and a pot of coffee started, he headed for the bathroom. The hot water cascaded over him as he stood in the shower, the steam rising and enveloping him in a comforting warmth.

Mitch returned to the kitchen with a large towel wrapped around his waist. The dark roast he started earlier had finished brewing. He poured himself a mug and headed off to get dressed. Just past five o'clock. He had plenty of time to drink this coffee, get dressed, and have another and something for breakfast before heading over to pick up Nicole.

They were clearing out the nursery today. That rocking horse was apt to be heavy. The rest of the furnishings, not so much, as long as they emptied them first and put the contents in boxes. Perhaps, if Nicole hadn't already put some from her parents' storage locker out in the recycling, she'd have a few to add to the stack. Mitch was ready for the day, anticipating the tasks ahead with excitement.

Nicole waited downstairs in the lobby for Mitch to pick her up. After her findings the previous night, she found it hard to sleep. Excitement had coursed through her. She found answers to some of her questions. Robert never made it back to Canada to meet his son. Did he manage to meet again with his German woman?

Nicole found a match when comparing Robert's service number on the Victoria Cross certificate to the one on the Canadian Expeditionary Force records. This proved that the two men were one and the same.

With the house now in Janet's hands, Nicole felt a sense of urgency to continue her research on Ancestry.ca. She needed to find her grandfather's birth date, hoping it wasn't too recent to be excluded from the records.

Nicole had woken early so she was ready when Mitch arrived to pick her up. She didn't want to keep him waiting. After all, he was giving up his time to help her. A few minutes after she arrived in the building's lobby, he pulled into the parking lot. She raced to his truck and waited at its side before the man even brought it to a stop.

"I've got it. I've got it," she babbled.

"Slow down. You're not making any sense."

Nicole climbed into the passenger seat. "I have Robert Holbrook's Victoria Cross. Some of his other medals and the certificate from the presentation of the medal to his wife. The military records I downloaded and the service number on the other document confirm it's the same man."

"I'd love to see the medals sometime. That's quite the bit of history you've uncovered."

"I found them in the envelope wedged behind the tall dresser in the nursery. I barely slept last night from the excitement of finding them. We might find other things, too. I'm so close to proving this man is a relative ..."

"Don't get too excited and ahead of yourself."

"You don't get it. Aunt Janet inherited the house.

My father is her brother and has never gotten along with his parents. There's just that gap in the middle I have to figure out. I hope there's more in the boxes I picked up from my aunt."

"Have you found anything interesting in the boxes you got from your father?"

"They were all Mummy's things. I still don't buy the china head doll coming from there thing. But there's no other logical explanation."

"Possibly not. But I'm sure you'll get it all figured out in time," Mitch said. "By the way, do you have any empty boxes from what you got from the storage locker?"

"No. Why?"

"It would be easier to remove the furniture if we emptied it first. No worries, I'll swing by the yard first and the Anderson house. I'm sure there are some at both."

Nicole settled back into the passenger seat. Mitch was right. She was getting carried away. She turned to him to say something, but no words came out. Why didn't she speak? It was so unlike her to be at a loss for words.

Their first stop was the yard. At first glance, it looked like the back of any building supply store with the shed and wood stacked inside.

Mitch climbed out of the truck and unlocked the gate. Storage containers lined one side of the property and he steered towards them.

"I'll only be a sec," he said, exiting the truck.

Nicole watched him unlock the first one and close it almost as quickly. The next one proved more satisfactory. He locked up and returned to the truck with three boxes.

"Next stop, the Anderson house. Unfortunately, those few boxes aren't going to get us very far.

Soon, he pulled the truck into a sweeping driveway. The house took Nicole's breath away. It was gorgeous. This couldn't be the place where the floor and ceiling caved in. It looked too pristine for something of that nature to happen.

"I'll just be a minute," Mitch said, putting the truck in park. "I'll leave it running so you'll have heat."

"Okay."

Nicole leaned back in the seat, her mind consumed with the puzzle of her family tree. She had made it her mission to find her elusive relatives on her father's side. Robert and June had a son, William. Fact. He obviously had children because her grandfather had the surname Holbrook. Or did whoever William marry already have a child? That would explain the friction between that man and her father.

Without her computer and Internet access, she could do nothing on that front. She could log in to Ancestry using her phone, but that small screen would make it difficult to view anything. She should think about where she was putting the furniture from the nursery.

She would put the rocking horse in front of her living room window. It was too special to be shut away in a bedroom. Chest of drawers? Her bedroom. Rocking chair? Someplace where the rockers wouldn't be sticking out, so people didn't get hurt if they hit them. Corner of the dining room, perhaps? The table and chairs moved towards the living room.

Mitch interrupted her thoughts when he opened the back door and tossed boxes on the seat.

"Let's go get this done," Mitch said, fastening his seatbelt. He put the truck in gear, and they pulled away from the Anderson house.

"I can't believe a house this beautiful would have the problems you mentioned," Nicole remarked, glancing at the elegant facade of the Anderson house.

"Water can do a lot of damage, and sometimes you don't realize there's a problem until it's too late. That's what happened here, supposedly."

"You mean she didn't notice the wet spot covering the ceiling in the room?"

"I don't think she used that room often. The plumbing is old, and the water pressure the pits, so I doubt she would have even noticed the leak."

"And you have her cat."

"Even though I'm in and out throughout the week, I'm not usually there on weekends. Mrs. Anderson is staying with her sister; I believe she's allergic. I couldn't send Raven to a shelter, so that's how I came to have a cat."

"That's sweet of you to do that for her. I'm sure she appreciates it," Nicole said with a hint of admiration in her voice.

Mitch nodded. His thoughts had shifted and focussed on where to put the furniture from the nursery. "I think the rocking horse should go back here," he said, his mind already visualizing the layout. "The other furniture will be all right in the box. The contents can ride inside. Do you have any idea what's in the dresser drawers?"

"No. Baby clothes and blankets is my guess. I hope there isn't anything weird like daggers or ... I don't know, just strange."

About half an hour after they left the Anderson house, Mitch turned into the driveway at the back of the property. When he drove up to the back of the house, it seemed rougher today than the day before. As the previous day, he turned the truck around and backed it to the porch, leaving room to put the tailgate down.

Chapter Thirty-Seven

FEBRUARY 5, 1918

June dried her eyes for the umpteenth time that day. She wore a black suit, white blouse, black gloves, and matching shoes. On her head was a hat of the same colour with a veil covering her face.

A soft knock on the front door preceded her mother's entrance. "Are you ready, June? Your father is waiting in the car."

June nodded then checked her appearance in the mirror once more. Underneath the veil, her eyes were red and swollen. Her young son, almost three was oblivious to the significance of the day. "Mommy, why do I have to wear a suit? Where are we going?"

"Come along, William. It's time to leave."

The little boy stood and came to his mother's side.

In a few hours, she would be presented the Victoria Cross for her late husband's bravery during the Battle of Passchendaele — a moment she dreaded despite being proud of Robert's accomplishments.

Mrs. Graham, a pillar of strength for her daughter, helped June and her grandson to the car before climbing into the front with her husband, a silent but reassuring presence.

The presentation ceremony was scheduled to begin at two o'clock that afternoon in the Opera House, a grand and imposing room on the upper level of the Brighton Town Hall. During the car ride to the venue, June picked at her handkerchief.

Ute slipped through the door as the ceremony began, her heart heavy with grief. She found a seat in the back row, making a futile attempt to hide her emotions. As much as she longed to be by Robert's wife's side, it was impossible. She'd remain at the back, her grief a burden she had to bear alone. No one could know of her deep connection to the decorated war hero.

Despite her efforts to be discreet, her tears betrayed her. Her bond with Robert, though brief, was profound and unforgettable. Though only a few hours long, their connection was undeniable and left a lasting mark on her.

As June stood to accept the Victoria Cross, Ute's sobs echoed in the hall. She struggled to contain her emotions, her hand over her mouth, as she fled the upper level of the town hall. The pain in her heart was unbearable.

Inside the beautiful opera house, June sat quietly with her parents. She held William in her lap.

When the ceremony started, the Mayor of Brighton, Mr. Herbert Carden, was the first to address the gathered assembly. "Welcome, attendees. We are here today to honour the bravery of one of our own boys, sadly a fallen one, Private Robert Holbrook. At this point, I would like to introduce Base Commander Thompson of nearby Cobourg to say a few words."

The man, tall and imposing in his military uniform, stepped forward, addressing the gathered crowd. "Ladies and gentlemen, we gather here today to honour an extraordinary individual whose actions in the face of unimaginable adversity have earned him a place among the bravest of the brave. The Victoria Cross, which we are about to present, is not just a medal but is the highest military decoration awarded for valour in the British and Commonwealth forces."

He continued. "The Victoria Cross, since its institution by Queen Victoria in 1856, has been awarded only to those who have demonstrated the most conspicuous bravery. Those with a complete disregard for their own safety, and an unwavering commitment to their comrades and country. It symbolizes the ultimate sacrifice and heroism, given only in the most exceptional circumstances."

The Base Commander's voice was monotone. June dabbed her eyes with her handkerchief.

"The Cross is made from the bronze of cannons captured during the Crimean War, and each one is a tangible reminder of the courage that soldiers like Robert Holbrook have shown in the service of their nation. It is a rare and deeply revered honour, bestowed upon fewer than 1,400 individuals since its inception. Today, we stand in awe of Private Holbrook's actions, which earned him this distinguished award and brought immense pride to our community and country. We cherish and celebrate his bravery, selflessness, and devotion to duty as a nation."

Base Commander Thompson continued. "And now, it is with profound respect and deep gratitude that I invite June Holbrook, on behalf of her late husband, Robert Holbrook, to receive the Victoria Cross in recognition of his extraordinary valour on the battlefield."

June rose from her seat and made her way to the front. Her steps were measured, and her expression solemn. As she stood before the gathered crowd, her eyes glistened with tears, reflecting her mixed emotions.

"Today, we honour Private Robert Holbrook, who showed extraordinary bravery at Passchendaele. His actions saved many lives, so we posthumously award him the Victoria Cross." The commander opened the box and presented the medal to the widow. She accepted it with a mix of pride and sorrow, her heart heavy with the memory of her husband's sacrifice.

Before June returned to her seat, Mayor Carden asked everyone to stand and sing God Save the King.

Chapter Thirty-Eight

Nicole climbed out of the truck, opened the back door, and retrieved the boxes that found their way to the passenger side of Mitch's truck. Strange things had happened to her here. Visions, daggers buried in the floorboards, the secret passage. Even the Freemason's symbol on the ceiling medallion. But those things didn't spook her as much as the ones at Kembleford Manor had.

Once inside the house, she headed straight for the nursery and took the small Beatrix Potter prints off the walls. Nicole recalled the Peter Rabbit stories. When she was a little girl, her mother read them to her after tucking her into bed.

Two dressers stood in the room. The tall one where she found the envelope with Robert's medals and other memorabilia wedged behind. A short one that might have doubled as a changing table stood like silent witnesses to the past.

Nicole started with the latter. She pulled the top drawer open. A square metal can of baby powder lay flat. Could you even buy baby powder now? Hadn't it been determined that it caused cancer? An open bar of soap sat on a saucer, and other bars remained in their wrappings. A glass bottle housed the shampoo. Glass bottles? Nicole had never seen shampoo in one. As far back as she could remember, they had always been plastic.

An assortment of large safety pins sat in a bowl.

Some opened and stabbed into the soap. She removed these items and placed them in a box, leaving the open diaper pins where they were. She had rubbed safety pins through her hair to make them slide through fabric easier. The soap must have done the same thing but through layers of flannel.

The next drawer held diapers — cloth ones. If Nicole had children, these would not be her choice. She would use disposables or a diaper service. These remained as white as the day June purchased them. June, or William's wife, must have bleached them within an inch of their lives to get them so clean. Nicole placed them in another box. The bottom drawer had small flannel blankets and nightgowns. She removed them and put them in with the other cloth items.

She took a marker out of her backpack and labelled the boxes. The pictures could have gone in the same carton as the toiletries, but Nicole didn't want to risk spillage and ruin them. If she came across similar items in the other dresser, she'd keep them together. Once Nicole had the smaller dresser emptied, she removed the drawers.

"I'm ready for this one to go to the truck," she called.

Nicole moved on to the cradle and removed the small mattress and bedding, boxed it up before she moved onto the crib. With the way regulations changed, this one was far from legal. Still, it was a family heirloom, a tangible link to the past. It looked easy to take apart, so they could do that and it would lie flat in the truck's bed. She had a small storage locker in the basement of her building and when dismantled, it would fit in there, leaning against the wall.

Mitch hadn't come into the room with her. He'd left the other boxes and let her do her thing. He was likely checking out some piece of architecture in the mansion.

She moved on to the larger chest of drawers. Sweaters, bonnets, and bootie sets. Knitted and crocheted blankets. Socks, underwear, and toddler clothing filled this piece of furniture. Once William grew older, his mother must have moved him into one of the other bedrooms. These articles were for infants up to toddler age. Which one of the other bedrooms was his?

How many other children lived here over the years? Did her father and aunt live here as children? They might — no, must have. There had to be a secret in this house. A secret buried deep within the walls, a secret that held the key to her family's past. But what could it be?

A movement in the corner caught Nicole's eye. She stood and walked to the window. It was only a crow. While she gazed over the property, something she hadn't noticed before became apparent. Depressions were in the ground over near the fence.

"Mitch, can you come to the nursery, please? Quick before the light changes."

Nicole pulled her camera out of her backpack and clicked off many photos. As she snapped pictures of the remains, she whispered.

> *I dwell in a lonely house I know*
> *That vanished many a summer ago,*
> *And left no trace but the cellar walls,*
> *And a cellar in which the daylight falls*
> *And the purple-stemmed wild raspberries grow.*
>
> *O'er ruined fences the grape-vines shield*
> *The woods come back to the mowing field;*
> *The orchard tree has grown one copse*
> *Of new wood and old where the woodpecker*
> *chops;*
> *The footpath down to the well is healed.*

"What is it?" Mitch asked, catching his breath from running up the stairs.

"Look, those depressions in the ground.

They were in the shape of a rectangle. It could mean it was a foundation at one time. What stood there years ago? Beyond it stood an old farm windmill. Was it just an outbuilding? A chicken coop? Engine shed or carriage house?

"In the censuses I looked up, the Holbrook's lived next door to the Grahams. Do you think that might have been where their house stood?"

"It could be. If so, it makes you wonder what happened to it. Looks like you've got yourself another mystery to solve. What were you saying when I came into the room?"

Nicole turned away from the window. "I'm not sure why I thought about it, but the poem *Ghost House* by Robert Frost popped into my head."

The light streaming into the room made Nicole's hair appear to be on fire, and a warm aura surrounded her. Mitch doubted his sanity for a moment. He didn't believe in auras and supernatural mumbo jumbo, but as sure as he stood there, a glowing, orangey aura embraced Nicole. It had to be the sun. There was no other explanation.

"If you're done packing up the drawers, we should get this stuff to the truck."

"Sure. Sorry, I got carried away."

Mitch placed his hands on Nicole's upper arms. "Don't worry about it. If you'd like, we can always check out that corner of the property before we leave."

"You don't have to pretend you're interested in what I saw just to appease me."

"Actually, Nicki, I am interested. Not necessarily for the same reason as you, but I am truly interested. So, what can go to the truck? Take the light stuff and come back for the heavy? Or the other way around."

"Let's get the rocking horse out and down the stairs first. It's going to be the heaviest. The drawers are out of the dressers, which should make them lighter."

Mitch moved to the hobbyhorse's frame and lifted one end. It was heavy, but didn't weigh as much as he figured.

"You get the other end. It's not too bad. Awkward, though."

Nicole lifted the large toy where he showed her, and they worked their way out of the room to the top of the stairs, where they rested.

"It had to have come up the steps, so it has to go

back down them," Mitch said, surveying the staircase and the animal's size. "Too big to go sideways. I think you'll have to go first."

"Not backwards, I'm not."

"Okay, then we'll take him at an angle, so you'll be sideways. I'll be a few steps after you, but I'll try to take most of the weight."

"Sure."

"You don't sound convinced."

"I'm not." Nicole tucked her hair behind her ears, cracked her knuckles and said, "Let's get this over with, then."

They managed to get the rocking horse downstairs without casualties, although they stopped frequently to rest. Crossing the house to the truck easy by comparison, until they had to manhandle it into the backseat of Mitch's truck.

Exhausted, they took a break and sat on the tailgate. Mitch high-fived Nicole for her efforts in getting the awkward thing downstairs. After that, the dressers, drawers and boxes would be easy.

Back upstairs in the nursery, Nicole turned to Mitch. "What do you think happened to the Holbrook house? Fire, maybe? That's a theory my brothers came up with."

"Possible," he said.

"What if Robert's parents died after he left to fight in the war, and his wife let the house go until it fell in on itself? This is 2022, and he shipped out in 1914 or thereabouts. That's a lot of time for an empty house to not fall down. Which means people lived in this one until the mid-1900s," Nicole mused, her voice tinged with curiosity.

"Plausible."

"Would you come with me the next time I visit my aunt?" Nicole asked, arranging the remaining things to be removed into piles.

"You don't want me with you, do you?"

"Why not?"

"I wouldn't know your aunt from Joan of Arc."

Nicole laughed at his weird sense of humour. She always liked that about him. But if he visited Janet with her, would her aunt put two and two together and come up with five? Think that they were a couple? She might. Perhaps, that wasn't such a good idea after all.

"Let's finish up so we can check out the corner of the property for clues."

Nicole followed in Mitch's footsteps to the corner of the property. Even the day she and her brothers first explored here, they never ventured into this area. She knew from the censuses she had looked up online, the Holbrook's lived next door to the Grahams. But did they live to the east or the west of the big house? This corner of the property might have only been the barn. That made more sense since there was a windmill. Any farms she had seen growing up, all had one, and they were closer to the barn than the house.

While she walked, the possibility of what had happened to the house filled her head. Did it collapse after being abandoned? Destroyed by fire? There may have been a chimney fire, an old wooden cookstove and maybe another wood burner. They still happen today. Would there be anything in the local newspaper or the library that would give her the desired answers? She paused, typed a cryptic note into the app on her phone, and tagged it as research.

Mitch stopped and turned around. "You coming?"

"Yes. I wanted to write myself a note to research what happened to the house."

"Don't get too far behind me. We're almost there."

Nicole watched as Mitch's gaze focussed on the nursery's window that faced this direction. She didn't have the same grasp of measurements as he did, but she knew it wouldn't be much farther. They continued towards the back corner of the property.

When she stepped down, something cracked under her feet. "Mitch, I think I've found something," she said, her voice filled with trepidation, fear creeping into her every word.

"Don't move," Mitch said.

He came to her side, squatted, and swept the long grass aside. "I think it's window glass. It's flat ... and dammit." He yanked his hand back and shook it. Blood sprayed from the wound and left a trail on the ground.

"Is it bad?" Nicole slung her backpack to the ground. She rummaged for a tissue or something to wrap around the wound until she had something more permanent.

Mitch inspected his hand, the metallic tang of blood filling his nostrils. It was difficult to determine where the blood originated by sight. Like a thousand needles, the stinging pain told him precisely where, but how deep or long had yet to be determined.

"Here. It's not fancy, but it will do in a pinch." Nicole handed him a crumpled tissue. "It's clean."

Mitch wrapped his injured finger with the offered paper.

"There's a first aid kit in the glove compartment of the truck. This will do until we get back there."

"I feel terrible. If it wasn't for me wanting to see if there were any clues to what this used to be and why it disappeared, you wouldn't have cut yourself."

"Better my finger than the bottom of your foot. Those shoes aren't designed for wandering through this stuff," Mitch joked, trying to lighten the mood.

Mitch kicked at the glass. His toe hit something larger. What? He nudged it with his foot. A rock. But not just any rock. This had signs of nineteenth-century mortar on it. This came from the foundation or a wall if the entire building was stone. Nicole had discovered something huge. They just had to find out what.

"You're awfully pale, Mitch. Are you okay?" Nicole asked, her voice filled with concern, her eyes reflecting her worry for him.

He swayed.

"That's it. I'm taking you to the hospital. You need stitches. I'll drive."

Chapter Thirty-Nine

"**L**ean on me. I'll help you to the truck," Nicole instructed.

"It's not that bad, Nicki. Trust me."

"So you're white as a sheet for no reason and can barely stand upright. That tissue I gave you is completely soaked through already."

At least everything they had come to remove from the house today sat in the back of Mitch's truck. Once she got him bundled into the passenger seat, she'd assess his hand and put a clean dressing on it.

"Hold your hand up above your heart. It won't stop the bleeding, but it might buy us some time."

It was her fault he got hurt. That shard of glass must have been sharp to do that much damage. Dirty, too, after years of lying in the grass and mud. His line of work meant he used his hands — both of them — a lot. He was self-employed. If he didn't work, he didn't get paid. Why did she have to spot the depressions in the land? The guilt ate her up inside.

Nicole finally got Mitch into the truck and fastened his seatbelt. Sighing with relief, she opened the glove box and removed the first aid kit, which contained alcohol wipes, gauze pads, a roll of gauze bandage, tape, and scissors.

When she removed the blood-soaked tissue from his injured finger, Nicole cringed. A jagged cut sliced the side of his middle finger. Another cut on his pinky and ring fingers but they didn't seem to be as deep. And another on the palm of his hand.

Mitch's pained groans filled the air, accentuating the severity of the situation. Taking a deep breath, she opened an alcohol wipe and began cleaning the wound.

"Take it easy, will you?" Mitch shouted through clenched teeth, his voice strained with pain.

"Sorry, but I had to clean it. It's not perfect, but better than before." Nicole opened a gauze pad and wrapped it around the wound. Then she wrapped the rolled bandage around that and taped it before placing Mitch's hand on his chest.

"Can you handle this beast?" he asked.

"Much better than you're able to in your state."

Before Nicole started the engine, she used her phone to Google the nearest hospital. Unfortunately, Brighton, where they were just outside, didn't have one. The closest was Trenton, so she retrieved the directions and put the phone in the cupholder.

Nicole had seen no one bleed as profusely as Mitch was at that moment. It scared her. She was determined to get him to the hospital before he got worse. She started the engine, put the truck in gear, and navigated the pothole-riddled driveway, doing her best to make the ride as smooth as possible.

Mitch was in a great deal of pain. He'd never admit it, but she could tell how he winced when they hit bumps. Nicole was thankful for the pavement when she finally got to the road. At least this portion of the ride would be smoother.

She sped down the road until she reached the primary thoroughfare. She had to get him there before it was too late. Nicole deemed heading north towards the motorway unnecessary. The two-lane highway between Brighton and Trenton was faster and more direct.

Her heart raced, tears blurred her vision and she dashed them away. The last thing either of them needed was for her to crash his truck. If she got a speeding ticket, she didn't care. The urgency of getting Mitch to the closest emergency department was all that mattered.

At the emergency entrance, Nicole brought the truck to a screeching halt. She leaped out of the driver's seat and sprinted to the passenger door. The bandage she put on Mitch's finger when she got him back to the truck was soaked, which indicated the extent of his injury. The wound didn't spurt like he'd cut an artery. There had to be another underlying cause for the blood loss.

Nicole helped him out of the truck and into the hospital. "My friend needs help. He's bleeding badly. He cut his finger on broken glass." She steadied Mitch, her heart pounding in her chest, as she got him to the nurse's TRIAGE. "You'll be okay. I'm going to move the truck. I'll be right back." Nicole bent down and kissed the top of his head before she dashed back to the truck to move it.

She hated to leave him, but couldn't leave the truck where it was. Nicole had pulled into the ambulance bay. There was no way she could leave it where it was.

Nothing like this had happened before on a visit to an abandoned property. It terrified Nicole. If the hospital staff couldn't stop the bleeding, Mitch might die. She couldn't bear living with that for the rest of her days. They had to save him. She was determined. If only she hadn't seen what may have been the foundation of a century-old house.

Once Nicole had the truck parked, she raced back to the emergency department. Mitch wasn't in the waiting area. That was a good sign. Hopefully, they'd taken him back and were in the process of treating him.

She approached the desk. "My friend. I brought him in not more than five minutes ago. He was bleeding badly from cuts on his right hand. Where is he?"

"They've taken him back for treatment."

"Please, can I see him?" Nicole's voice trembled with worry.

"Are you related to him?"

Nicole paused before answering. She wasn't related to Mitch and had just referred to him as her friend. "He's more than a friend, actually. I'm his fiancée."

"Are there any other family members? Mother, father, siblings?"

If they searched for next-of-kin, it had to be serious. Mitch was an only child. That was likely why he fit in so well with her and her brothers. His parents, both gone. Killed on holiday. He had no one.

"No." The weight of that word felt like a knife piercing her heart. He had her and she would do everything she could in her power to keep him safe.

"Where's Nicole?" Mitch asked the nurse who attended to his injured hand.

She didn't answer, so he repeated the question and added. "The person who brought me here? Where is she?"

Still no answer. Instead, the nurse persisted with her barrage of questions. "Any history of profuse bleeding from a minor injury? When did you have your last tetanus shot? Are you on any medications that would impair your blood's clotting ability?"

Mitch focussed on the door they brought him through. Nicole had to be on the other side of it. Why wouldn't they letting her come through? Damn hospitals and their rules.

"Sir? You haven't answered my questions."

"No. I don't know, and no. There, you've got your answers. Can you see if you can find Nicole and bring her back here?"

The nurse walked away, but not towards the emergency department waiting area. He was about to get off the gurney and look for her when Nicole burst through the door. The sight of Nicole melted his stress. When she reached him, she hugged him.

"Hey, not so tight," he said.

"Sorry." She stood and dashed the tears away from her eyes.

Mitch took hold of her hand. "I'm not dying."

Meanwhile, the nurse returned with a basin. She removed the temporary dressing and submerged Mitch's hand in warm, soapy water.

Nicole pulled a stool over from the corner and sat beside him. "I had to tell them I was your fiancée so they'd let me come back here."

"It's not such a bad idea." Mitch reached up and pulled Nicole's face towards him and kissed her.

Chapter Forty

Valter debated meeting his wife when the train arrived. Did it say he knew her secret? Or would it be better to act as if nothing happened until he got home? His mind was a whirlwind of conflicting thoughts and emotions. Whatever he did, the china head doll box sat in the middle of the table with the lid off. Wait and dig herself into a hole, he mused. It would be worth the price of admission.

After the boys had left for school, Valter retrieved the incriminating evidence from its hiding place under the bed and placed it on the kitchen table. He considered leaving the love token where he had hidden it, relishing the thought of his wife's panic when she couldn't locate it. But he knew the truth needed to be revealed, and the sooner, the better. The urgency of the situation was not lost on him.

He debated leaving a note telling her he knew her dirty little secret and leaving it on top of the doll, but the object itself, being out in the open, said that. It didn't require any further information.

His shift at the bakery usually started at four in the morning, but Heinrich said he could begin once they left for school because he had to care for the boys. Valter's shift today started at nine. He took a last look around the room and left for his job.

The train ride home was a gruelling ordeal. The car was packed with jubilant passengers, their celebrations contrasting the war that still raged on without end.

Ute was proud of the send-off the Canadian Military had given Robert. The only thing that would have been better was if they presented her with his Victoria Cross, but that went to his widow. The child with her had to be the one Robert mentioned in his letters — William. The name suited the boy. He wasn't a Willy. With his wide eyes and a shy smile, William seemed to take in everything around him, including Ute.

When the train arrived in Toronto, she had to run to catch the one that would take her the rest of the way to St. Jacobs. Otherwise, she'd have to wait for another, which was out of the question, since it didn't run until the following day.

At least on this last leg of her journey, her fellow passengers were more subdued. For the rest of her trip, she settled into the wooden bench seat, which was more uncomfortable than a church pew, with its hard, unforgiving surface and lack of cushioning.

Once she arrived at St. Jacobs, Ute took the same route she used when she left for the station. It was quiet this way, and little chance of her being seen by neighbours. She got all the way to her house unseen. It wasn't until she opened the back door that one of her neighbours called out to her.

"Yes, hello, Mrs. ... sorry, I don't remember your last name," Ute said.

"Miller. Ada Miller."

"Yes, now I remember. So sorry of me to forget."

"I see you've been away for a few days."

How did she know that? Of course, Ute carried an overnight bag. "Yes. But I'm back now." Nosey woman. It was no one's business but hers where and when she went.

Ute opened the back door and stepped into their small kitchen. It couldn't be. She stepped closer to the table and gasped. It was. Valter had found her hiding place.

"Well, my dear, I see you've found the little

surprise I left out for you," he said when he stepped through the door. "This urgent trip out of town was to a presentation of a Victoria Cross to a Canadian soldier's widow. I know everything. I also found the letters you had hidden under the wrappings. For you to remember our night together."

Ute's mouth gaped open. What did she say? What could she say? Valter had found the doll and read the letters from Robert.

"That explains your behaviour that night. The night you acted like a common whore wanting me to bed you. I'm not stupid, my dear. Even before I discovered the doll, I knew. When you came home from Lützkampen, you still had bits of hay in your hair. If you were merely delivering bread to cousins, you wouldn't have. That tells me you had a dalliance. Did he force himself on you?"

"No. No. Robert wasn't like that." The words had barely left Ute's mouth when she realized she'd walked right into Valter's trap. He forced her to confess.

"What do you think I should do to you? My scheming, lying wife? I have a few trains of thought about that. I could beat you. It would be what you deserve. Force you from our home. Again, being what you deserve. But I think what would hurt you most of all is if I destroy this ... this ugly thing." He picked up the doll and brought his arm back.

Ute's eyes grew wild with fear. "No, Valter, please. Anything but ... please don't destroy her. Whichever one of our sons has a daughter, she'll get it. That's what I'd planned from the beginning."

Valter enjoyed the power he held over her at this moment. How had he been so blind all along. Until he read the letters, he wasn't one hundred percent certain his wife had relations with another man. He was furious. Never in all the years of their marriage had he been that angry with her.

He let her come close to him, and when she reached for the doll he held in one hand, he punched her in the stomach with the other. Ute dropped to the floor. He stood over her with one foot on her torso preventing her from rising, then he kicked her a few times to finish her lesson. When he finished, he spit on the doll and threw it beside her.

"Oh, and that was only today's lesson. You'll continue to get one as long as I have the strength to give it."

Ute didn't make a sound. She daren't. Besides, she didn't want to show him she was in pain by crying. Why did Ute have to fall for Robert? It was easy. He was handsome, kind, and caring. Valter had never attacked her like this before. These beatings would only get worse.

Once she ensured her husband was gone, she picked herself up from the floor. Her stomach hurt, her back hurt. So far, he'd damaged her in places the children wouldn't see.

Ute picked up the doll and inspected it. Relieved that it hadn't broken when it hit the floor, she put it in the box and returned it to the bedroom. It was bad enough that Valter had found it, but the thought of Friedrich and Walter finding it, too, didn't bear thinking about it.

Chapter Forty-One

A man in green scrubs with a stethoscope around his neck interrupted their moment when he approached.

"I'm not interrupting anything, am I?" he asked.

"N-no." Nicole jerked back upright.

"I'm Doctor Andrew Bennett." The physician introduced himself as he lifted Mitch's hand from the red-stained water.

"It's not an overly deep or long cut. I doubt it will even need to be sutured. But the blood loss concerns me. You're not taking NSAIDs at the moment? Ibuprofen products."

"No."

The doctor asked questions about Mitch's medical history. The family's, too. Nicole couldn't offer any suggestions why he bled so severely. When asked, she told the doctor how Mitch came to cut himself.

"We'll see you get a tetanus shot before you leave, but I want to run a few tests to rule out something serious." He walked to the corner and picked up the phone.

Nicole wasn't sure who he called or why. He spoke in medical terms to the person on the other end, then hung up and returned to speak with them.

"What is it, doctor?" Nicole asked.

"Given the severity of the bleeding, I want to check for hemophilia and leukaemia. We'll draw some blood and test it here. I see you live in Belleville. Do you have a family doctor?"

"Yes. Asha Patel."

"We'll forward our findings to her. Should the results warrant it, you'll have to go for a bone marrow biopsy and a flow cytometry."

A young woman with various vials and syringes appeared and began drawing blood.

"You'll mark them urgent, Leslie?"

"Yes, doctor."

"We should have them in a few hours."

Mitch couldn't have hemophilia or leukaemia, could he? The news dumbfounded Nicole. Mitch was always so healthy. The man rarely caught a cold. Now, the possibility loomed that he had a potentially life-threatening disease? Tears pricked the backs of her eyes, and she turned away. She refused to let Mitch see her cry. Together, they would figure out a way to beat it.

She'd heard of hemophilia, although she knew little about it other than your blood didn't clot properly, and it was mostly males who suffered from it.

Nicole stood and walked to the foot of the gurney, where she remained with her back to Mitch. Until she regained her composure, she couldn't face him. Instead, she chewed on the cuticle of her left thumb and worried it until it bled.

Doctor Bennett bandaged Mitch's hand. The gash on his middle finger was the worst. The others were scratches by comparison. After he finished, the doctor left them but pulled the curtain around the small area where Mitch and Nicole waited. They might have to return to the waiting area rather than take up treatment space if something came up.

"Come here, Nicki," he said softly, extending his arm towards her.

She returned to the stool and rested her head on his chest. He wrapped his arms around her, feeling the warmth of her body and inhaling the scent of her shampoo. He couldn't put his finger on what it smelled like other than a delicate floral aroma. His bandaged finger throbbed. That had to be a good sign. He'd have to worry if he didn't have feeling in it.

The prospect of suffering from either of those ailments stunned him. He felt fine most days. The occasional one, he was tired, but that usually depended on how challenging the previous day's work on the job site was. Mitch, dedicated to his trade, wasn't about to have a pity party. He would not curl up and die, either. He'd do like he'd always done. Get on with it. That's what you did. Foremost, he had a job to finish for Mrs. Anderson; once it was out of the way, he'd worry about his future. One he hoped would include Nicole.

One nurse stopped by and told them they'd have to go to the waiting room. Ambulances were en route, with casualties from a multi-vehicle collision.

Nicole pulled out her phone, since COVID had put an end to magazines to leaf through. The spacious room looked empty because many chairs had been removed to maintain social distancing. She had come in with Mitch — she'd stay with him and close to him. Nicole moved her chair next to his, her heart heavy with worry. She couldn't concentrate, her mind filled with the uncertainty of Mitch's condition. She tried to put on a brave face for him, but because of how he looked at her occasionally, she hadn't succeeded.

"I can't spend too long with you, but your blood work all came back normal. I'm going to send the report of your stay here to your family doctor, and she might want to order more tests. I'm sorry, I can't give you more information now because I'm needed in the ER."

The doctor's words echoed in Nicole's mind, leaving her with more questions than answers about Mitch's health.

Nicole let out a sigh of relief. By the sounds of things, Mitch didn't have leukaemia or hemophilia. But his family doctor would run more tests to rule out the disease. Still, she'd take this nugget of news as excellent.

"Let's go home. I've seen enough of this place for one day," she said, standing and shrugging on her coat.

Mitch grabbed his and tossed it over his

shoulder. As they approached the exit, his free arm wound around her shoulders in a comforting gesture, a silent reassurance that they were in this together. It felt right; it felt like home.

When they exited the hospital, it was dark. Had they been in there that long? It didn't seem like it. When she returned from moving the truck, Mitch was already in the treatment area. But they had to wait for the results of the blood tests, and that took time.

She'd drive back as far as her place; if she deemed Mitch was up to it, he could drive to his apartment from there. She was the one making the decisions now, the one taking charge of their situation.

Was there anything in the truck she wanted to take to her apartment tonight? Not wanting to risk splitting the cut open again, she decided it would wait until the next day. With luck, she might enlist the help of her brothers.

Half an hour later, Nicole pulled the truck up in front of her building.

"You okay to drive the rest of the way?" she asked.

"Ain't dead yet."

"Not funny." This was one time Nicole didn't find Mitch's sense of humour endearing or amusing. "Can we leave the furniture and the rocking horse in the truck overnight and unload it tomorrow after work?" Nicole asked, her concern for Mitch's well-being clear in her voice.

"I don't think I have to pick anything up, so it should be fine."

"I'll take the boxes in tonight, though."

Using his good arm, Mitch opened the tailgate and slid the cartons to the back of the box. Without a word, Nicole grabbed one and headed to her building's lobby. She returned for the second one.

"Don't even think about it, Mitchell Kane," Nicole warned, her tone a mix of exasperation and fondness, as she strode back to the building.

The woman had eyes in the back of her head. She must. Otherwise, she wouldn't have seen that he tried to lift it. Mitch left it where it sat, but jogged ahead to get the glass door for her.

"I'm using my good arm so you don't need to get bent out of shape."

Nicole turned towards him, rolled her eyes, and then placed the second box on top of the first one in the lobby.

He had no idea what the boxes from the nursery held. When Nicole packed them, he had been inspecting the pocket doors downstairs and the freaky ceiling medallion. Who would want to have a Freemason symbol on their ceiling? A Freemason, someone high in the organization, the local chapter head, or something like that. He supposed it proved power and influence.

While he pondered that, among other things, Nicole walked past him and collected the last box. If he was going to make his move, he needed to do it soon. He followed her back to the entrance of her building.

She had just straightened up from placing the carton on top of the others when he wrapped his arms around her, leaned down and kissed her full on the lips. In the back of his mind, he figured she'd pull away, but she didn't. Her arms encircled his waist, and she returned the kiss. At that moment, Mitch's heart raced, and he thought he was the luckiest man in the world.

Nicole broke the embrace first. Her eyes searched his as if looking for an explanation. His fingers remained entwined in her hair, and he gently backed her against the door, held her closer, and kissed her again.

Nicole pulled back. Where had that come from? Until the moment their lips locked, she thought kissing Mitch would be like kissing her brothers. It wasn't. It was far from it. But was it right? They were such good friends. The fear of ruining their friendship loomed large in her mind, casting a shadow over the unexpected feelings she now grappled with.

"I-I need to take these boxes to my apartment," she said. Her nerves jangled. In all the times, she'd spent with Mitch, she never thought this would happen. Heat rushed to her cheeks. That embarrassed her.

"Do you want a hand taking them up?" Mitch asked.

"I-I'll be fine. You don't need to split your finger open again and get it bleeding." Nicole's voice was strained. She wanted him to leave. She needed time to process what had just happened between them.

"I'll call you tomorrow, and we'll figure out how to get the stuff out of my truck and into your apartment."

"Sounds good."

Connor might help them. Cooper definitely not. She could handle the dresser drawers on her own, but the rest of the pieces of furniture and the rocking horse were more than a two-person operation. With Mitch cutting his finger and it bleeding so profusely, he shouldn't do anything to get it bleeding again.

The hobbyhorse was inside the truck's cab, and the pieces of furniture were in the back, covered in tarps. Mitch's apartment building provided secure, underground parking. Those things would be fine for the night.

Nicole stood in the lobby and watched until Mitch drove out of sight.

Chapter Forty-Two

Mitch locked the truck and strode to the elevator, his mind swirling with doubts. Had he crossed a line with Nicole earlier? The fear of ruining their friendship gnawed at him. The prospect of awkwardness loomed, not just for a few days, but possibly for years. He blew it.

Raven's excited meows greeted him as he opened the apartment door. He had grown accustomed to the warmth of her welcome instead of an empty flat. The thought of the cat returning to her owner, Mrs. Anderson, only added to his isolation.

Meanwhile, his finger began to throb again, a sharp reminder of his recent injury. He made his way to the bathroom and opened the medicine cabinet. Advil, extra-strength. Mitch dry-swallowed two of them and returned the bottle to the cupboard. As he left the bathroom, a sudden realization struck him. The doctor had asked if he was on any medication that would affect his blood clotting ability. Not now, but earlier in the year, he had been popping these high-test pills like candy when he tore the ACL in his left knee. Mitch should have had it looked at and operated on, but no work, no pay. He endured the pain. Would there still be enough of those pills in his system? What did the doctor call it? NSAIDs. Ibuprofen products. That was it. At least, the blood tests had come back normal. The physical pain from his injury, coupled with the memory of the medication, added to his current worries.

Mitch reached for his phone, intending to text Nicole about his discovery. But as his finger hovered over the screen, he hesitated. What if she misunderstood? What if this only made things worse? He returned the phone to the coffee table and moved to the kitchen. He opened the fridge, but nothing inside appealed to him, not even the cold bottle of Coors Light.

Nicole lugged the last box up to her apartment and sat it on top of the others she'd brought up already. Some from her parents' storage locker in the hallway remained untouched.

The day had started out great. She and Mitch had made progress getting the nursery furniture packed up and loaded into his truck. Then things took a downhill slide. First, he cut himself and bled. The agonizing wait for the results of the blood work at the hospital. But the most confusing was her reaction to Mitch's kisses. Almost as fast as she responded to the first one, she pulled away. They could have overstepped a mark and ruined their friendship.

It was late, and she hadn't eaten since breakfast. Food first, then get ready for bed. What to eat? Something fast. Did she have anything meeting that requirement she wanted to eat?

She peered into the fridge. A small tub of Boursin cream cheese caught her eye. Not sure how long it had been in there, Nicole pulled it out, took the lid off, and sniffed. It was fine. Did she have crackers? No. Eat it on toast, then. She pulled the loaf of bread out of the freezer and removed two slices, which she dropped into the toaster.

A cup of tea with her snack. Nicole had tea bags but wasn't sure where she'd put them. She filled the kettle and set it to boil. There were bags of breakfast tea in the canister, but there was also Earl Grey and green tea in the apartment. She craved Earl Grey. It took her a few minutes to source the box of the blend she wanted. It was in the cupboard over her fridge. Not a place where she stored many grocery items, but plastic dishes and whatnot.

Her toast popped, and she slathered the cheese onto it. When the kettle boiled, she made her tea and took the plate of food and the mug into the living room.

The boxes from her aunt's storage beckoned her. Did she have the energy to go through it tonight? No. It would be waiting for her tomorrow.

Chapter Forty-Three

U te spent little time in the bakery. She was so sore from Valter's repeated beatings; it was hard to move. Instead, she took to her bed as soon as the boys left for school and her husband was long since at work.

A knock on the door roused her from her rest. It took forever to get out of bed to answer it. Every move put her in agony.

When Ute finally got to the door, Mathilde stood in the opening.

"Whatever is wrong? You've not been to the bakery in four days. Heinrich and I are worried. Valter said you were ill. I came to check on you and see if you needed anything."

Ute gestured for the woman to come in. When she did, a searing pain shot through her ribcage. He had broken at least one of her ribs in this latest beating. It had been bad enough that she passed blood because of the kicking he gave her in her kidneys.

"Please, Mathilde. You mustn't say a word."

Her cousin-in-law helped Ute to a chair.

"What is it? Please tell me. I want to help."

"It's such a mess." Ute shifted in her seat, hoping to find a more comfortable position. "The year before we came to Canada, I met and fell in love with a Canadian soldier. We had ... relations. Just once, but we were so passionately in love with one another; if it weren't for the war, the situation might have progressed."

Were her ears playing tricks on her? Did Ute say she'd had an affair with a Canadian soldier? In honesty, she couldn't blame the woman from what little she knew of Valter since they'd come to Canada and worked in the bakery alongside her and her husband.

"Ute, I don't know what to say."

"Say nothing. Let me finish. My soldier died in the Battle of Passchendaele. He received the Victoria Cross for his heroics. The ceremony was earlier in the week. That's why I left for a few days. I had to go. After our night of passion, he bought me a china head doll to remember him and our encounter. While I was gone, Valter found it and the letters my soldier had written to me. And, he tricked me into admitting it. Valter's beaten me within an inch of my life every day since I've been back."

Mathilde rushed to Ute's side and hugged her. "Oh, I'm sorry. I didn't mean to hurt you."

"Valter had stopped looking at me in that way not long after Friedrich was born. I'd given him two sons. That's all he cared about."

"Can I see your injuries?"

"We'll go into the bedroom." Ute struggled out of her chair and walked rigidly across the room and into the one she and Valter shared.

Mathilde gasped when she saw how battered Ute's body was. Her back, her ribs, her stomach and breasts were all black and blue. "I must tell Heinrich. He can help."

"No, please," Ute begged. "The beatings will only get worse. It's my cross; I must bear it for what I did."

"You had a visitor today, I see," Valter sneered when he entered the kitchen.

"Yes, Mathilde stopped in. She was worried since I hadn't been at work."

"I hope you didn't tell her anything. You know what happens to people who talk out of turn."

"You don't frighten me, Valter. You can't hurt me anymore than you already have with your daily beatings. I give up. I don't want to fight. Please, can this stop?"

Enraged, Valter grabbed his wife by the throat and squeezed. She clawed at his fingers. The bitch drew blood. It dripped down his hands to the floor. She would pay for this. He put more pressure on her throat. He'd squeeze the life from her.

Suddenly, a pain struck Valter in his chest. Cold sweat formed on his forehead and dripped down his face. He couldn't breathe. His hands lost their grip on Ute's throat, and he collapsed on the floor. His vision blurred. Was this what it felt like to die?

Ute stood over her husband. By now, his eyes had rolled back into his head. He'd stopped breathing. He was dead. She felt no remorse. No grief. Only relief. No more would she have to endure one of his beatings.

The hardest thing would be to tell her sons their father had died. They didn't need to know he was trying to strangle her. She checked her reflection in the small mirror in their living room. Ugly bruises, the shape of fingertips, formed around her neck.

Ute summoned her courage and walked to the bakery. Every step anguished because of her broken bones and bruises.

When she opened the door and entered, Mathilde and Heinrich raised their heads.

"Valter is dead. He can't hurt me anymore."

Oh, no! Did this mean Ute had killed Valter? She didn't blame the woman after the way he'd beaten her black and blue. But murder? Ute wasn't that sort of person. Mathilde rushed to the woman's side.

"My lips are sealed," she whispered in Ute's ear. "You have my sympathy. No one deserves to be treated like you have these past few days. I will tell the boys if you like."

"No. I'm their mother. It's my job." Ute's sense of responsibility was a heavy burden on her shoulders.

Ute struggled back to the door and left the bakery.

Mathilde stifled a sob, unable to imagine the pain Ute was in. Heinrich joined her and put an arm around her shoulder.

Ute perched on a chair. It was impossible to get comfortable, but she managed to find a position that lessened the pain. Now, to wait for the boys to return from school. The funeral director had been and removed Valter's body from the middle of the room. She had cleaned up the blood from the scratches she'd given him when she fought for her life. Her sons didn't need to see that.

Shortly after four o'clock, Walter and Friedrich bounded in. At this time of day, it wasn't unusual for their father to not be home. He usually worked until six o'clock.

"Walter, Friedrich, I have news. Please, come sit."

The boys did as they were told.

"Your father had a heart attack this afternoon," she told them. No sense sugar coating it.

"Will he be all right?" Walter asked.

"No. I'm sorry, but he's dead."

"Vater dead? No," Friedrich cried and ran from the room.

"Mutter, are you all right?" Walter asked. He put his arms around her neck and hugged her. Ute tried her best not to flinch under his touch.

"He was a good father to you boys. You must never forget that."

Chapter Forty-Four

NOVEMBER 28, 2022

Monday morning dawned dull and overcast. Nicole checked the weather app on her phone. If the temperature dipped low enough, they might receive lake-effect snow; otherwise, it would be rain. She walked to her living room window and pulled the drapes aside. So far, it had remained dry, but heavy, black clouds loomed off to the southwest.

Her mind wandered back to the previous evening. Nicole had always had a special relationship with Mitch. They were close, having grown up together in the same neighbourhood and attending the same schools. Not quite sibling close, but cousins. The fact he kissed her twice with such passion remained unnerving. She wasn't a prude, and she certainly wasn't a nun. She'd dated over the years. Made mistakes along the way.

The biggest mistake she made was getting involved with one guy when she was nineteen-twenty years old. She couldn't even say his name. It happened when she studied commercial art in college. That relationship was terrible. He manipulated her, filling her with so much self-doubt and confusion that she almost dropped out of school. Her art was garbage. She had no talent. She was wasting her time in school. No one would ever hire her.

Nicole had tried to keep things a secret from her friends and family, but they knew something was wrong. When they asked, she denied it and said everything was fine. It all came to a head when she was so filled with self-loathing that she attempted suicide.

During her hospitalization, Mitch stayed by her side every day, trying to help her regain her confidence. It was a long, hard slope to dig herself out of the hole this guy put her in. Cooper was still friends with Mitch then, and they, along with Connor, paid the guy a visit. They never told her what they did, but he left town right after that. His departure lifted a weight off her shoulders; she felt a sense of freedom she hadn't experienced in a long time. No one had seen or heard from him since. Good riddance.

Mitch was caring, considerate, and gallant. He looked out for her. Cared for her. Spent hours soothing her when she sobbed uncontrollably over the mess she'd made of her life. He brought her back from the brink, which was something neither her parents nor brothers could. His unwavering support was a warm blanket in the cold storm of her life.

Mitch lay in bed, his mind a whirlwind of conflicting emotions. His feelings for her, always present but unreciprocated, now seemed to be a source of turmoil. What was his next move?

At the hospital, when Nicole said she'd lied to the staff and said she was his fiancée to gain access to the treatment area, the idea appealed to him. He was willing to make it happen if she wanted it. But the thought of Cooper's reaction weighed on his mind. Cooper wouldn't be pleased if Mitch and Nicole became engaged. He was a jackass at the best of times anymore, so being with her would only add fuel to the fire. It would be wrong to use her just to drive her brother crazy, but the temptation was strong.

Mitch had been Nicole's rock, a steadfast presence in her life through thick and thin. He had pulled her out of the abyss of despair that the gaslighting prick had thrown her into. She had been his pillar of strength when tragedy struck his family.

He was fourteen when his parents perished in the plane crash off Nova Scotia in 1998.

Mitch had to have a heart-to-heart with Nicole.

He needed to express his feelings, even though his actions had already spoken volumes the night before.

"Okay, I'll get up and feed you," he said to the cat.

After she arrived at the office, Nicole made herself a coffee while she waited for her brothers to arrive. She was curious about what happened to the old Holbrook house. While on her own, she sat at her computer, typed house *fires near Brighton, Ontario, between 1914 and 1980* into the search bar, and hit enter.

Her search yielded more results than she had expected, filling the screen with a wealth of information. She refined her criteria to focus on the fire at the *Holbrook home near Brighton, Ontario, between 1914 and 1980*. This time, the search narrowed significantly, piquing her curiosity even more.

With the house almost completely gone, save a few rocks and broken panes of glass, it had to have burnt in the 1920s or 30s, perhaps even the 1940s, but not after that. Nicole scanned the list of hits her search had returned. While some said they were missing the name Holbrook, others included it. She concentrated on those. What was the name of the road? She opened a new tab, brought up Google Maps, and zoomed in until she found the desired area. Tenth Line Road and Graham Side Road. Was it named after the owners of the mansion?

Nicole returned to the tab with the fire results and added the names of the roads to her search, but eliminated the name. With the location listed, she wouldn't need to add anything else.

One result stood out. **Fatal Fire on Graham Side Road**. Nicole clicked on it.

Brighton Ensign
Nov 11, 1939
Fire engulfed the home of Claude Holbrook and his wife in the early hours of yesterday morning. The fire department responded to the blaze, but found it too far advanced to save the structure. It is believed the fire started in the chimney of the kitchen's wood stove.

However, one of the firemen said he smelled the odour of an accelerant such as kerosene. While the chimney fire isn't ruled out, the fact that arson may be involved adds a layer of intrigue. The investigation will continue.

Tragically, once the fire had been extinguished, firemen found the lifeless bodies of Claude Holbrook and his wife Elizabeth upstairs in their bedroom. They had succumbed to the smoke, unable to escape the engulfing flames.

That explained what happened to the house. Unfortunately, with no picture, the mystery of the home's appearance lingered. It didn't appear to have been as grand at the Graham mansion, but from the footprint visible from the nursery window, it was still a substantial house.

The sudden slam of the back door announced Nicole's brothers arrival, abruptly interrupting her investigation.

"So, what did you get up to on the weekend, Nicki?" Connor asked.

"Not much. Returned to the Graham mansion. Aunt Janet asked me to collect everything but furniture or dishes. Said I could have them. And everything from the nursery."

Nicole had mentioned nothing about going out to Brighton. Or talking to their aunt.

"Anyway, guys, I just found this newspaper article online. It explains what happened to the Holbrook family home." She picked the sheet of paper up from the printer and handed it to her brother.

"What? Deliberate? Why would anyone want to burn down their house?"

"Do you think they burnt the wrong one down? They wanted to destroy the Graham mansion. After all, it had some freaky things in it," offered Cooper.

"I don't know. But I need one of you guys to come and help unload the things I brought home. I took some boxes up to the apartment last night, but there are still photographs, paintings, and nursery furniture. I had asked Aunt Janet for the rocking horse. Trust me, it's heavy, and she told me she had no use for anything in that room."

"Where is this stuff?" Connor asked.

The room became quiet. He had a good idea where the stuff was. He'd help, if for no other reason than to find out what all happened over the weekend. So far, his sister had only told them what she wanted them to hear. She was hiding something, and he had a fair idea what. Now, he had to wait for Cooper to leave so he could find out.

About five minutes later, Cooper's cell phone rang, and he left the outer office to take the call.

"Okay, sis, spill."

"M-Mitch took me."

"I thought so."

"You don't have a problem with him helping me, do you?"

"No, but you know who will."

Nicole's face turned crimson. More happened than just Mitch helping clean out a house. How could he get her to tell him? Or did he want to know? What his sister and Mitch got up to when they were together wasn't any of his business. Was it? For now, he'd drop it.

With Cooper still out of the room, Nicole took a deep breath and said, "I spent almost six hours at the hospital in Trenton with Mitch last night." She stood and paced. "I discovered the marks in the ground from the foundation for the house in the article I printed. We walked over to investigate once we had everything loaded in his truck."

"And?"

Nicole chewed on the cuticle on her right thumb. "He cut himself on a piece of broken glass. Window glass. It didn't look that bad, but he bled so much."

The recollection of the scene made Nicole woozy, and she staggered.

Connor leapt to her aid and sat her in one of the office chairs. "You okay?"

"I think so. Anyway, at the hospital, once the emergency staff got the bleeding under control, they ran a bunch of tests. One was for leukaemia."

"Wow. And?" Connor asked.

"Came back negative."

"That's good, isn't it?"

Nicole heaved a sigh. "Yes. But I don't want him to split his finger open again, helping me. It's bad enough he cut it in the first place because of me."

"Isn't he working on the Anderson house again today? Every chance, he'll do something there to break it open."

Mitch wasn't one to take time off when he was working on a project. Injury or no injury. Even when he tore his ACL, he kept working. Nicole worried about him breaking the cuts open, especially with how they bled.

She stood and walked to her desk and picked up her phone and opened her text message app. Her fingers hovered over the buttons. Did she send him a note to tell him to be careful? Nicole put her phone back on the desk. Five minutes later, she picked it up again. Her hands shook when she tried to type a text message. Wait until her nerves settled. But what if they didn't? She broke out in a sweat. What was so difficult about sending a friend a message? Before yesterday, nothing. Finally, she typed a message.

Be careful working today. Don't hurt your hand.

Nicole should get some work done, not spend the day fretting about Mitch. But she couldn't help it. Their relationship took a serious turn last night. One she wasn't sure it should have. Until she talked to him, she didn't want to tell her brothers anything. Especially Cooper.

"I'll hitch a ride to yours after work and help you get the things into your apartment. Okay?"

"Thanks, Connor. I knew I could count on you."

Nicole sighed again. Did Mitch have questions about the turn in their relationship, too? She picked up her cell phone again.

Connor willing to help after work.

Mitch should be able to understand the message. The original plan had been to unload the rest of the things from the truck this evening after Nicole got home. Just the two of them. But now, she'd enlisted her brother's help.

The day dragged on. Nicole's mind flitted from one thing to another, unable to concentrate. Even the simplest of tasks became daunting. Frustrated with how things had spiralled out of her control, she stormed away from her desk towards the kitchenette at the back, her frustration seeping through every step.

"What's wrong with her?" Cooper asked when he returned. "She nearly bowled me over when she turned the corner."

"I'm not entirely sure," Connor said, his mind wrestling with the knowledge of Nicole's hospital visit and the tests for leukaemia. It wasn't his place to reveal, but the weight of the secret felt heavy. Nicole would be the one to tell him when Cooper needed to know.

As it was, he didn't want to tell his brother he was going to Nicole's after work to help her and Mitch unload some things from the Graham mansion. He didn't know until his sister mentioned it earlier today. With Cooper's philosophy of taking nothing, leaving only footprints, he'd go ballistic when he heard Nicki had taken objects from the place — despite having their aunt's permission.

Nicole was keeping something from him, and he wasn't happy about it. But knowing his sister the way he did, she'd tell him everything when she was good and ready.

Chapter Forty-Five

Nicole heaved a sigh when the workday finally ended. As she packed up her belongings and shut down her computer, her cell phone pinged. She picked it up to see who had contacted her. A message from Mitch appeared.

Should be there about 5:30.

"Go on home without me, Coop. I'm helping Nicki with a few things at her place. I'll see you later," Connor said, following Nicole through the offices to the back entrance.

That should keep her brother at bay. There had been bad blood between Cooper and Mitch for some time. She didn't need it to get worse. And it would. Tenfold, at least, if he knew about the weekend.

"I'll order us pizza after we get the stuff shifted from the truck into my apartment," she said.

"So tell me, what does Aunt Janet have to do with the Graham mansion?"

"I drove out to see her at the place she's been living in since she had her accident."

"Whoa. What accident?" The news piqued Connor's curiosity, and Nicole saw the questions forming.

She had assumed both of her brothers were aware of the accident and that their aunt lived in an assisted living facility. "Oh, God, this is turning into such a mess. I visited Aunt Janet. I haven't been able to put it all together yet, but according to her, our grandfather Holbrook bequeathed the Graham mansion to her. Dad got mad that she inherited the house and not him. I'd found the fancy marriage certificate in the desk the day we explored the place, which led me to search on Ancestry." The shock of the revelation remained fresh in Nicole's mind.

"Wait, you mean the Graham mansion is owned by a relative?" Connor's surprise was clear.

"Yes. At first, Aunt Janet was upset that we had been inside looking around. But she got over it and told me everything was mine but furniture and dishes. I asked about the rocking horse. She told me to take all the nursery furnishings because she had no use for it."

Nicole pulled into her parking space, shut off the engine, and turned to her brother, whose mouth gaped open.

Nicole had been carrying a secret of monumental proportions, a weight pressing down on her for days, if not weeks. No wonder she was so visibly nervous.

Connor's heart swelled with a profound sense of pride. His sister had unearthed a significant part of their family history, a discovery that filled him with a deep connection to their past.

Within minutes, Mitch pulled in with his truck and parked close to the building.

"So, I hear you had some excitement yesterday," Connor said.

Mitch's eyes darted from Connor to Nicole and back. She appeared to be on edge, too.

"The broken glass. Cutting your finger. It was more than that, wasn't it?" Connor probed, his voice low and intense.

Relief washed over the man's face. "You could say that," he said.

Something was going on between Nicole and Mitch. If Connor was a betting man, he'd swear something serious, not that bleeding like a stuffed pig wasn't.

"How's the work coming on the Anderson house?"

"Slow. Have a subcontractor coming in this week

if the rest of the supplies arrive. That's been the biggest delay. Waiting for pipe. Waiting for lumber and drywall. I have to re-plumb the entire house. She's living with her sister. Her cat is living with me."

Mitch, a pet owner. When they were kids, he never had a pet of any kind. But that might have been down to his parents. Connor and his siblings grew up with animals. Mostly dogs, but a pair of Guinea pigs lived with them for a while.

"Nicki is going to order us pizza," said Connor.

"Ah, her go-to for slave labour," Mitch said and chuckled.

Mitch opened the back passenger door of his truck. "Let's get this beast out and upstairs first."

Connor nodded and walked around to the other side of the truck. He opened the door. "You pull, I push?"

"Sounds good. Nicki can get the building doors."

With one good tug and Connor pushing from the other side, the rocking horse easily slid out of the truck. Now, to get a grip on it in a place where neither of them would get pinched if the thing swayed and inside it would go.

Mitch turned so that he walked frontwards to the building, holding the hobbyhorse behind him. It was much easier than when he and Nicole crab-walked it down the stairs and dragged it out of the mansion.

When they approached the outer door of Nicole's building, she pulled it open and held it for them to enter the lobby. While they waited for her to unlock the security door, Mitch sat his end of the rocking horse down. He inspected his bandaged hand. Still no blood. That was a good thing. He'd checked it periodically while working at the Anderson house. Through his peripheral vision, he watched Connor put down the other end of the heavy and awkward object.

Getting this thing into his apartment would have been much easier. Put it on a cart, wheel it through the garage to the elevator, and up to his floor. Mitch didn't look forward to the day he'd get voluntold to take the steed out of Nicole's flat.

About an hour later, they had everything out of the truck and into Nicole's apartment. She put the dressers in her bedroom, the paintings and other pictures on top of the boxes in the hallway, and the rocking horse by the window as planned. The only piece of furniture that didn't come up to the apartment was the crib, which went into her locker in the basement.

Mitch and Connor had collapsed on the couch. At least they still got along with one another. She'd like to find out what occurred between Mitch and Cooper, but he didn't have a clue either when she asked Mitch about it.

Nicole entered her living room carrying three bottles of Corona and handed two to her donkeys. "Pizza is ordered. I got two extra-large specials. Should be here in about half an hour."

"So you started to tell me about your visit with our aunt," Connor said.

"Right. So, it seems that June, who married Robert Holbrook, a war hero, remained in the house. Her son, William, after her." Nicole took a sip of her beer. "There's a gap, but from what I can tell, our grandfather took over the house next. He and our father never got along. Fought constantly over anything and everything. So, when our grandfather died, he left the house to Aunt Janet." The family history was like a puzzle with missing pieces, and Nicole was determined to fill in the gaps.

"Have you spoken to Dad about any of this?"

"Tried. He's not interested. Doesn't want me digging into it either."

Nicole stood and walked into the hall. A few minutes later, she returned with the yellowed newspaper article from one box she had brought home from her aunt's storage. "Handle it carefully. If I had cotton gloves, I'd make you put them on to touch it." She unfolded the brittle sheet of newsprint and laid it flat on the coffee table.

"What about the medals you told me about?"

Mitch said.

"Right." Nicole put her beer bottle on the floor under the edge of the low table and walked to the dining room. The envelope sat in the middle of her table, the contents on top.

"Here you go."

Chapter Forty-Six

NOVEMBER 28, 2022

While the conversation remained on topics other than something related to Nicole or Mitch, both seemed at ease in one another's company. But when it came to a lull, the atmosphere in the room changed. It became tense, and they couldn't look each other in the eye. A mystery hung in the air, a puzzle waiting to be solved. Now, to find out what. But how?

"These are quite the medals. I've seen some World War Two ones, but never ones this old. Especially a Victoria Cross.What are you going to do with them?" Mitch asked.

"Not sure. Shadow box? I'd also like the certificate to go in, but I'm unsure how it will work. I must be careful that it doesn't stick to the glass or it will ruin it."

"Any other treasures you haven't told us about?" Connor pressed.

"No. I still have more stuff to go through from Mummy's boxes. The pedigree chart I showed you and Cooper at work that day was the last thing I looked at. Who knows what other treasures lie hidden in those boxes?"

So much for that. Connor hoped she'd let something slip.

"So far, I've only seen the letters with the china head doll. The last one in there wasn't for Ute, even though it came in the envelope addressed to her."

"I remember that. Somehow, the soldier put a letter to his wife into an envelope meant for his lover,"

Connor said.

"I hope to find something in the boxes from Aunt Janet's. The one I got the newspaper clipping from looked well organized, so it shouldn't be hard to find anything. I want to find the letter he wrote to Ute and mailed to his wife."

The intercom interrupted their conversation. The pizzas Nicole had ordered arrived.

"Okay, guys. Over here. I don't want the things on the coffee table to get ruined." Nicole placed the two boxes in the middle of her dining room table and returned to the kitchen for plates and napkins.

The three sat at the table, and Connor opened the top pizza box. The guys each grabbed a couple of slices before Nicole grabbed a single one for herself. The two men worked hard, so they deserved it. As she brought her hand back, it brushed against Mitch's, and she jumped like she'd been scalded. At least her brother hadn't noticed. He was too busy stuffing his face. Mitch had, and one glance at his eyes almost finished her.

Nicole took a few deep breaths and sat. The gooey, stretchy, cheesy goodness made her tastebuds dance. The pepperoni was spicy, adding a bit of heat. The red onions and a spice she couldn't place completed the savoury meal. The only thing she had removed from the pizzas was green peppers. The food momentarily took her mind off the turn in her relationship with Mitch.

She stole a few glances at Mitch's hand. It was clean. Well, as much as possible when working on a job site all day and helping her move. The important thing was it hadn't started bleeding again. Anything red on it now was tomato sauce from the pizza.

"Anyone want another Corona?"

"Not me," said Connor.

"I shouldn't since I'll be driving later," said Mitch.

"That's good, because I think these were the last three," Nicole said, giggling.

"You're a tease, Nicole Holbrook," Mitch said.

The smile on his face threatened to melt her on

the spot.

The three didn't take long to polish off the two pizzas.

"You sit. I'll take the plates to the kitchen," said Mitch.

Before Nicole had the chance to protest, he had the plates stacked and in the kitchen. He returned to retrieve the empty pizza boxes.

She was bursting with words, but her brother's presence stifled her. She longed to express her gratitude, but the words remained trapped in her throat.

What was that expression? Name of a song, too. Stars in her eyes? His younger sister sure had them now every time she looked at Mitch. Three's a crowd, and worse when the third wheel is a sibling. Connor felt the tension in the air. He didn't dare tell Cooper what he witnessed between Nicole and Mitch tonight. She would when Nicole deemed it proper to tell their brother. It wasn't his place to do it.

They spent about an hour after their meal sitting around the table, their shared interest in urban exploration providing a safe haven for their conversation. It was a topic they all found fascinating, a common ground that kept them together.

"Any more ideas about how you ended up with the china head doll from Pike Falls, sis?"

She shot him the look. Oops. Not the question to ask.

"Well, if the little girl died ..."

"She did," Nicole snapped.

"Sorry. When the little girl died, do you think her parents returned the doll to the person who gave it to her?"

Nicole, elbows on the table, buried her face in her hands. That was the wrong subject to broach. Connor didn't want to upset his sister. He stood and walked behind her and hugged her.

"It's about time I left, anyway. I'll see you at work tomorrow, okay?"

Nicole stood and walked her brother to the door.

He shrugged on his jacket, then leaned over and whispered, "Your secret is safe with me." Another hug, and he was out the door.

It was an awkward time. Now, it was just Nicole and Mitch. She was so used to them being friends — they had been for years — she wasn't sure what to do now. Their relationship had always been platonic, and she had considered nothing beyond that. If it were anyone else, the butterflies wouldn't be there. Maybe they would, but their wings wouldn't be beating so hard and fast.

Until yesterday, it was friendly and protective whenever Mitch had put his arm around her or kissed her on the forehead. And then, in an instant, it all changed. His touch felt different, his gaze more intense, and his words carried a weight she had never felt before. How could she deal with that? Mitch had followed her to the door to see Connor off. "What did he whisper in your ear?"

"N-nothing." Nicole sidestepped him, her movements uncertain, and returned to the living room, where she started picking up the things on the coffee table they had looked at before supper.

Arms encircled her waist from behind. Hot, moist breath puffed on her bare neck.

"Not only are you a tease, Nicole Holbrook, but you're also beautiful." Mitch spun her around to face him.

Those dark brown eyes. Nicole could lose herself in them. She had always admired Mitch, his kindness, his humour, his unwavering support. But now, as he looked at her with such intensity, she felt a mix of confusion, fear, and a strange fluttering in her chest. Tidying would have to wait.

Her hazel eyes glistened with unshed tears. One escaped, and Mitch wiped it away with his thumb. "What's wrong?"

"I'm scared, Mitch. What if we've crossed a line and can never get back what we had before yesterday?"

"Do you want to go back to that?"

"Yes. No. I don't know." Nicole's voice wavered with uncertainty.

Mitch pulled her close to him. The warmth of her body against his was soothing and more. He stroked her hair, then lifted her chin so he could look her in the eyes.

"I won't make you do anything you don't want. You should know that by now. Whatever happens, we'll never lose our friendship since we were kids. I promise you that." Mitch's voice was firm.

Nicole broke out of his embrace and turned away from him. Maybe he had gone too far, too fast, when he kissed her after his trip to the hospital. Mitch raked his fingers through his hair and sighed. He'd fought these feelings for Nicole for a long time, primarily because of Cooper. Yes, the man thought he was protecting his sister, but with the length of time Mitch had been friends with the Holbrook siblings, Cooper should know by now he'd never hurt Nicole. His internal struggle was tearing him apart.

What a mess.

"Nicki, please." He placed his hand on her shoulder. She turned around. "I have a confession. Before you say anything, hear me out. I may have overstepped the mark kissing you last night, but I was afraid if I didn't soon give in to my intentions, you'd be with someone else. I love you, Nicole Holbrook. I have for a long time."

Despite the undeniable attraction, Nicole's stubbornness kept her from admitting her feelings for Mitch. Whenever he put his arm around or kissed her forehead, the little frisson of excitement was a secret she held close, one she was not yet ready to reveal.

"I-I don't know what to say," she whispered.

"Then say nothing." Mitch leaned down and kissed her.

At that moment, they were the only two people in the world. She leaned into him and wrapped her arms around his waist.

After the kiss, Nicole's lips were numb from its intensity. "I love you, too, Mitch." There, she'd admitted her love for him. As long as there was excitement and not the familiarity of a cozy pair of slippers or bathrobe, things between them would be fine.

"What did Connor whisper in your ear when he left?" Mitch asked again.

"He said my secret was safe with him. I guess he sensed the change in our relationship dynamics. I wasn't ready for my brothers to find out until I was ready to tell them." The uncertainty of the situation hung in the air.

The clock chimed ten o'clock. How had that much time passed? Okay, it took some time to get everything unloaded and upstairs into the apartment and more or less put away. Then, they had to wait for the pizza delivery. So, that much time may have elapsed.

"I should go," Mitch said.

"Do you have to?"

"I better. I'll see you tomorrow evening."

Nicole walked Mitch to the door. He planted a soft, lingering kiss on her lips before he left. She didn't want him to leave, but was afraid of how far things might go if he stayed.

He didn't want to leave either, but he couldn't trust himself to not take things too far if he'd stayed. That would ruin everything. Mitch wanted to be certain Nicole wanted intimacy as much as he did before he made that move.

Another cold shower when he got home, but it wasn't the first time he'd done that. And he was certain it wouldn't be his last. He had Raven to thank for insisting he went home, even though the cat was never mentioned.

Connor wouldn't tell Cooper about what he witnessed tonight at Nicole's. If he mentioned anything, it would be helping them move stuff from the truck upstairs and looking at the medals and certificates.

To get his thoughts off Nicole, he reviewed in his mind everything that still had to be done at Mrs.

Anderson's house. The upstairs bathroom where the leak started had new floor joists installed. The plumbing in that room was complete. Sheet the floor and drywall the ceiling in the room below, although that could wait.

The new bathtub was to arrive this week, so hopefully, it came on time, and it wouldn't be a brute to manhandle up the stairs and into the bathroom. Mitch called Mrs. Anderson with regular progress reports. He should have called her earlier, but it was too late now. Phone calls after ten o'clock almost always meant bad news.

Nicole, her mind racing with the revelations of the evening, found herself unable to sleep. She dressed in warm, cozy pyjamas and slipper socks, a futile attempt to calm her nerves. The well-organized box containing the newspaper clipping now seemed to mock her. She retrieved a bundle of letters addressed to June Holbrook and padded to the couch, her heart pounding.

They were from Robert, and the content was mundane. How were things at home? How was William? Are you coping all right with me away? Normal, family stuff. Then there was the next one on the pile. She had to do a double take. The envelope addressed to June contained a letter to Ute. The contrast between the mundane and passionate letters added to the emotional conflict Nicole currently experienced.

30 June, 1915

My dearest Ute,
We have been under heavy attack, but things are quieter today, so I thought I would write to you. I'm sorry we only had one night together. You are such a beautiful woman. I try to hold your image in my mind. Sometimes, you blur away, and I see my wife's face instead. Not that it's a bad thing, June is a wonderful woman, but she's not the same exciting lover as you.

Nicole shivered. This man, this soldier, was indeed in love with Ute. The contrast between the passion in the letters to Ute and the lifeless ones to June told of the emotional turmoil he must have been in. War and the possibility of death led people to do things they wouldn't normally do. But here was another letter to Ute filled with passion.

Perhaps, I only think of you that way because of our circumstances inside a barn in the hay mow in Lützkampen. I yearn to be with you that way again, but in a proper bed. Someplace where I can admire your beauty. Perhaps in a hotel room or a room at an inn. A hotel seems more anonymous, so there would be no danger of your husband finding out about us.
All my love,

Robert
xoxo

The letters to his wife were flat and lifeless. There was not even some excitement when he mentioned his son. Given the timing of William's birth and their marriage, June was pregnant on their wedding day. Did he feel trapped? Marry her out of obligation and never love her? She laid the letter on the coffee table.

It had been folded in the envelope for so long that it wouldn't lie flat, so she placed two of her blown glass paperweights on the diagonal corners so the handwriting remained visible. Nicole snapped a picture with her phone and then sent a message to Mitch with the photo attached.

Look what I just found!

While Nicole waited for Mitch to return her text, she looked at the following letter in the stack. Unopened. Every one written by Robert from that point onwards remained unopened. The temptation to open them was almost too much to bear, but Nicole placed the ones she'd read back on top of the pile and secured them with the ribbon.

Chapter Forty-Seven

T he day of the funeral had arrived. Ute, her body a canvas of fading bruises and darkening injuries, was a portrait of inner turmoil. Her ribs, aching with each breath, were a physical manifestation of her emotional conflict. She should have sought medical help, but the fear of awkward questions held her back.

Rain and snow mixed in with unforgiving winter winds made the day of the funeral cruel. The community huddled in the church and listened to the minister's eulogy. He praised Valter's virtues, unaware of the man behind the facade.

Because of the ground being frozen, the gravediggers couldn't prepare the grave for the coffin. Instead, they interred him in the vault until spring, when they would bury him after the thaw. Winter had robbed Ute of the chance to stand over his casket in the ground and spit on him. Instead, she stayed in the church and wept, but not for Valter, but for Robert.

Chapter Forty-Eight

NOVEMBER 29, 2022

Mitch hadn't replied to her text message before she went to bed the night before, so she checked her phone. Still no message. Did that mean he'd changed his mind about their relationship? Nicole had expected a response within minutes of her sending it. If he was busy or hadn't made it home yet ... Did that mean he'd been in an accident on his way home from her apartment?

Worst-case scenarios raced through her head. He lay somewhere because he bled to death thanks to the gash on his finger, which was down to her wanting to explore the remains of what might have been the Holbrook farm. Nicole's phone pinged, and she snatched it up. Mitch. He'd finally replied to her text.

Sorry, didn't see it until now. Battery on phone died. Quite the interesting letter.

Nicole sighed. All those worst-case scenarios were for naught. Mitch was fine. His phone was the dead thing. She threw back the covers and swung her legs off the mattress.

Something on the nightstand caught her eye. It wasn't there when she climbed into bed. The only things on its surface then were her water glass, phone, reading lamp, and box of tissues. Nicole picked up the object — a photograph of an older house with a farm windmill behind it. She turned the picture over to reveal the backside of a postcard. Someone had written on the back, but she was unable to read it in the dim light, so she switched on the lamp.

A pencil had been used, and the handwriting was horrendous. She needed better light to decipher the chicken scratch.

Found something weird on my nightstand. It's a photo postcard. Not there when I went to bed.

She picked up her phone and the picture and headed to the bathroom, her curiosity piqued. The light was better there, but that wasn't her main reason for stopping.

Once in the kitchen, Nicole started a pot of coffee and laid the postcard face-down on the counter. The bright overhead light forced her to blink when it first came to life, but her eyes had now adjusted to it.

More of the writing showed up. Nicole kept a magnifying glass in a drawer, so she pulled it out and used it to enlarge the writing. It looked like *Claude & Lizzie's house.* Who were Claude and Lizzie? She dashed into the living room, where her backpack sat in the corner. She pulled out the documents she had printed from Ancestry when she started searching. Claude and Elizabeth Holbrook with their son Robert. That had to be a photograph of the Holbrook family home.

Nicole snapped a picture of the postcard and attached it to a message to her brothers.

This is the Holbrook house next door to the Graham mansion.

This piece of evidence would go to work with her later. She had sent Mitch the letter last night. Her brothers needed to see it, too. With a determined click, she attached it to another message, ready to continue her quest.

Letter from Robert to Ute sent to June by mistake.

Nicole had solved two mysteries within twenty-four hours. First, the identity of the Holbrook house, and second, the letter from Robert to Ute mailed to June in error. Would her aunt be able to identify the house in the photograph? Probably not, since it burned to the ground long before Janet and her father were born.

Unless, the woman had seen a photo of it similar to this one. She had to send the picture to Mitch, too.

The Holbrook house where ... she backspaced. Mitch didn't need to be reminded of his misfortune there.

The Holbrook house.

Nicole left the message at that.

Did she dare bunk off from work again? She could work at home — she had done it before — and nothing was pressing that had to be done in the office. The clients had approved her designs for the *Cheese Board & Café* artwork, and she had digitized them so everything was on the system at work and ready to be inserted in the headers for the website and other locations.

While Mitch wasn't interested in genealogy, he specialized in historic homes and other buildings and had a keen interest in urban exploration. The letter was an eye-opener — a man madly in love with a woman he couldn't have. Except he did. For Robert's sake, it was a good thing he was halfway around the world. His wife would have killed him. In the end, the result was the same, but the war got him.

The picture of the house and windmill intrigued him. There was no room for a barn on the corner of the property where the house stood. It might have been across the road. The house, before it burnt, stood near the corner. What secrets might be revealed about the house that no longer existed? The possibilities were endless.

When he saw the footprint of the house from the nursery, Nicole was reciting a poem. What was the name of it? Ghost House. Mitch looked it up on his phone.

It didn't warrant an archaeological dig, but a metal detector might be useful. Mitch googled them, found one that would do the trick, and ordered it from Amazon. Even though he lived in a secure apartment building, he was never home during the day. He had it shipped to the Anderson house since that's where he'd spent most of his time lately. Guaranteed two-day delivery, so he'd have it for the weekend, and the prospect of their metal-detecting adventure thrilled him.

If Nicole came with him, he'd ensure she wore better footwear than her canvas running shoes. It was bad enough that he had gotten cut. He typed out a quick message to her and hit send.

Ordered metal detector. We can try it out on Saturday. Wear decent shoes. Not your runners.

That would work, provided it didn't snow between now and then. It had been relatively mild for this time of year, so the ground wasn't frozen. If it snowed, their metal detecting would be put off until spring.

What would they find in and around the Holbrook family home? Metal detecting was something she and her brothers had never done. But it went against the take nothing, leave only footprints mantra. If you went to the trouble to scan the ground and dig up your findings, you'd want to take them with you.

The house no longer stood, so they wouldn't break that unwritten code of urban exploration, although other explorers took objects. Others who entered the empty properties vandalized them. They had been lucky with the last two places — Kembleford Manor and the Graham mansion — they remained in decent repair.

As Nicole sipped her coffee, she brought out another stack of documents from the first box from her aunt. Some contents, like grocery lists written on the detachable leaves from calendars, made her question why they were kept. Nothing was written on the front of the pages. But then, she found a document on heavier green paper, folded in half. At the top, it read CERTIFIED COPY OF AN ENTRY OF MARRIAGE.

The marriage took place on January 2, 1940, in the church in the parish of Deal, Kent, England. Interesting. Nicole read further. William Holbrook, aged 25, bachelor and Canadian soldier living in the village of Deal. The bride was Alice Bates, aged 21, spinster and barmaid, who also lived in the same village.

She'd found Robert's son's marriage certificate —

well, at least a copy of it. This discovery might unlock a significant part of the family's history. Had someone tried to research the family before and been stymied by some members, not wanting their secrets to be known?

Nicole folded it and set it aside. Another official-looking document lay under it. When she unfolded it, she discovered an original birth certificate for Grayson Holbrook, born on November 11, 1940, in Deal, Kent, England — her grandfather's birth certificate. This document and the marriage certificate were not just historical records; but part of her family's story, and they were going to work with her.

Her smartwatch vibrated on her wrist. She would be late for work. Nicole raced around the apartment, gathering the things she needed to take to the office, getting dressed, and doing the rest of her bathroom ablutions. There wasn't time for all her makeup, so she settled for a slash of eyeliner and mascara.

Chapter Forty-Nine

Nicole breezed into the office as if on a cushion of air, excited about the things she had found; the fact that the photograph of the house materialized out of the blue didn't factor into the equation.

"I sent you the letter that Robert wrote to Ute but mailed to June. And the picture of the house. Well, the rest of the letters from Robert to June in that same stack were never opened. I'm willing to bet they're full of grovelling, apologizing, and general sucking up."

"Yes."

"I've found more, but I'm holding off until Dad's here for the big reveal," Nicole announced with excitement.

"I'll give him a shout," Cooper said, leaving his siblings in the main office.

Connor sidled over to Nicole, his curiosity piqued. "Why do I think there is more to your mood than your big discovery that you can't share with us until Dad gets here?"

"I don't know what you mean," she said, trying to sound innocent.

"That's Dad called. He'll be here shortly. I told him you had something to show him."

Unable to contain her excitement and nervousness, Nicole sat at her desk and fidgeted with a pencil. She was excited with her findings, but nervous about how her father would react to her findings. Her father, who had always been guarded about their family's past, was about to be confronted with a part she had uncovered.

Time seemed to stretch endlessly, but only half an hour passed before their father finally stepped into the office, his presence adding a layer of tension to the already charged atmosphere.

"What's so important you had to drag me out at this time of day?" Frank asked, as he pulled the office door open. Even without the man speaking, Nicole knew someone had come in because of the scraping of the door.

The tension was so thick it could be cut with a knife, and the scowl on Frank's face spoke volumes about his mood.

"Did you know your great-grandfather, Robert Holbrook, was a war hero? Killed during the Battle of Passchendaele in World War One. Awarded the Victoria Cross, too," said Nicole, keeping her voice calm and steady. "I found an envelope containing it and the certificate that accompanied it and his other war medals in the nursery at the mansion."

Her father's brow furrowed.

Did this mean he had no idea his ancestor was a war hero? The expression on his face seemed to say that.

Nicole continued. "While we're talking about Robert, did you also know he had a relationship with another woman soon after he was sent overseas?"

Frank's colour changed from its everyday shade of pale to crimson. "Dammit, Nicole, I told you not to interfere in things you know nothing about. Or have any business knowing. It's in the past."

Despite the tears threatening to spill, Nicole held them back, refusing to show weakness in front of her father.

"I suppose that sister of mine told you. I visited her shortly after that damn doll turned up. Told her not to tell you anything. But Janet always knows best. She told you, didn't she?" He stepped forward and pointed an accusing finger at her face.

"Geez, Dad. Take a chill pill," Connor said, stepping to his sister's side. He rubbed her back.

"No, Dad. Aunt Janet told me nothing. I found some letters in the bottom of the china head doll box. I saw her, and she didn't say a word. Instead, she gave me the key to her storage unit in the basement and told me to take everything there. I found things out reading letters from Robert to June, and one sent to June meant for his lover, Ute."

Frank paced back and forth like a caged animal, one arm folded against his stomach, the other still pointing his finger.

"Connor, Cooper and I explored the Graham mansion. That house you're so miffed about not being left to you in your father's will. I found a marriage certificate in a desk drawer."

This wasn't Nicole. Not his daughter. He didn't recognize this young woman standing before him, speaking over him. Whoever had taken over his daughter's body could leave at any time.

Frustrated, Frank raked his fingers through his salt and pepper hair. He removed his glasses, tossed them on one a desk, and pinched the bridge of his nose, a sign of his growing impatience.

"I suppose you're not finished, are you?"

"As a matter of fact, I'm just getting started," Nicole declared, reaching into her backpack and pulling out the things she'd brought from her apartment.

"This is the picture of Claude and Lizzie Holbrook's house, which stood on the corner next to the Graham mansion. Their son, Robert, married George and Myrtle's daughter, June. That union produced William. And it appears June was pregnant when she and Robert married. But that's another story."

Heat rose to Frank's cheeks, his anger simmering just beneath the surface. How dare his daughter speak to him in that tone? If she was younger, he'd have her over his knee.

"William went overseas at the beginning of World

War Two. He was stationed in the village of Deal. That's in Kent, England, in case you didn't know. He married a young barmaid from the town. Here's their wedding certificate, certified copy anyway."

Frank reached for it, but Nicole pulled it away from him, afraid if he got his hands on it, he'd rip it to shreds.

"And the next piece of evidence I have is your father's, our grandfather's, birth certificate. He was born in England. Did you know that? Do you even care?"

"Of course, I care. Why do you think I've been trying to keep you from digging all this up? It will come to no good, I promise you."

"So far, it's come to a lot of good. I know why you never took us there as kids. You didn't get along with your parents. They were against you and Mummy marrying. And you were mad at Aunt Janet because your father left the house to her and not you."

Nicole stood on her tiptoes, almost nose to nose with her father. Connor reached his arm across in front of her and pulled her back.

"Don't do it, sis," he whispered.

"What's with the freaky Freemason ceiling medallion? Or the Baphomet that I found buried under the floorboards of an upstairs bedroom?" Nicole asked.

Frank turned so red he looked ready to explode.

"Don't worry, Dad. With or without your help, I'll get to the bottom of it."

"Nic ... I'm warning you. Let it go." Again, the accusing finger pointed in her face.

"I also know that the Kembleford Manor Hotel in Pike Falls was part of our history on Mummy's side. So, there are secrets all around us. We're not immune to them."

Nicole turned her back to her father and leaned against her desk. She vibrated. Whether it was from fear or adrenalin remained unknown. This didn't work out the way she planned. Not by a long shot. Connor wrapped his arm around her, and she buried her face in his shoulder.

The front door opened. Even without looking in that direction, she knew her father had left the building. The door scraped when it opened and closed.

"You okay, sis?" Connor asked.

"I will be, thanks."

"I've never seen Dad so bent out of shape before. You hit a nerve," Cooper said.

Frank, his determination burning within him, climbed into his car and slammed his hand on the steering wheel. Why didn't Nicole leave well enough alone and let sleeping dogs lie? It had to be his sister. She had to be the one who encouraged his daughter down this path. He started the engine and sped out of the parking lot. He had some words for Janet, and nothing was going to stop him.

A few skeletons remained hidden in the family closets, but Nicole was on the verge of discovering them. He didn't want that. The thought of everything he'd fought for since childhood being destroyed was unbearable.

He sped towards the assisted living facility where his sister lived since her accident. If he caught her off guard, she might let something slip. If only.

Frank brought his vehicle to a screeching halt in Willow Glen Manor's parking lot, slammed it into park, and rushed to the door, his heart pounding in his chest. Every second precious as he pressed the lock button on his key fob.

Breathless, when he arrived at reception, he panted, "Janet Holbrook. I'm here to see my sister."

"Please sign the visitors' register," the receptionist said.

He scribbled his name and his time of entry.

"She's upstairs in her room. You can take those stairs or the elevator there."

Frank opted for the stairs. He'd have to wait for the lift. And who knew how many old and infirm people would arrive on it.

Frank burst into his sister's room, his voice

echoing off the walls. "What are you playing at, Janet? What have you told Nicole?"

"Not a word, I can assure you."

He leaned over, his hands gripping the arms of her wheelchair. "You're lying. I know you are. Just like you did when we were kids, to get your own way." Frank sprang back from the chair and spun around.

"I have no idea what you're talking about. Why don't you calm down? We can talk about it like rational adults." Janet pleaded with her brother.

"That's rich coming from you."

"Honestly, Frank. I think you've lost the plot. You come here ranting and raving and not giving me any clue what your tantrum is about."

"Christ, Janet. You should know. You told Nicole. You defied my wishes and told her things about the family."

"All right, I admit I told her about you and our parents, but nothing else."

"Then how did she know of these other things?"

"I gave her the boxes from my storage locker. What happened after she removed them wasn't down to me. Nicole's a smart girl. She'd figure it out without any help. And, in case you forgot, she and her brothers are urban explorers. They wandered through the Graham mansion before Nicole even came to see me."

"You vindictive, manipulative bitch. Thanks to you, you've turned my kids against me."

"I did no ..." Janet gripped her chest. Her face paled, and beads of sweat formed on her forehead. Suddenly, she pitched forward out of her wheelchair and collapsed on the floor.

Within minutes, staff from the home arrived in Janet's room. One carried the portable defibrillator.

"Her fall detector went off. What happened?"

"I-we ..." Frank turned away. Despite everything that happened between him and his sister over the years, he didn't want it to end like this.

Someone began CPR on Janet while the person who brought the defibrillator readied it for use. They shocked her with no result.

The ambulance arrived, the EMTs entered the room, and took over from the home's staff.

It was to no avail. Janet Holbrook was dead.

Chapter Fifty

NOVEMBER 29, 2022

Nicole slumped into her chair with her brothers on either side of her. What had she done? She'd never challenged her father like that before. But something was not right about his side of the family. What other reason could there be for the man to be so adamant about leaving things alone.

One of the local courier companies arrived. Among the packages they delivered was a cardboard envelope addressed to Nicole.

She pulled the tab, pulled the contents out, and set the mailer aside. It was a letter from Aunt Janet.

Nicole tore open the paper envelope and yanked out the letter, which had been written the previous Friday.

Nov 25, 2022

Dear Nicole,

I want you to have this as proof should anything happen to me. It's only a matter of time before your father shows up here shouting the odds.

When I die, the house is yours. I've updated my will, which is on file at my lawyer's office. His business card is enclosed with this letter.

You don't want to think ill of your father, I know that, but you should learn a few things. In one of his spats with your grandfather, Frank pushed him down the stairs. That was a terrible fight. It was down to our parents not wanting your dad to marry your mother. To our shame, we all covered up for him and said that our father tripped and fell down the stairs. The fall fractured his skull, and he spent the rest of his days in a coma.

Nicole paused. She found it difficult to see through the unshed tears. Her father almost killed his father. It didn't sound logical, at least not until today. The wrath she witnessed earlier was minor compared to what her aunt said in this letter.

"You okay, sis?" Cooper asked.

She reached over and squeezed her brother's hand. It was a pleasant change to see him so concerned. Typically, it was Connor who asked about her well-being. But this letter was turning their world upside down, too.

Nicole took a deep breath and continued reading out loud.

Remember, I told you I tripped over Bruiser when I took my tumble down the stairs? I lied to you that day. I did that to protect you. You didn't know what your father was capable of. It wasn't Bruiser who caused my fall. It was your father.

Nicole gasped. Her father wasn't capable of these heinous acts. At least, not the father she knew before today. She handed the letter to Cooper. "Please keep reading. I can't."

By the time I took my fall, your grandfather had died, and I had inherited the house, something your father never got over. I think guilt over what he'd done to me made him help me get into Willow Glen. But I don't trust him. Not for a minute.

Nicole, Connor, and Cooper, should anything happen to me, and I die before my time, please believe there were extenuating circumstances involved. Those being my brother, Frank Holbrook. Notify the authorities on my behalf because I won't be able to do it.

I pray to God that your mother was never aware of this dark side your father carried around with him. If the cancer and COVID hadn't killed her, his actions would have.

I'm sorry you had to find out about your father like this, but it was the best way I could think of to tell you. If you look up newspaper articles on your grandfather's and my accidents, you'll find them online — at least the Holbrook spin on the mishaps.

Love
Aunt Janet

The father she'd known all these years was a monster. No wonder he didn't want her digging into the family's history.

Along with her two brothers, they joined together in a group hug and wept.

"I think we should close up for the day. There's nothing that won't keep until tomorrow," Cooper said, his voice trembling. He still reeled from the contents of his aunt's letter. His father, a man Cooper had always looked up to, was a fraud. The revelation was like a lightning bolt, shattering his perception of his father. He wasn't the caring, compassionate man he portrayed, but a cold-blooded monster. If not for the fact his grandfather and aunt both survived their accidents, he would have been a murderer, although his grandfather did eventually die as a result.

"I agree," said Connor. "What about you, Nicki?"

"I don't want to go home alone. Dad's actions today scared the life out of me. He's so angry; what if he tries to hurt me like he did our grandfather and aunt?"

"Come to ours. Safety in numbers. We'll keep you safe." Cooper drew his sister into a hug.

As they began shutting down equipment and lights, a police cruiser pulled up in front of their office. This happened often, but usually the officers visited the coffee shop at the end of the strip mall or had business elsewhere. Today, they entered CNC IT Solutions, adding to the tense atmosphere.

"You Nicole Holbrook? And you two are her brothers?"

"Yes," all three answered in unison.

"There's been a mishap at Willow Glen Manor."

The assisted living facility where Aunt Janet had gone. Cooper had never visited her, but remembered the name.

"What kind of mishap?" Cooper asked.

"One Janet Holbrook, we believe to be your aunt, died earlier of a massive heart attack."

The letter, a crumpled and tear-stained piece of paper, held the weight of Aunt Janet's accusations. As luck would have it, they hadn't shut down the colour copier printer.

"Nicole, where's the letter?"

She handed it to him, and Cooper made a copy.

"It arrived today. Only my aunt who wrote it, and my sister and I have touched the letter," he said, handing the photocopy to the officer.

"Your aunt has made some serious accusations against her brother. Do you think your father is capable of committing these assaults?"

"Until today, no. But Dad showed up here this morning spewing fire and brimstone at Nicole because she found out some information on our family history on our father's side. Nothing that man does would surprise me anymore."

"I realize you'd prefer to keep the original copy of the letter, but do you think we could have it instead? Let our forensic people examine it. Sometimes, you can tell a lot from a person's handwriting."

"Like they were made to write it?" asked Nicole.

"Yes."

"Take it."

"We'll get you a proper receipt for it."

Nicole dropped into the nearest chair. Today had turned into a giant nightmare. Going to her brothers' apartment so she wouldn't be home alone eased her mind, but she'd rather spend the day with Mitch.

"Come on, sis," Connor said, offering his hand to help her up.

Cooper had already locked the front door after the police left and was headed back to set the alarm.

"Best not keep him waiting. You can use my room at the apartment. Text or phone Mitch, sleep, whatever you need to do."

"Thanks."

Nicole walked to the back, with Connor supporting her. After reading the letter and receiving the police visit, her legs were wobbly.

Outside, he helped her into the front seat of Cooper's SUV. That was different. She usually rode in the back. Her brothers were as shocked as she was and every bit as afraid for her. Nicole never dreamt her father would do anything to hurt her — until today.

Was her father with Aunt Janet when she had her heart attack? Did he upset her to the point she had it? These questions swirled in her mind. When she visited, she'd seen no prescription bottles on the table or nightstand. But then, didn't most retirement/assisted living places administer the drugs to ensure the residents took them?

At that moment, Nicole craved Mitch's presence more than ever. She yearned to be enveloped in his powerful arms, to hear him assure her of her safety. Connor seemed to understand the change in her relationship with Mitch and was supportive. But what about Cooper? Would he be as accepting when he found out?

If everything continued on course, things could be wrapped up by the weekend at the Anderson house. The fixtures had been delivered on time. The drywall man was doing a fantastic job on the ceiling where the old tub fell through. It was not just smooth drywall, but it had made a series of arcs with the trowel, and it was much nicer than the old lath and plaster ceiling covered with paper.

Mitch's phone vibrated in his pocket. He pulled it out, expecting it to be a text message, but it wasn't.

Nicole was phoning him.

"Are you all right? Only you don't normally phone."

"Oh, Mitch," she cried. "It's such a mess."

His heart clenched at the torment in her voice. "Slow down. What's a mess?"

Nicole related the earlier events, including the letter's contents. He hadn't seen Nicole's father in a long time, but he didn't seem to be the type she had just told him.

"Where are you?"

"I'm at Cooper and Connor's apartment. They're here, too. I'm safe."

"I'll come and get you."

"No, please don't. I'll be fine here. I just needed to hear your voice."

"Nic ..."

She had already disconnected the call.

Mitch's protective instinct towards Nicole surged. All these years, a man he had looked up to had been revealed as a monster. She'd be safer at his apartment. Her father didn't know its location.

Going to get her would mean Cooper finding out about their relationship before Nicole could break it to him. The tension between Mitch and Cooper ran deep. To hell with Cooper. Nicole's safety was paramount.

He looked into the room where the drywall man worked and told him he'd be offsite for a few hours but would be back to lock up. With steely determination, Mitch climbed into his truck and raced to the Holbrook brothers' apartment.

Connor's voice was firm as he answered the intercom.

"I'm here to get Nicole and take her to my place. If she's there, she's safe because your father doesn't know where I live," Mitch said. His words carried a weight of responsibility, a determination to keep Nicole safe at all costs.

Mitch's understanding was evident. Not that his father visited frequently, but he knew the location of his children's homes. But they lived in secure buildings. How much did that count for? Anyone could ring another apartment with some excuse, get in, or follow someone else through the door.

Things would get messy, though, with Cooper not liking Mitch anymore for whatever reason. Still, his sister's welfare was at stake. He released the latch to let Mitch pass the security door and held his breath.

"Wait there," Connor said when Mitch reached the apartment's entrance.

He then walked to his room and knocked on the door. "Someone to see you, sis," he whispered.

Nicole's eyes were red and puffy, and her mascara had run. "Who?"

"Go find out." He winked.

Connor followed his sister to the door. She threw herself into his arms when she saw who awaited her. The tension in Connor's neck and shoulders eased.

"Thanks, Conn," he mouthed.

He did the right thing, letting his sister go with Mitch. In his gut, he knew it was right.

"Who was at the door?"

"Some sales scam. The guy must have rung his way through the security door." Connor hated lying to his brother, but swore to Nicole that he would keep her and Mitch's secret. And he had so far.

Chapter Fifty-One

U te stared at the china head doll she passed down to her granddaughter, Grace. She recalled the day with clarity when she handed the doll to Mary and Walter to be put away for their infant daughter when she was old enough to understand its value and care for it.

Dear Mother Ute,

It is with heavy hearts that we share the news of Grace's passing. She left us on August 31st, a victim of a tragic drowning. The sight of this doll serves as a constant reminder of our profound loss. We believe it belongs with you now.

We have moved out of Kembleford Manor. Too many strange things happened there. You might think me insane, but I think the vindictive spirit of Ophelia Kembleford lured Grace to her death. Besides the strange goings-on, Grace's death was the final straw. I can't live in a house where my child died. Walter is having a difficult time coping with her passing, too. She was his little sunshine, as you know.

We plan to return south, whether in Quabbinville or the St. Jacob's area where you live. I don't yet know. I just know we want to be near family.

Please, Mother Ute, take good care of the doll. Grace named her Clara, and we want her to remain a cherished part of our family history.

Your loving daughter-in-law,

Mary

Now, her granddaughter was dead. She'd drowned at the Kembleford Manor Hotel. No one seemed to know how she ended up in the boathouse that day, let alone how she ended up in the water. Mary had written a brief note and put it in the package with the doll.

When she gave the doll to her granddaughter, she kept the box in which it came. It was about the size of a large shoebox. Not that she bought many pairs for herself, but having two young boys, they were always outgrowing footwear. And the winters in Canada were far more harsh than in her homeland, so the boys needed winter boots, too.

Ute had saved the newspaper clippings of Robert's death in the Great War. They told of his hometown. She would package the doll up and send it to his widow. Perhaps, by now, she had a granddaughter who would appreciate it.

Chapter Fifty-Two

NOVEMBER 29, 2022

The last thing Nicole expected was for Mitch to drop everything and come pick her up. It went well beyond his remit as a friend, but she was still thankful to be with him.

"You can stay at mine for as long as you need," Mitch said, his voice filled with empathy. "You'll be safe there. Your father doesn't know where I live. I'm sorry about your aunt. Guess I won't get to meet her after all."

"Thanks. I'm still trying to wrap my head around everything Aunt Janet said about my father, that he pushed Grandpa Holbrook down the stairs. And her, too. I never thought he was that twisted and bitter. You don't suppose she lied, do you?" Nicole asked.

"Having never met your aunt, I can't say."

"It wouldn't surprise me if my father had something to do with the Holbrook house, too, except it's long since gone."

"Is there anything you need from your place? We can swing by on the way to mine."

"No. I'm fine for now. Maybe tomorrow."

Nicole stole a glimpse at Mitch's bandaged hand. It appeared clean from where she sat.

"Was that Mitch's voice I heard?" Cooper asked.

"Yes. Nicole has gone to stay at his apartment for a few days."

Cooper half expected his brother to make up a story, so it surprised him when Connor fessed up.

"Before you get bent out of shape and go off half-cocked, it's a good thing."

"Why's that?"

A can of beer landed in his lap, tossed from the dining room. He opened it and took a sip. It might be a bit early for drinking, but it hit the spot with how things had played out earlier in the day.

"Dad knows where Nicole's apartment is."

"Yeah, so? That's why we brought her here."

Connor pulled the tab on his beer and slugged some back. "But Dad also knows where we live. He has no clue where Mitch lives. I don't even know. So, if Nicki is there, that's the safest place for her."

Cooper snorted. His sister safe with Mitchell Kane? He severely doubted it. But the fact the man's apartment's location was unknown to their father made sense. He hated to admit his brother was right.

Mitch had better hope he did nothing to hurt Nicole because Cooper would come down on him like a ton of bricks. His sister said many times she didn't need protecting. He begged to differ with that. She got involved with that guy at college, and he nearly destroyed her.

Likely just as well, because he had the same possessive, protective streak as their father. Did he blame Mitch for what happened? Was Mitch the one who gaslit his sister? Mitch was away at school himself when it started taking some trades course. Just like he and Connor were at college, at home in Belleville. They were in their last year, and Nicole was in her first. But she had opted to go to an out-of-town school. Supposedly, it had a better program for what she wanted.

Had he been unfair to Mitch? Maybe. But if that guy hurt Nicole, there would be no telling what would happen.

"Can we go back to the Graham mansion?" Nicole asked, wringing her hands in anguish. The entire day had been a nightmare, yet she was excited about what she found. Her father's bizarre behaviour towards her that morning spooked her.

"It's a bit late now, but yeah. What's on your mind?"

Nicole paused before speaking again. "When I first went with my brothers to explore the mansion, I saw and heard things. Not scary things like at Kembleford Manor. Yes, there were ghosts, but not evil ones. At least none that had manifested themselves to me." She turned in the seat.

"I'm not sure I follow," Mitch said as he started the engine.

"I'm now starting to think something bad happened, maybe when my father was a little boy. I mean, the Freemason symbol on the ceiling medallion is freaky; you must admit that."

"I'll give you that. Not exactly the kind of decor I'd want in my house."

"So, what if my grandfather was the leader of a chapter of Freemasons? They met at his place in the room with the medallion. The Baphomet was part of their ceremony."

"Okay, but I still don't know where you're going with this, Nicole." Mitch's confusion was clear as he signalled to turn at the next intersection.

"What if, I can't believe I'm saying this, but what if my father walked in on their meeting and saw something he shouldn't have?" Nicole's voice trembled with fear.

"Like what?"

"A ritual gone wrong? I don't know. If I walked in and saw something like that, it would push me over the edge."

"I have to go back to the Anderson house and lock up. Do you want to come with me, or do you want me to drop you at my place first?"

"I'll go with you. I don't want to be alone right now."

"Okay." Mitch pondered what Nicole had said to him. He knew nothing about the Freemasons except for their symbol. He drove on to the Anderson house on the outskirts of town in a historic area.

When Mitch pulled into the driveway, the drywaller was loading his equipment in his van. Once he loaded his things, Mitch locked the house and shook hands with the man.

When he returned to his truck, he turned to Nicole and said, "We can go to the Graham house tomorrow."

"Thanks. You don't think I'm crazy, do you?"

What could he say? She wasn't crazy. What was the term? Medium? Spirits tended to appear to her and channel their energy through her. He never saw the things she did except in her sketches. Mitch found it hard to believe in the supernatural, but Nicole's experiences were undeniable.

"No, I don't think you're crazy," Mitch reassured her, his voice steady and calm.

About ten minutes after they left the Anderson house, Mitch pulled into the underground parking lot at his apartment building. His protective instincts kicked in, and he knew Nicole would be safe there.

A shadow near one pillar startled him, but once he pulled into his parking spot, it was gone. It must have been a trick of the lights.

Raven trotted to the door to meet them upstairs in Mitch's apartment. Nicole bent down, picked up the cat, and walked to the balcony doors. In the darkness, the lights from the streets and sidewalks around the harbour reflected on the water. This view captivated her. Mitch must pay a fortune in rent. Hers on her small apartment in a secure building near her brothers and their office was outrageous, but it gave her a roof over her head.

Even if her father became infirm, she doubted she'd move in to look after him. Something must have happened to him when he was a little boy. Of that, she was positive. But what? Did his parents physically abuse him? Worse, was he sexually abused by one of them? Now, with her aunt dead, she had no one to ask. Her father wouldn't tell her anything.

Pots and pans clanging and clattering in the kitchen pulled her out of her reverie. She kissed Raven's head and placed the cat on the floor. Nicole could picture herself living here. Snowflake, the name she'd christened the rocking horse with, would stand by the balcony doors.

During their childhood, if Mitch wasn't at their house, she and her brothers were at his. They lived on the same street. The Holbrooks lived in a three-bedroom semi. The Kanes, across the road and down a bit, in a larger detached two-storey brick house.

Mitch's parents never put on airs and graces. Yes, they had money. She didn't remember what his father did for a living, but his mother was a stay-at-home mom who always welcomed the neighbourhood children with warm smiles and, if requested, hugs.

After the plane crash, Mitch's aunt, who had never had children, moved into the house and raised him. Between this woman and his mother before, they did an excellent job. He was kind, gentle, caring, and loving. He proved that by bringing her to his place.

"Spaghetti work for you?" he asked, his head inside the fridge.

A container of something frozen sat in the sink in water.

"Yes."

"Go sit, turn on the TV, whatever. I'll get supper going for us."

"Let me help, at least."

"No." The answer was firm, but not rude.

"Then I'll wash up afterwards," she said. Mitch would not wait on her hand and foot while she was his guest.

Mitch relented and let Nicole set the table, except for the plates. He plated the meal in the kitchen and carried it through. "Sorry, no salad or garlic bread," he said when he placed the spaghetti on the table.

"That's okay. This is more than enough for me. As it is, I still owe you a home-cooked meal."

"Don't worry about it. I won't hold you to

something like that."

"I want to."

"Okay." Mitch held his hands up in surrender. He'd been more than happy with takeout pizza at Nicole's. What mattered, he was in her company. That was all that mattered.

After their meal, Nicole did the dishes — she washed, to ensure is injured hand stayed dry, although a pair of rubber gloves sat in the dish rack, and he dried — and they went to the living room. Mitch searched the guide for a program for them to watch. After the day Nicole experienced, he wanted something light. Comedy would be an excellent choice. He wasn't a fan of Rom-Coms, but even one of those would be all right. He sacrificed an evening of darker shows for her comfort.

"Stop there! I love this movie," Nicole said. The guide was on *The Holiday*.

"You sure?"

"Yes."

Mitch selected the movie, which was just starting, and they settled in on the sofa, snuggled together.

Soon, soft snoring sounded beside him. Nicole had fallen asleep, her body finally succumbing to the exhaustion of the day. With everything she'd been through, it was a wonder she could.

Without getting up, Mitch grabbed the blanket from the back of the couch and spread it over her, his actions a silent promise to protect her even in her sleep.

"Mmm," Nicole murmured.

"You're awake. You fell asleep during the movie. I think we best find you something to wear to bed. You can sleep in my room, and I'll crash on the couch."

She couldn't put Mitch out of his bed. He'd already done more than enough for her.

"My drafting table takes up the other bedroom, so I don't even have a bed in there," he said.

Was that to make her feel less guilty about putting him out of his?

"No, I'll stay out here. It's fine."

Was she trying to convince him or herself? It

wouldn't be the first time she sofa-surfed at someone's flat. She'd stayed over at her brother's many times. But this was different. This was Mitch.

Mitch worked his way out from under her. He disappeared and returned a few minutes later with a T-shirt.

"I don't wear pyjamas, but I thought you'd like to cover up some."

Now, that was a revelation she hadn't expected to hear.

"I would offer you a pair of flannel pants, but I think they'd be too big for you. Bathroom is right through there if you want to get changed."

Nicole remained at the *I don't wear pyjamas* statement. She blinked several times, took Mitch's clothing, and headed into his bathroom. Nicole took her time so that if he was changing, she didn't happen upon him in a state of undress. She folded her jeans and sweater and carried them out into the hall.

Mitch met her outside his bedroom door, where he took her things and sat them on a chair. He wore plaid sleep pants like she'd seen her brothers wear, but nothing on top. Ripples of excitement rushed through her, and she broke out in goosebumps. Her heart raced as she tried to control her breathing.

"You're cold. Come here," he said.

Nicole found herself enveloped in his arms. The warmth from his bare flesh both soothed and excited her.

Mitch walked her into his room, a cozy space with warm, earthy tones, and pulled back the blankets. "In."

"But ..."

"No buts." He leaned down and kissed her on the forehead. Once settled, he pulled the duvet back over her, walked to the door, and turned out the light. "I'll leave the door open for you. There's a nightlight in the bathroom. I hope it won't keep you awake."

Mitch didn't mind giving his bed up to Nicole. He'd prefer to share it with her, but that step was up to her. He wouldn't pressure her into something and ruin everything they had. The ottoman that doubled as his coffee table contained bedding, so Mitch lifted the top. He pulled out a sheet and spread it on the couch so it would be under him as well as over, then two pillows. The blanket he'd covered Nicole with during the movie, would be the top layer. Once he had the couch made up, he settled in for the night.

He couldn't get what Nicole had done that was so terrible that her father went crazy. There had to be something related to the house or an ancestor that sparked his wrath. But what? What he'd seen of the house was architecturally interesting. Steep gabled roof, high ceilings, pocket doors, the tower, and the floor furnace. The latter he had come across in his renovations of older houses. Outdated

Nicole had mentioned the secret passage, but he hadn't entered it. He knew where it came out; he'd seen the gouges on the floor caused by its opening and closing. The pocket doors with a hidden switch to close that room off from the rest of the house. From what he could tell, there was no other way into that room.

He had just begun to doze off when a scream pierced the silence. Raven, who had settled on the couch beside him, leapt off, her fur on end and green eyes as big as saucers. It took a second for the source of the sound to register. It came from his bedroom. Nicole. Was she okay?

Mitch raced into the room. Nicole thrashed on the bed, mumbling something incoherent. He knelt beside the bed, reached out and touched her shoulder. Her eyes opened. Wide and wild. She shrank away from him.

"Nicole, it's me, Mitch. You're safe. It was just a bad dream." He sat down beside her. She shivered, so he drew her close to him. Whether from cold or fright, he didn't know, but she needed his support.

"No one is going to hurt you here, Nicole. I promise you that." He stroked her back as he held her close. "Can you tell me what it was about?"

She took a shuddering breath. "I-I," she said, gasping.

"What?"

"It was another secret passage. Blood-soaked Freemason regalia hanging in it."

"You mean at the Graham mansion?"

"No. Yes. Same passage. Steep ladder-like stairs. It had to be the one the guys, and I used to get from the tower to the main level of the house."

"I'll get you some water," Mitch offered.

"Please don't leave me."

"I'm only going to the kitchen. I'll be right back."

As much as he hated to leave her, he needed to. He got her the water, and he grabbed his heavy blanket off the couch on his way back. She could sleep under the blankets. He'd sleep on top. Perhaps, she'd manage some sleep if she wasn't alone.

Chapter Fifty-Three

NOVEMBER 30, 2022

Nicole woke early to an arm around her and the length of a body close behind her. What? Did they? She removed the limb and slipped from under the covers and across the hall to the bathroom.

Mitch comforting her after the nightmare was all she remembered. That and he brought her a glass of water. Had he put something in it? Roofied her? Her clothing remained intact. Why couldn't she remember?

Her clothes were in Mitch's bedroom. She should have grabbed them before she came in here. Get dressed and sneak out, and no one would be any wiser. But now, she risked sneaking back into his room to retrieve her clothes.

Nicole opened the bathroom door a crack and peered through the opening. The apartment was still in darkness. Good. She tiptoed across the hall, snatched her clothes off the chair, and returned to the washroom.

Raven yowled and hissed. She stepped on the cat's foot. So much for stealth. Nicole carried on. Hopefully, Mitch slept soundly and didn't hear the animal's outburst. She got dressed, folded the T-shirt neatly, and left it on the counter.

Her shoes were in the front hall. She had to get there with no further disturbances. Her coat? Where had Mitch put it when he brought her here? No way she could leave without it. She'd freeze to death before she got home. Her backpack. She'd left it with her shoes.

Nicole started across the living room. About

halfway through, the lamp in the corner switched on, and she froze.

"Where are you going, Nicole?"

That voice. It sounded exactly like Hannibal Lecter talking to Clarice in *Silence of the Lambs*. The tone, the cadence. What kind of nightmare had she walked into?

"You didn't answer me, Nicole."

"Home," she cried. "You roofied me or something."

Mitch was at her side within seconds. "I didn't drug you. Nothing happened. After you woke screaming from your nightmare, I stayed with you. I thought if I did, you might not have any more dreams."

"But ..."

"You were under the duvet. I was on top of it, covered with the blanket I used out here."

In her heart, she knew he would never do anything like that. Tears started to flow. Wracked with guilt over what she had accused Mitch of, she wanted to crawl away and die. How did things go so bad in so short a time? Her aunt was dead. She suffered a heart attack. Was her father there at the time? If the police told her, she didn't remember. Now, she'd accused Mitch of having roofied her. What a mess. He'd never forgive her for that. She didn't deserve to be forgiven.

Mitch was in disbelief. Nicole, the woman he cared for deeply, had accused him of such a heinous act. He couldn't fathom it; the weight of her accusation was heavy on his heart. No drugs were involved unless his body heat could be considered one.

"Mitch, I am so sorry. I know you'd do nothing like that to me. Between finding out my father is a monster, my aunt is dead, and then the nightmare, my head's all over the place. Please forgive me."

He couldn't deny that the past twenty-four hours had been a nightmare for Nicole. He almost empathized with her, understanding why she might have accused him. But forgiveness? It was a possibility, but not an immediate one. Mitch turned away and walked to the bedroom. He needed to be alone for a moment. Process the accusation. He returned about five minutes later.

Nicole looked so innocent standing there. He'd never take advantage of her the way she said. He cared for her and respected her too much. She seemed so fragile, so unlike her usual self.

"Do you still want to go back to the Graham mansion today?" he asked, his voice flat.

"Yes, but can we go to my place first? You said before I needed proper shoes, and I'd like to get some clean clothes."

"I'm going to have a quick shower. Make yourself a coffee. Everything is in the kitchen. Milk's in the fridge."

She nodded.

Her phone. Where was it? Nicole found her backpack and rummaged through the pockets. It wasn't in there. Had she left it in her coat? That didn't do her any good because she didn't know where Mitch put it last night.

She padded to the kitchen, found the coffee-making supplies, and started brewing a pot of medium roast. Her heart skipped a beat when she saw her phone on the counter beside the Keurig. Relief washed over her as she picked it up, feeling the familiar weight in her hand.

No messages from her brothers. They knew she'd be in safe hands here. She knew it, too, but she had to accuse Mitch of something terrible. Should she message her brothers? Not bother to mention the misunderstanding, but the events of the nightmare and the secret passage.

Did either of you see some bloodied Freemason regalia in the secret passage at the Graham mansion?

Maybe she hadn't dreamt, but recalled seeing something in that spooky confined room.

Not me.

Connor replied first. He came down the stairs, if you could call them that, last. Cooper had been in the passage the longest, so was more apt to be the one who saw anything.

Me neither.

That ruled out a recollection. It had to be a nightmare if Nicole's brothers had seen nothing untoward. They had been trapped in the room the passage opened into until Connor stumbled on the switch to open the pocket door. Mitch was there when the chandelier shook. Something happened in that house, possibly even that room, and she was determined to find out.

Mitch joined her, still towelling his hair. He pulled mugs from the cupboard and placed them by the coffee maker, but didn't speak to her.

"I sent my brothers a text message," Nicole said.

A look of horror crossed Mitch's face, his eyes widening in shock.

"About my nightmare and the bloody Freemason regalia. Had they seen anything in the secret passage we discovered?"

"And?"

"They both said no."

The Keurig machine in Mitch's kitchen wasn't as ordinary as the one in the office at CNC IT Solutions. This one brewed by the mug or carafe. Nicole found the larger pods in a basket next to the machine and made a pot of breakfast blend.

"You want anything to eat? I've got sliced bagels in the freezer and we can toast them." Mitch's voice lacked its usual tone. There was no compassion in it. Flat. Speaking only because it was necessary. Yes, she'd hurt him when she made the accusation.

A toasted bagel sounded wonderful. Why was Mitch letting her stay? After what she'd accused him of, he should have chucked her out on her ear. He hadn't, and for that, she was grateful. And he still offered to take her back to the Graham mansion.

"If you're having one."

Mitch reached into the freezer, pulled two bagels out of the sleeve, and popped them into the four-slice, wide-slot toaster.

After what she'd accused Mitch of, he should be furious. He wasn't. His love for her was a constant battle with his anger. The bagels popped, and he put them on two plates and handed them to her. After that, he took the cream cheese out of the fridge, and they walked to the dining room, where Nicole had placed their coffee earlier.

"Do you think we'll find something there we missed before?" Nicole asked as she spread the topping on her bagel.

"Hard to say. If you're talking about finding the things you saw in your nightmare, I don't think so. But then, what do I know? I'm not and never will be a Freemason." His uncertainty was apparent, his tone a little too abrupt.

Chapter Fifty-Four

SEPTEMBER 30, 1947

While William didn't fight in the Great War, the one that cost his father his life, he took part in the Second. He spent most of his time in England, protecting the country's southeast from attack by the Germans. While not injured, he returned to Canada as a changed man. And with a wife and son. After the war, William struggled with the memories of the battlefield, often waking up in a cold sweat. He found solace in his family and his work, becoming a successful business owner in Canada.

William and Alice met in a rather unconventional manner. Despite the fear, now that everything was safe, he could sit back and laugh about it. He was on a temporary leave and wandered the streets of the seaside town of Deal in Kent. All was quiet until the air raid sirens began wailing. He didn't know the place well. Where were the shelters? People ran helter-skelter in the streets but knew where they were going, so he followed them and ended up in the cellar of a quaint village pub.

A young girl, in her early 20s at most, took charge of the people sheltering in the cramped space. In true British fashion, as he was about to find out, she distributed cups of tea and calming words.

As unexpectedly as the sirens started, they stopped. People climbed the stairs, heading for home. William was the only one left. He preferred coffee but took the offered cup. When he took his first sip, he almost spat it across the room. There had to be half a cup of sugar in it. It tasted vile.

He stayed behind with her. They chatted about life, the war, and what would happen when it ended. William discovered her name was Alice, and she worked as a barmaid in the establishment above the cellar they sheltered in. Alice shared her experiences of living in a war-torn town, the constant fear of air raids, and losing loved ones. He told her about his father and what he knew of him, as told to him by his mother, and about him being awarded the Victoria Cross.

Soon after that night ended, when he was on leave, William spent time with her. Whether it was across the bar or if she had the night off, they strolled the streets of the town. One thing led to another, and they were married in the Town Hall.

His mother came round to Alice. He was sure the change of heart was because of her becoming a grandmother. William and his wife welcomed a baby boy into the world in 1940 at Deal Cottage Hospital. After arriving in Canada, they had a daughter. Now, he sat in the waiting room while Alice delivered child number three. An heir and two spares. The two older children were with their grandmother, and by this time of day, she should have them both tucked into bed.

June worried about the length of Alice's labour. William took her to the local hospital before breakfast that morning. It was now going on ten o'clock. Her two older grandchildren were fed, bathed, and tucked into bed.

Their house had a phone line, but they shared it with eight other families. William may have tried phoning from the hospital been unable to get through because the line was in use. She walked to the front door and pulled the lace curtain on the window aside. There was no traffic on the road that ran along in front of the house.

She walked to the back door. The air was cool and still, and carried the distant sound of a dog barking. But then, headlights in the distance grew brighter as the vehicle approached. Soon, they glared into the house, blinding her. She hoped it was William coming home, but until the engine was off, as well as the headlights, she couldn't tell.

A haggard-looking William exited the car and staggered towards the house with exhaustion dogging his every step. The outside light over the back door was on all the time. June realized how tired he was when he got within its powerful glow.

"Hi, ma," he said, walking into the kitchen.

"Well?" June asked.

"Twins. One of each. Any coffee going?"

"Sit yourself down at the table, and I'll get you some. Have you eaten?"

When she didn't receive an answer, she turned around. William had his arms folded on the table and his head on them, fast asleep. He didn't look comfortable, but she refused to wake him. Let him sleep. William was like his father. Could sleep anywhere at any time. This trait of his, a reminder of his father, always surprised June. It surprised her he hadn't slept at the hospital, but being worried about Alice and the unborn baby, which was now two babies, he wouldn't have. At least Alice had him near her when she went into labour. When William entered the world, his father fought in the Great War overseas.

Chapter Fifty-Five

NOVEMBER 30, 2022

While at her apartment, besides showering and putting on clean clothes, Nicole pulled her hiking boots out of the closet, added a new sketchbook to her backpack and grabbed her camera and the extra charged battery.

"Will this do?" she asked.

"Yes."

Nicole looked all around as they returned to Mitch's truck. She half expected her father to turn up and continue his rant from the previous day, but there was no sign of his vehicle. That was a tremendous relief.

"Are your brothers expecting you at work today?"

"I shouldn't think so," Nicole said, clambering into the truck.

Mitch remained unusually quiet. She'd hurt him and badly with her accusation.

"Will you at least talk to me, yell at me, hit me, do something," she pleaded.

"I would never hit you. Okay, you want me to yell? Okay, I'll yell. What you accused me of hurt, Nicki. You cut me right to the bone. I thought we had something. Trusted each other. But that? What kind of fucking bastard do you think I am? I'm not anything like Brad, who damned near killed you."

He mentioned that name. Her ex from college who beat down every bit of confidence she had. Mitch swore. Really swore. The occasional damn shit and hell crossed his lips when she was around, but never anything this strong. Tears pricked the backs of her eyes. She couldn't stop them, nor did she want to. Fair play. She'd hurt Mitch with her false accusation, so he broke her by bringing up a time in her life she'd tried to forget.

Mitch didn't regret yelling or using foul language, but the mere mention of Brad's name filled him with deep regret. To him, that was far worse than what Nicole had accused him of. He stole a few sideways glances at her as he drove, then reached over and took hold of her hand. She turned and looked out the window when he did.

They had both said some hurtful things to each other. Rightfully or wrongfully so, they hung in the air. But despite the hurt, there was a glimmer of hope for reconciliation. Could they start over? At least get back to what they had before the night at the hospital?

Today's traffic was heavy, with commuters making their way to work. To get there faster, Mitch opted to take the motorway rather than the route he usually took.

It made little difference to their time on the road, but Mitch finally pulled the truck into the driveway at the rear of the property.

After he shut the engine off and unfastened his seatbelt, he leaned over and pulled Nicole towards him. His heart was heavy with regret and longing for reconciliation. "I didn't mean to bring up his name. I was hurt and angry," he whispered.

She nodded and buried her face in his shoulder.

Inside, the house seemed different today. Colder, but then it was colder outside, and the heat wasn't turned on. Except it wasn't that kind of cold. This was a ghostly cold.

Nicole headed straight to the room where the secret passage opened. She stood in the archway between the two rooms, but a creaking sound made her take a step forward. What if the pocket doors closed, and she was between them? She'd be crushed. Those doors wouldn't have had any safety features built into them like today's automatic garage doors.

Suddenly, she was transported back in time. She didn't know when, but a meeting of Freemasons took place in this room. A man in robes, gold thread stitched in intricate designs, and regalia stood behind the desk. The medallion he wore around his neck glowed in the candlelight. Other men, dressed similarly, sat in chairs which lined either side of the room.

Nicole pulled her sketchbook out and drew furiously. She needed to capture everything. A shuddering sound echoed. The door to the secret passage opened. An inductee? Another man dressed the same as the others pushed a man with a cloth hood over his head, hands bound behind his back, and what resembled an adult cloth diaper, into the room.

The scantily clad man was made to kneel before the desk. The dagger! The one she first discovered under the floorboards of an upstairs bedroom. The man, she assumed the leader of this group, held the Baphomet dagger up in front of him. "By the light of knowledge, we bind our brother to our cause." A blessing? For the weapon or the man? He brought it down and pressed it against the naked chest of the man kneeling before him. A trickle of blood ran down the bare flesh.

When the vision appeared in front of her, Nicole stood on the inside of the closed pocket doors. She was in the room with the Freemasons. The doors creaked open and a small boy ran into the room. "Father," the child exclaimed. The shock of the interruption caused the man to push the dagger up to the hilt in the man's chest, and he collapsed backwards. Blood oozed out from around the wound. No one stood. No one tried to assist him.

As the small boy ran out of the room, Nicole recognized him as her father, at about five or six years old. She closed her eyes, unable to believe what she had just witnessed. The shock caused her to drop her pencil and sketchbook. When she opened her eyes, no one remained. She returned to the present once again.

Her father had witnessed a murder. The

revelation hit Nicole like a thunderbolt, leaving her stunned and struggling to process the enormity of the secret she had unearthed. Tears threatened to spill from her eyes, but she fought to keep them at bay. No wonder the man didn't want her to dig into the family history. Given her father's age, her grandfather was the leader of this chapter of the Freemasons. And the one who murdered the inductee.

Nicole staggered to a chair. It was too much to take in. Who were the other men in the room at the time? Who was the victim? Did anyone miss him?

She jumped when Mitch put his hand on her shoulder. "My grandfather was a murderer," she whispered, as if saying it out loud would cause something terrible to happen to them.

"Who's the child? The boy who interrupted proceedings?"

"You saw my sketches?"

"I watched you capturing the details you saw in your mind's eye."

"My father."

"How old?"

"Five or six, I believe," Nicole said. She had seen pictures of both of her parents as children.

"What year was he born?"

"1963."

"So, this murder happened between 68 and 70."

"What are you getting at?"

"I wonder if something was in the papers back then."

"Somehow, I don't think anyone ever reported it. Don't ask me why; it's just a gut feeling." Nicole turned towards the entrance to the secret passage, a mysterious portal that seemed to hold the key to their family's dark past. "I think our answer is hidden in there," she said, pointing to the wall where she and her brothers had emerged when they explored the empty house.

Nicole bravely led the way to the tower room where she and her brothers had first discovered the secret passage. The memory of one of her siblings joking about blood on the dagger's blade now seemed eerily prophetic. She assumed it was the blood of the young man, judging by the firmness of his skin and muscle tone.

Her hiking boots on the metal spiral stair treads echoed at a deafening level, adding to the tower's mysterious atmosphere. Inside the tower room, Nicole found the key to the secret passage hanging on a nail next to the door.

"It's dark and nasty in here," she said, unlocking the door and returning the key.

The door resisted Nicole's efforts; even Mitch's powerful push didn't open it.

Nicole backed up to the wall on the opposite side of the tower room. What if the door flew open and Mitch lost his footing and fell? The drop would kill him. Why did she insist on trying to find out what dark and hidden secrets lie within the walls of this old house?

He tried again, this time with a forceful kick. The door finally gave way, crashing open in a shower of splintered wood. Nicole turned away and put her arm across her face to shelter her eyes. She didn't want dirt or splinters in them.

The smell wafted, no burst from the confines of the room — musty, stale, and oppressive. It made her gag and was far worse than when Nicole explored it with her brothers. Another odour lingered, but she couldn't place it.

While she struggled to breathe, Mitch pulled a headlamp out of his pocket and turned it on.

"Ready?" he asked.

Nicole had to do it, but it wasn't something she wanted. She nodded, and stepped onto the top rung of the ladder in the vertical tunnel.

The beam from Mitch's light flickered across the room as he looked up, down, and sideways.

"What's that?" Nicole asked when the beam of light hit something that wasn't there before.

Mitch held his head still, the light beaming in the

location Nicole had said she saw something — a stone. Most of this vertical tunnel had been constructed from stone, so this didn't surprise him. What did was that it was the only one that wasn't mortared into place, a peculiar discovery that piqued his curiosity.

"Can you go down a couple of rungs so that I can have a foothold?"

Once Nicole was down below him, he stepped onto the top rung, and pulled a pocketknife out of his jeans to work this loose rock out of place far enough that his fingers were able to remove it the rest of the way. It was awkward standing on one side of the narrow passage with an arm around the ladder's rail to help support his weight. Mitch played with it, working it back and forth until he lost his grip, and the rock fell to the bottom of the passage with a thud.

He concentrated the beam of light into the opening. Something was in there. He reached in and felt around, hoping some critter didn't bite him. Then his fingers touched it. Leather? Mitch pulled his hand out to allow the light to do its job. A book of some sort. He stuck his hand back into the opening and grabbed it. An old book, its leather cover worn, and its pages yellowed with age. It felt heavy in his hand, as if it held secrets waiting to be discovered.

"I'll hang onto this until we get downstairs," he said, tucking the object into one of his jacket's large pockets.

"Okay."

Nicole clung to the rails a couple stairs below him. She hadn't lied when she told him the steps in this passage were as steep as a ladder and the treads not much broader. The precariousness of their situation was clear. You'd never get approval for something like this nowadays. Tread, riser, and slope all dictated in the building code for new builds, for good reason.

Over halfway down, Nicole shouted, "Stop! What's that on the wall? It looks like fingernail scratches."

Mitch focussed the light on the area she pointed at. Scratch marks, but animal or human? The possibility of something more sinister sent a shiver down his spine.

Nicole couldn't pull out her sketchbook because the of the confined space. Besides, she'd left her backpack downstairs, but she pulled her phone out of her pocket and took pictures. The flash was blinding. Until his eyes adjusted from that, Mitch stayed put. Missing a step from this height could be fatal.

Were those human claw marks in the beam? In her vision, the inductee was led into the room downstairs from this space. Shivers ran down her spine at the thought. Nicole breathed a sigh of relief when she finally stepped onto the floor inside the confined space. A pile of rubble sat between the *ladder* and the wall. She didn't pay any attention to whether it was when she came with her brothers. At the time, she didn't know a murder had taken place in the building.

She turned on the flashlight on her phone and moved some of the bigger pieces of debris until her hand touched something other than cement, dust, or cobwebs.

"Mitch, can you shine your light here, please?"

He turned and bowed his head so the light shone where she'd asked.

That wasn't stone. Nicole brushed some more of the chalky debris away. She screamed and jumped back when what she had uncovered turned out to be a skull. "Oh my God! Do you think it was him? They shoved him in here, thinking he was dead, but he wasn't? Those marks may have been from him clawing at the walls, trying to escape. The stab wound didn't kill him but he died trapped in here."

Mitch put his arms around Nicole and pulled her to him. Her mind raced despite being in the comfort of her friend. This poor man who was stabbed then trapped in here, who was he? Not knowing anything about the Freemasons and their rituals, she wondered if what she witnessed in the past was normal? Even if she found one of the men, he'd either be dead or too old to wouldn't remember. The only person who would was her father. Did she dare take her findings to him? If so, she wouldn't go alone, and she wouldn't have the original sketches. She'd photocopy or scan them at work.

Chapter Fifty-Six

June opened the door to the postman on the front porch. Other days, he dropped the mail and left, but not today.

"Sorry to disturb you, Mrs. Holbrook, but this package won't fit in your letter box," he said.

"Thank you." June took the package and retreated into the house. Whoever had sent it to her had used special delivery. That would explain the service. She turned the box over in her hands. No return address. Odd. The label, addressed to her, Mrs. June Holbrook, Graham House, Brighton, Ontario. There were no other Holbrooks in the area other than her son, William, and his children.

June carried the box to the kitchen and placed it on the table. She took a pair of scissors out of the drawer to cut the string, but stopped. Instead, she worked away at the knot until she untied it, then removed the cord and put it away in a drawer. She might need it someday.

Once she removed the cord, June unwrapped the object. Again, she folded it for reuse if needed. Having lived through the depression, she wasted nothing. When she lifted the lid off the box, she gasped. Who would send her a china head doll? A sheet of paper lay folded on the doll's chest. June lifted the page, unfolded it, and read the note. The handwriting looked familiar, but she was unable to place it. All she knew was that she had seen it before.

The note was simple, yet heart breaking.

My granddaughter is dead, so I have no need for this anymore. Perhaps you have a granddaughter, or in the future you might have a great-granddaughter you can pass it down to.

Then it dawned on her. The same person who had anonymously sent the sympathy card after Robert's death wrote this note. June was sure of it. She took the paper to the front room where she had put the card, along with her parents' framed marriage certificate.

The handwriting matched. Was this the woman Robert had the affair with? The one whose letter she received in error? At that moment, she wanted to smash the china head doll to smithereens.

June dashed to the kitchen where she had left the package and picked up the doll. She drew her arm back as if to hurl it at the wall, but something stopped her. She couldn't explain it, but it was as if an unseen force took her by the wrist and prevented her from following through with the action.

"What's this, ma?" William asked.

His mother stood, transfixed on the open box in front of her. The letter dangled in her fingers. He took it from her and read.

"Who sent you this, ma?"

"I-I don't know. There's no return address on the wrapper." June dropped onto the chair and sighed. She knew in her heart it was the woman her husband had the affair with after he was sent to the Western Front in Belgium, but how did she tell her son that? Her son that hung on every word she ever told him about the man. How he was a war hero. His Victoria Cross. She couldn't ruin that image he had of his father. That would be cruel. She couldn't ... wouldn't do that to her son.

"Are you going to the hospital today?" she asked.

"Later. Off to the barn now. Bye, ma." William walked to the back door and paused. He turned back towards his mother. "You going to be okay?"

"Yes, I'll be fine."

Since she'd found out she was knitting for a boy and a girl, June knitted day and night. That way, she'd have the two sweater sets finished in time for Alice to bring the children home from the hospital. She used the same pattern for both. While feminine for a boy, it wouldn't make that much difference because he'd outgrow it long before he knew the difference between boys and girls. She had finished the pale pink for her newest granddaughter. It was just the baby blue one for her grandson that wasn't. The bonnet and booties were, and there wasn't much left to do on the sweater.

William had never mentioned names. Not even how much the children weighed. She'd pin him down before he went to the hospital. Alice and the children had been there since she gave birth. They would come home in the next day or so. My, how things had changed since William was born. A midwife delivered him, right in this house in June's bed. She hoped William was able to afford the hospital stay. The farm made decent money, enough to keep the growing family in food and clothing. Fresh milk from the dairy herd and eggs from the hens, too.

Grayson, at age seven, was a lot like William at that age: mischievous, daring, and interested in vegetable gardening. Susan, only a year old, had much simpler interests. And she was far too young to be given the responsibility of caring for a china head doll.

Chapter Fifty-Seven

NOVEMBER 30, 2022

"We need to notify the authorities about the body we've found in here," Mitch said. He'd never experienced an urban exploration of an abandoned property that came close to this one on the bizarre level.

"Not yet."

"We can't not report it."

"I know, but another day isn't going to mean much. The poor soul won't be any less dead. I want my father to see the sketches I made first. See if he can explain. Then, we'll notify the police. I want to gather my stuff and see Connor and Cooper. Show them what I found today."

He mulled it over. Whoever the dead man was, he'd been that way for over fifty years. Another twenty-four to thirty-six hours wouldn't mean a thing to him. "Okay, but once that's done, we call the authorities."

Nicole nodded.

Nicole and Mitch entered the quarters of CNC IT Solutions offices through the front door. Her car was still parked out behind since they had taken her to their apartment. Connor witnessed Cooper's face colour changing. "Play nice, bro," he said, then turned to Nicole. "What's up, sis?"

"This." She spread her sketches out across the tables.

"What is it?"

"Some sort of Freemason initiation, I think."

Cooper joined them.

"Hear me out, guys. I think this is our grandfather," Nicole said and pointed to the man she'd drawn holding the dagger. "I have no idea who the half-dressed guy with the hood over his head is kneeling in front of him, nor do I know the identities of anyone else in the room. That is until ..." She laid out the following image. "I think this little boy is our father when at about five or six years old."

"What are you getting at?" Connor asked, his voice trembling with the shock of the sketches done by his sister and her narration.

"I think an initiation or even something more sinister happened that night. Our father interrupted, and this guy was killed. If he didn't die immediately, then he did when they locked him in the secret passage. Mitch found a logbook of sorts; we've not looked at it yet. I saw scratch marks on the walls and found a skeleton behind what passed for a staircase."

Nicole picked up her sketches and walked to the copier. "No one gets my originals. I'll make copies, and that's what I'll share," she declared.

"So, what's your next move?" Cooper asked. His sister's sketches and photographs from the hidden passage unnerved him. Why hadn't he spotted those things when they explored the house? Had he, this entire ordeal his sister just went through would never need to happen.

"Can you phone Dad and ask him to come here?" Nicole asked.

Cooper didn't believe what he heard. When the last time their father was in the office, it turned into mayhem. Vitriol spewed at his sister. No, he wouldn't be the one to make the call. "After last time, I can't believe you want to be in the same room with him."

"A lot of things I wasn't aware of then. Maybe now, knowing Dad witnessed a murder as a child, he might be more receptive to what I have to say. Still, I want to make photocopies of these. Those are what I'll show to him. My sketches will stay hidden."

"If you're sure. I don't want to see Dad go off on you again."

Mitch stepped up and put his arm around Nicole's shoulder. "If he does, he'll have me to deal with as well as you two."

His sister looked towards the man's eyes, and a look of gratitude passed over her face. Had Cooper been wrong to fall out with Mitch? After all, the guy looked after her when things got weird at Kembleford Manor. Maybe all his posturing to keep the man away from her was wrong.

Cooper made the call but did not mention why they needed his father at their office. Once that was done and out of the way, he sidled over to Mitch. "I think I owe you an apology. You've been good to Nicole. Kept her safe in a place where the old man didn't know where she was."

"You're okay, man. I know where you're coming from. If I had a sister, I'd be protective of her, too."

Frank burst through the office door about half an hour after Cooper had called him. Nicole turned her face into Mitch's shoulder after the look her father cast her way said she was dead to him. Or if not, she would be dead soon.

"Dad, Nicole discovered something today. I know you didn't want her digging into your side of the family. But before you go off on her, at least let her tell you what she found," Connor said.

He squeezed his sister's shoulder and stood beside her when she began. Nicole leaned towards him, gathering his strength.

"Dad, your father was a Freemason, wasn't he?" Nicole asked.

Her father nodded, but the scowl hadn't left his face. She laid out a couple of her sketches. "You witnessed this, didn't you?"

He looked at her sketches and his figures distorted. Nicole could only imagine the torment seeing them brought to him.

"But ... how?"

"Mitch took me to the house today, and this vision appeared to me," Nicole whispered. "You witnessed your father kill a man." She revealed the next image she'd sketched of the scene.

Her father dropped to his knees and covered his eyes with his hands. Tears fell and escaped below his fingers.

Nicole knelt beside him. "It's okay, Dad. I understand why you were so angry with me. Your father is gone and can't hurt you anymore. I assume he abused you, and that was just part of your hatred towards him, as if him killing a man in your presence wasn't enough."

"He wasn't dead. Yes, he was bleeding badly, but he was alive when they shoved him into that, that, god-awful space."

"You stumbled into a Freemason ritual, didn't you?"

"I've tried so hard over the years to forget it all. But it didn't work. Can you imagine what it was like as a child when you saw your father stab a man?"

"I found what I believe was the weapon buried under the floorboards in a room upstairs."

"You're probably right." Frank wrapped his arms around her and wept. "You understand now why I didn't want you researching the family?"

"Yes. But I received a letter from Aunt Janet. It arrived by courier, dated last Friday. In it, she said you pushed your father down the stairs, and from then until he died, he remained in a coma. She also said you pushed her down the stairs. It wasn't her cat she tripped over like she'd told everyone."

Nicole nodded to her brothers and stood. It was over — at least this portion of her life was.

Cooper pulled out his cell phone and made a call. Soon after, police cars with flashing lights pulled up in front of their office.

As they were about to lead Frank away, Nicole stepped up. "I have a question if that's okay."

"Yes, go ahead."

"Did Mummy ever know what you did to your father and Aunt Janet?"

"As God as my witness, no. And before you ask, I never harmed a hair on your mother's head. I loved her; she got me through the darkness and into the light."

Nicole looked at the officer and mouthed, "Thank you."

The police took her father away.

The revelation left Connor reeling. He knew of his sister's unique ability to perceive things beyond the ordinary. However, the intricate sketch of a Freemason ritual, with the words subtly woven into the scene rather than in a speech bubble, left him utterly dumbfounded.

A hand found its way onto his arm. He turned to see his sister's eyes looking into his.

"Are you okay?" she asked. "It's a lot to take in."

That was putting it mildly. Grandfather involved in a murder. Father witnessing said murder. You couldn't write a book or a screenplay better than this. He nodded and then hugged Nicole. He felt a hand touch his shoulder and opened his eyes. Mitch had placed his hand there. Solidarity between friends and family.

But where was his twin when all this was happening? He stood by the front door, his face a mask of shock. He was ready to face the news alone, just like their father. Was he becoming like their father?

At that moment, Connor was filled with regret for not having spent more time with his aunt. Her sudden death from a heart attack had made it too late. If only he could have heard her perspective on their father's past, it might have shed light on the current turmoil he was experiencing.

Chapter Fifty-Eight

Nicole had convinced Mitch to accompany her back to her apartment. She held the letter her aunt had sent tightly against her chest, the lawyer's business card in her other hand. Should she act on the letter's instructions? Was her aunt in a sound state of mind when she wrote it? The questions swirled in her mind, creating a storm of uncertainty.

Staying at his flat wouldn't be the same now that the renovations and repairs had been completed at the Anderson house. Raven had gone back to where she belonged. Nicole missed the cat. It had a unique personality. Usually, cats were aloof and only attached themselves to one person. This one had grown to love Mitch and her.

"Are you going to be okay?" he asked.

"I think so. You can stay if you like. I won't toss you out on your ear."

Mitch leaned over and lifted Nicole's chin. He placed his lips on hers, softly at first, but the longer they kissed, the harder he pressed.

It wasn't what Nicole had anticipated, but she loved how she felt when Mitch kissed her. She pulled away from him before his intense dark brown eyes completely disarmed her.

"We need to phone the police and tell them what we found. We might even have to return to the house and meet them there. The dagger is here. They'll need it, too."

Nicole scoured the room for the trunk she brought home from the Graham mansion. It wasn't in the hall with the boxes.

"I think you had me put it in the bedroom. I'll check," Mitch said, walking towards Nicole's room.

Standing in her room was weird. He was a stranger, and this was her inner sanctum. Her private place. The two dressers from the nursery were in here with the drawers back in them. The rocking chair and cradle were in here, too. It didn't seem strange when the furniture had been moved in here because they were both in the room. Right now, it was only him.

"Found it," he called out.

Within seconds, Nicole stood in the doorway. Mitch leaned against the taller of the two dressers and pointed to the top. The trunk sat on top of it.

"I don't remember putting it up there, do you?" Nicole asked.

"No, but I've learned not to question things, not being where they should be when I'm with you."

"Can you lift it down, please? I need it where I can get into it."

Mitch set the trunk on the floor. Nicole unlatched the catches and lifted the lid. The wedding gown and veil lay on the top in a green garbage bag. She lifted it out and handed it to him. Beneath that, a stack of framed pictures. Nicole removed them and set them aside. An object in a blanket came out next. She unwrapped the bundle enough to reveal the dagger's handle with the occult carving, then re-wrapped the weapon and laid it on her bed with utmost care.

Nicole placed the framed pictures in the trunk one at a time. Between two of them was a folded, yellowed newspaper clipping.

"What's that?" Mitch asked.

"I don't know. When I took the pictures out of the wardrobe, I grabbed them all at once. This had to have been in between them then."

Nicole set the document aside and returned the artwork to the trunk. Last, she retrieved the trash bag containing the wedding gown and veil, placed it back in the trunk, and closed the chest.

"You should see if you can get the bridal outfit dry-cleaned. It's yellowed over the years and is pretty dusty." Mitch's nose tickled, and he sneezed.

"We'll leave the dagger on the bed for now. Let's sit on the couch and see what this is all about."

Nicole led the way to the living room and, with care, opened the newspaper article preserved from the Brighton Ensign. "Wow! Do you think this is our body in the secret passage?"

Mitch leaned forward to take a closer look. "It might be. Let me see your sketches. At least the one with your father in it."

Nicole retrieved the drawing Mitch asked for. "October seems to be right. Look what your father is wearing."

The hulking house wasn't warm, but her father wore long pants, a long-sleeved shirt, and a sweater vest over it.

Brighton Ensign
LOCAL MAN MISSING: POLICE SEEK INFORMATION
Date: October 12, 1968
Edward Hartwell, Staff Reporter
Brighton, Ontario — *The sudden disappearance of a local labourer has left family members and authorities searching for answers. Thomas Carrow, 28, was last seen on the evening of October 10 near Graham Side Road, where he had been employed as a carpenter on a private estate formerly belonging to the Graham family.*

According to witnesses, Mr. Carrow left work that evening without his belongings and failed to return home. His wife, Margaret Carrow, reported him missing the following morning after he did not appear for breakfast or retrieve his tools.

"Thomas would never leave without telling us where he was going," said Margaret, visibly distressed. "He's a devoted husband and father. This isn't like him at all."

The estate where Mr. Carrow worked, a Gothic Revival mansion owned by the Holbrook family, has drawn scrutiny in recent years for its enigmatic history. While police have not indicated foul play, speculation abounds within the community because of the building's notorious reputation for secrecy and whispered tales of unusual gatherings.

Authorities are appealing to anyone with information regarding Mr. Carrow's whereabouts to come forward. The search continues in earnest, with local volunteers combing the property's grounds and surrounding woodlands.

When questioned, a spokesperson for the Holbrook family stated, "We are cooperating fully with the investigation and hope for Mr. Carrow's safe return."

A Troubling Pattern?

This is not the first unusual incident tied to the Holbrook estate. Reports from years past speak of unexplained phenomena, missing individuals, and whispered accusations of clandestine activity.

"We always hear strange things about that place," said one local resident who wished to remain anonymous. "People go in, but not everyone comes out. It's enough to make anyone uneasy."

Mr. Carrow is described as 5'10" with dark brown hair and a sturdy build. He was last seen wearing a lined plaid flannel shirt, jeans, suspenders, and work boots. Anyone with information is urged to contact the Brighton Constabulary.

The mystery surrounding Mr. Carrow's disappearance deepens with each passing day, leaving a community desperate for answers and fearing the worst.

"We should take this to the police, along with the dagger. But before we do that, I want to scan it in case it doesn't return. I wish I had photos of my father as a child."

"You might and just don't know it. They might be in the stuff that came from your parents' storage locker. Do you want me to help you look?"

"Would you? You've done so much for me

already."

"Point me in the right direction."

"The ones at this end of the hall."

Nicole had taken the newspaper clipping to her scanner and started it. When she returned to the sofa, Mitch was waiting for her with the boxes.

"This is the box I started looking through, but stopped when I found the pedigree chart that showed Mummy was a descendant of Albert Kembleford. That's what this is rolled up in the corner."

"I'd found a diary before that belonging to Lavinia Kembleford. She had it bad for Bartholomew Randall, who married her sister, Ophelia."

"Things haven't changed over the years," said Mitch.

She had to agree because she'd seen several movies in which the sisters vied for the attention of one man. Nicole pulled out other documents, but nothing that offered a clue about what she sought. These were bills of sale, the foreclosure letter—well, at least a copy that wasn't blood-soaked—and English birth certificates for Albert, Patience, and James.

"This stuff is way too old. Let's try the next box." With a sense of anticipation, she returned the paperwork she'd taken out and closed the box again.

The next box brought them closer. It held another copy of the photograph of Claude and Lizzie's farmhouse. Some of her grandmother's — her mother's mother — things were in here, too. A delicate, silver jewellery box on feet. Nicole opened it. It was a wedding set. The engagement ring with a matching wedding band in white gold and a plain band.

Unopened envelopes in her mother's handwriting, addressed to each of her children. Nicole dashed a tear away when she recognized her mother's hand. She set them aside to look at later. Some loose photos were in this box, but at a quick glance, they were mainly of Nicole and her brothers.

Finally, the last box. Photo albums. The first one held pictures of her parent's wedding. They weren't professionally done; it looked like a friend had taken them. Another was of her and her brothers as children, after the baby book stage. Her graduation from the commercial art course. Her brothers' graduations.

Another album contained pictures of her father and mother before they were married, but interspersed with older photos. Some of them as children. Nicole scrutinized them.

There it was! A picture of her father at about the right age. Wearing the outfit she'd sketched him in. The only thing she hadn't captured was that he wore brown corduroy trousers. She removed it from the album, feeling a wave of relief wash over her.

"I'll scan it, too."

"Why? The police have your father in custody. They don't need a picture of him as a kid."

"The OPP might need it when we take the newspaper article and the dagger to them, along with copies of my sketches. It proved that the kid in the picture was my dad."

Nicole's father had been taken away by the Belleville city police, not the Brighton OPP. "Make sure you have a copy of the letter from your aunt leaving you the house when we take the documents. If we're lucky, we'll be able to talk to the one who found us there and knows you had permission."

"Let's go get this over with." Nicole scanned the letter from her aunt before they left.

"You got everything?" Mitch asked.

"Photocopies of my sketches, including in the secret passage, actual photo of my father, the dagger, and the letter from my aunt. I think that's everything."

Mitch escorted her to his truck. He was amazed at how well Nicole was holding everything together. He'd be a basket case if he'd witnessed any of that. If it wasn't for Nicole standing by him after his parents were killed in the plane crash, Mitch might have gone off the rails. He was grateful to her for that. He might have loved her since then.

He remained quiet on the drive to the OPP station

near Brighton, his mind consumed by the mystery. Pondered what they would make of Nicole's sketches. The newspaper clipping and the revelation of the body in the secret passage. There had to be a better way of getting into that room than going up to the tower and back down. The floor was scratched so there had to be a switch somewhere nearby. Mitch hadn't looked that closely. Something similar to the switch inside the door, but where?

Nicole strode into the lobby and pressed the intercom button. "I have some information about a man who went missing from the Graham mansion in 1968. I think I know where he might be."

"You do, do you?"

"She does," Mitch said.

"You better come through," he said, pushing the button to release the door.

As they entered, the cop who tried to bust them that day walked by. It was the one with the orange hair. He hadn't gone far when he stopped and turned around.

"I recognize you two. My partner and I caught you red-handed inside the old Graham place. I heard what you said to the desk sergeant. You better come with me." He led the way to what appeared to be a conference room. Maybe where they met first thing on their shifts and received their assignments.

Despite June's surname becoming Holbrook and the house remaining in that family until today, people still referred to it as the Graham place. The only time it was mentioned with the name Holbrook was in the newspaper article.

"You'll think I'm crazy, but I see things from the past." Nicole's confident voice betrayed her inner fear. She hoped she could get through this without falling apart. At least the cop she was in the room with wasn't the dark-haired one with attitude.

The police officer nodded and smirked.

"No, it's true. Like these." Nicole spread the copies of her sketches out on the table. "That little boy in this one. That's my father. She placed the photo of her father on the sketch beside the child in it."

The smirk disappeared from his face.

"Now, there is a secret passage that runs from the tower room into this one where the stabbing took place. In it, behind the ladder, hidden amongst the debris, is a skeleton. At least part of it. There are scratches on the walls like the man stabbed during the ritual was locked in there alive, and he struggled to get out."

Nicole spread more sketches out, taking advantage of the time to collect her thoughts before she continued.

"I think the dead man is the one who disappeared from there in October 1968."

Nicole unfolded the newspaper clipping and laid it out, too. "It was between two pictures which were stacked in an upstairs wardrobe." She swallowed hard. Presenting these artifacts was more difficult than she imagined.

The last item Nicole placed on the table was the dagger. "I found this under the floorboards of one of the upstairs bedrooms. I'm pretty sure when you have it analyzed, you'll find human blood on the blade. Blood belonging to the missing man. When I discovered it, I immediately put on a pair of nitrile gloves, so I didn't contaminate it."

Nicole placed the knife, wrapped in the blanket she found it in, on the table. The cop used his pen to move the covering aside. Even it had stains on it that might have been blood. He disappeared, then returned wearing a pair of gloves. The weapon was unwrapped, revealing the occult symbols on the handle and the rusty-coloured stain on the blade.

"The Carrow case was a conundrum for the lads back then. It was before I became a cop. Hell, I wasn't even born yet. It's a cold case. If what you've shown and told me here today pans out, we might finally close the damn thing."

Nicole smiled. If the body in the secret passage turned out to be the Carrow man, she helped to solve it.

"Can you meet our forensic team there? Show them the entrance to the passage where you found the human bones?"

"Yes. We're on our way to my house now."

"Your house? You told us it belonged to your aunt when we caught you there."

"My aunt died suddenly, but before she did, she sent me this letter. She'd left the house to me. There are still the legalities of it all." Nicole held out the letter from her aunt. "My father is in police custody in Belleville. City force."

Nicole wore a gratified smile when they left the police station. "I'm proud of you, you know. A lot of people are intimidated by cops, but not you. You kept your cool, stated your facts clearly, and they believed you," Mitch said.

"I was scared stupid. I didn't know if he was going to believe me or arrest me."

Mitch hugged her, then picked her up and spun her around. All the while, she laughed wildly.

"I suppose if we're going to meet them there and show them where the entrance is, we best get a move on. I haven't found the switch that opens the bottom door."

"Cooper found the one on the floor inside the door. I'll text him and ask if he remembers it. Might give us something to look for in that room."

Nicole took out her phone and typed.

A few minutes later, she received the response. She turned the phone for Mitch to see.

Round and turns. I think I had to turn it to the left to get the door to open.

Before he handed the phone back to Nicole, another message came in.

Why?

"Do we tell him or let him stew for a while? It's up to you," Mitch said.

"You're evil, but I like that idea. I'll let Cooper know when we get there."

When Nicole and Mitch arrived at the mansion, the forensic team was onsite, and running crime scene tape around the perimeter of the property.

"You the ones who will show us where the remains are?"

"Yes. One of you want to come with us?"

Nicole led the way. The screen door at the back hung askew again. That would have to be fixed or removed. She knew a contractor who specialized in renovating and/or restoring old homes. Would he be interested in the job? Far more work needed to be done, starting with changing the locks on the front and back doors. Nicole didn't have the keys to either and wasn't sure if her aunt's lawyer did. Might as well start with new.

"In here," she said, entering the room with the freaky ceiling medallion. That was definitely coming down. "The door is here, but we're not sure how to open it from this side."

Mitch moved closer. "Given Cooper's description, it might be mistaken for a light switch."

Nicole moved closer to him. "The other light switches are push button, but they all have ornate wall plates."

She scoured the wall around the area where the access panel scratched the floor. The fireplace. It could be the same colour as the stone, so blend in. Nothing. The scratches on the floor showed the door opened out away from the fireplace.

"What's that?" Nicole asked.

"What?"

"Up there. Is that it?" If you weren't looking for it, you'd never see it, the thing was so cleverly disguised, it blended into the wall.

Mitch had almost six inches on Nicole. "Stand back just in case this thing flies open." He reached up to the spot she pointed to and turned the small knob.

A great shuddering sound filled the room, followed by the creak of hinges that needed to be oiled.

"That will be all. You two can leave now. We'll take it from here."

"If it turns out to be the man who went missing in 1968, will you let me know?"

Chapter Fifty-Nine

Nicole decided the information couldn't be relayed properly in a text message, so she phoned Cooper. "Put it on speaker so Connor can hear, too."

"Okay, sis."

"Well, Mitch and I went through the secret passage starting from the tower. Near the bottom, we found scratch marks on the studs and other areas of the walls. Behind the ladder, a human skull lie in a pile of debris. There was also blood-soaked Freemason's regalia, and Mitch found a journal buried in the wall behind a loose rock."

They were too shocked to respond, Nicole decided. "We sorted through some of the stuff from the house, and among the pictures, we found a newspaper clipping from 1968 about a man who went missing from the area. I've taken everything to the OPP in Brighton and we met their forensic team. They're in the passage right now, doing their thing."

"Wow!" Cooper finally said. "I don't remember seeing any of that stuff you mentioned."

"That's crazy," Connor added. "If it turns out the bones belong to this missing guy, our baby sister will have solved a cold case."

His statement took her aback. She had thought little about it. Even when the cop at the police station said that the case was still open, it had been cold for a long time.

"Come on, Nicki. Let's get out of here."

Mitch led Nicole to the back door. Besides the police presence, several onlookers crowded around the barrier defined by the yellow and black police tape. "Likely hoping to see a corpse get taken out in a body bag."

"Gross."

"Your bones will go out that way."

"Still gross. What did you do with the journal you found?"

"Forgot about that. It's still in my pocket. I'll give it to the first cop I see. It should prove to be interesting reading." Mitch pulled the book from his pocket and opened it. It wasn't written in English. It was some kind of code. Something that only another Freemason would understand.

"What is it?" Nicole asked.

"You tell me." He held the book out for Nicole to see.

"I have no idea what that is. Code, symbols?"

Mitch's truck was outside the cordoned-off area. The cop at the barrier scowled at them. "Here, you might want this. Might lead to more deaths associated with this place, if you can figure out the language."

Voices echoed up and down the line of spectators, repeating his words.

"You provided them with enough fodder for rumours for at least a year," Nicole said, smiling at him.

"Maybe when this has all blown over, or at least the police are gone, we can try out my metal detector. With everything else that happened, I totally forgot about it."

Nicole collapsed against him in a fit of giggles. He didn't think what he'd said was that funny. Not funny at all.

"Have you lost your mind?" he asked.

"No. But, now that I own this place, everything we took to my place can be returned. It's hilarious, don't you think?"

The recollection of getting the things downstairs,

especially the rocking horse, didn't tickle Mitch's funny bone. It was hard work moving that stuff.

"I'm thinking of renovating and moving in. You don't know of a reputable contractor who would be interested in the job, do you?"

"Well, I'm not sure if you could afford him."

"How much would he charge?"

"Not just the money. There's the terms and conditions that go along with it."

"Okay, and what are they?"

"Close your eyes." Mitch got down on one knee and produced a box from his pocket. "Condition number one is you say yes to my question."

"And what question is that?" She asked and giggled.

When he was satisfied her eyes were closed, he opened the box.

What was Mitch playing at? Terms and conditions. Her eyes had to be closed. He was up to something.

"Nicole Holbrook, will you marry me?"

Mitch didn't just ask her to marry him, did he? When she opened her eyes, a diamond ring sat in the box in his outstretched hand. He did propose. It wasn't her imagination. Tears streamed down her cheeks.

"Yes, yes, I'll marry you," she blurted out, her voice trembling with surprise and joy.

He stood and slid the ring onto her finger. It fit perfectly, a symbol of their perfect fit in each other's lives. How did he know what size? When did he get it? His proposal was a bolt out of the blue. She hadn't expected it. The ring was beautiful. It looked like it was custom made and must have cost a fortune. She wasn't worth that after some of the things she'd done, especially the roofie accusation.

Nicole threw her arms around his neck, and they kissed. She never dreamt this would happen. But now, in this moment, she realized she might have loved Mitch all along.

Back at her apartment, Nicole picked up the letters written to her and her brothers by their mother. Did she open hers? After her marriage proposal and being on cloud nine, Nicole didn't want to read something that would bring her down to earth with a thud. Still, she needed to know what was in hers, so she ripped it open.

May 1, 2020

My sweet Nicole,

You were a ray of sunshine in my life. After your brothers were born, I didn't think I'd ever be a mother again. And then you came along. What a blessing! I've always cherished you, my sweet Nicole, and I want nothing but the best for you.

I won't be there for you when you get married or have children. The oncologist tells me I only have weeks to live. Cancer is such an odious disease. But none of us gets out of life alive. Maybe it's a blessing? At least I know when my time will be up — more or less.

I hope you find a good man who will be kind to you and treat you well as you should be. I've always liked Mitch. He'd make an excellent husband and father to your children when the time comes. He cares for you a great deal. I've seen it in his eyes.

Nicole looked at him. Was her mother with her now? Did she know of Mitch's recent marriage proposal?

Use the talents you were given. They're a gift. You might not always see them as such, but they are.

Talents? She used her artwork every day. Was her mother talking about her ability to see ghosts and events of the past?

Be kind to your father. He had a terrible upbringing, and he doesn't know that I know, so please don't let on to him.

I love you and your brothers so much. I hate to leave. I wanted to see the three of you married with your own families and be a grandmother. But that won't happen now.

I'm tired so I must rest. But know I am at peace with what is coming, my dear Nicole.

I love you with all my heart and soul.

Mummy

Tears of both sorrow and revelation ran down Nicole's cheeks. All these years, she had never known her mother liked Mitch and would have loved to have him as a son-in-law. The mix of emotions overwhelmed her."W-want to read it?" Nicole held the letter out to Mitch.

"It's personal. It's between you and your mother."

"You're mentioned in it."

Mitch furrowed his brow.

"I'm going to invite Connor and Cooper over and give them their letters." Nicole stood and walked into her bedroom.

Mitch seized the opportunity when she left the room and read the letter. The revelation hit him like a ton of bricks. All these years, he had been oblivious to Mrs. Holbrook's belief that he was suitable son-in-law material. With Nicole's *yes* still echoing in his mind, he now felt the burden of living up to her mother's expectations.

When Nicole returned to the living room, she held a fistful of tissues. "I spoke to the guys. Told them I had letters from Mummy here for them." She blew her nose.

"You sure you want to do this?"

"Yes."

About ten minutes later, the intercom buzzed, signalling Nicole's brothers had arrived. Mitch was uneasy about being in Nicole's flat when Cooper arrived, but he was trapped now. Leaving would only raise suspicion.

"Hey, Mitch," Connor said. "Didn't expect to see

you here." He walked through and sat on the opposite end of the couch.

Cooper mumbled something, but Mitch didn't hear all of it.

Nicole entered the living room from the hallway, holding two envelopes. "These letters from Mummy were in a box from the storage locker. You can read it now or take it home to read. I've read mine already." She handed them to her brothers.

She stepped over Connor's feet and sat between him and Mitch on the sofa.

"Look, this is family stuff. I'll go so you can have this time for yourselves."

Mitch stood, grabbed his coat from the rack, and headed to the door. Nicole waited for him. How'd she get there ahead of him? Ah, it came to him. The galley kitchen. While he went around one way, she came the other.

"You don't have to leave. You're family, too," she said. Her eyes searched his.

"Not yet. But soon. You and your brothers need this time just the three of you." He leaned down, kissed her cheek, and left the apartment.

"Mitch didn't leave on account of us," Connor said.

"Paperwork to catch up on." Nicole's face reddened when she spoke. "Anyway, the letters. Mine was dated May 1, 2020, so about six weeks before Mummy died."

She pulled it out of her pocket and read it aloud, inviting her brothers into their shared emotional journey.

Connor pulled his envelope open and scanned the contents. His eyes grew blurry as he read. "Do you want me to read mine out loud, too?"

"Only if you want."

"Mine is dated the same date."

My dear Connor,

When I went to the hospital, I thought I was only having one baby. The way you were positioned, they could never pick up the second heartbeat. Imagine my surprise when you came. You may be an identical twin, but your personality differs from your brother's. You're more laid back, easygoing, and fun. If a practical joke was to be played, you were behind it.

I won't be there when you get married or have children. The oncologist tells me I only have weeks to live. But then, no one gets out of life alive. We all die. Some of us just have a better idea of when.

I love you, your sister, and your brother so much. I hate to leave. I wanted to see you three married with your own families and become a grandma. That won't happen, but my love and hopes for you will always be there, guiding you.

Be kind to your father. He had a terrible upbringing, and he doesn't know that I know, so please don't let on to him.

I'm tired so I must rest. But know I am at peace with what is coming.

I love you with all my heart and soul.

Mummy

Maybe his sister's idea of reading the letter at home would have been better. Instead, he was reading his mother's thoughts and fears in her apartment.

He sucked in a ragged breath and pinched the bridge of his nose.

Cooper took a deep breath. His siblings had shared their letters from their mother. Was he up to the task? What did she have to say about him? He opened the envelope and skimmed over the contents.

"Same date as your letters."

My dear Cooper,

When you were born, I thought it was just you, but Connor had other ideas. You probably think it's hokey that your names start with the same letter. It might be, but that was what we did back then.

You were always the driven one. The protective one. And sometimes, maybe even a bully. I'm not sure what happened between you and Mitch, but make amends. He's been a good friend to you three.

Because you and your brother were identical, I had to dress you differently to tell you apart. That was another thing they did at the time — they dressed twins alike. I knew once you got older, and your personalities came out, but not until.

And don't forget, end this feud you have with Mitch.

"The rest of it's the same as yours." He looked at Nicole. "What's all this about ending my feud with Mitch? Make amends. I'd almost swear he's a part of the family."

Nicole cleared her throat. "Well, he is almost. Besides the fact we grew up together and did almost everything together, Mitch has asked me to marry him."

Connor jumped up. "Congratulations, sis," he said and hugged her.

Mitchell Kane as a brother-in-law. He was tempted to say over my dead body, but one look at his younger sister told him everything he needed to know. And Mitch took her in so she'd be safe in an unknown location when their father was on the warpath. More importantly, she was happy. Mitch wasn't *his* first choice for Nicole, but he figured she could do worse.

Chapter Sixty

The police had finished investigating the secret passage and removed the bones. Pending a thorough reading of the journal Mitch found, they might be back. Nicole and Mitch had returned to the house, making a list of things that needed to be done.

"First things first, the place needs re-wiring," he stressed. "And the plumbing, it's a disaster waiting to happen. We can't afford a situation like Mrs. Anderson's."

"That's for sure."

"We could remove cookstove in the kitchen and move the fridge and stove in the utility room into that space."

"I like that stove, Mitch. It goes with the age of the house."

"The floor furnace needs to go, and a new front door fitted. Have you seen the gap under the current one? Snow or rain likely blows in during storms; it's that big."

"I get it. A more efficient heating system. And new windows and doors. Insulation because you can bet this place has none or very little."

"You catch on fast."

"One thing I want removed is that ceiling medallion. It's creepy. And I don't want the pocket doors between the rooms. Just a big archway."

The two continued through the house, with Mitch

making notes of things that needed to be done to bring the house up-to-date and the cosmetic things Nicole wanted. He agreed with her about getting rid of the ceiling medallion. Only a Freemason would like one with that symbol.

Mitch's expertise shone through as he discussed the pocket doors. He suggested removing the switch and framing in the archway, even musing about finding some vintage wood in his yard. His experience with older houses, where owners often wanted modernization, shone through in his plans for the old-style trim.

The house was cold enough today; he could see his breath. Even though the floor furnace had to go, he walked down to the basement and started it up. It would have to stay operational until a modern, efficient furnace was installed along with a heat pump. The low temperature wasn't doing the pipes or anything any good.

While they were indoors, snow had started to fall. If it kept up at the rate it came down, there would be no metal-detecting in the next few days. Maybe now, not until spring. If Mitch was going to do the work on the house, not until after he was finished.

EPILOGUE

JUNE 10, 2023

Six months to the day, after the police finished their investigation into Thomas Carrow's disappearance, they determined he was, in fact, the person whose bones Nicole found in the passageway.

She never heard if anything came from the journal Mitch handed over. With the way the entries had been written in code, even the police might never find out what it said. Hopefully, only one person died in an initiation or ritual gone wrong. But she didn't have time to think about that now. In a few hours, Nicole would walk down the massive staircase in her wedding finery to marry Mitch.

Her father was jailed for the assaults on his father and sister. Although she suspected it, they hadn't proven conclusively that he had caused his sister's fatal heart attack. Since her dad wasn't available to give her away, she'd asked Cooper, who, for the longest time, held a grudge against Mitch. She still didn't know what caused that.

Mitch's family doctor had run a battery of tests on him, but they all came back normal as well. Was it the amount of Advil remaining in his system that caused the excess bleeding, or was it something more sinister? Long-buried secrets that lingered after the original Holbrook home burned?

Connor was Mitch's best man. The wedding was casual, except for what Nicole wore. She'd had the wedding gown found in the tower room dry cleaned and any damage from improper storage repaired. The gown, with its history and the pictures she'd seen in the house of the blonde woman wearing it, gave her a tangible connection to her past. She was sure the gown belonged to June Graham, her great-great-grandmother.

Just before the start of the ceremony, Cooper came upstairs to get her. Nicole stood in the nursery — all the furniture and Snowflake, the rocking horse, returned to their rightful places. Clara, the china head doll, sat in the rocking chair. Something, whether or not supernatural, brought the doll to Nicole. Ute Birkhoefer had returned it to Robert's widow to be passed down through the generations.

Nicole placed her hand on her stomach. She wasn't yet, but she hoped she would soon be, and the room would be brought to life once again.

"Ready, sis?" Cooper asked.

"Yes."

The small living room across from the staircase was set up for the ceremony. Mitch had finished the last of the repairs two days ago, and they spent the day before their nuptials painting and decorating. In a few minutes, she would become Mrs. Mitchell Kane. Or perhaps, Mrs. Nicole Holbrook-Kane. The uncertainty of her future name added an intriguing twist to the moment, but she didn't care as long as he was part of the equation.

Mitch turned when the footsteps sounded on the stairs. Nicole looked radiant in the Victorian-era gown. He took in a ragged breath. Connor patted his arm.

Soon Nicole stood at his side. They had planned a simple non-religious ceremony and had secured an officiant from Belleville, willing to travel to the house on the outskirts of Brighton. There weren't many guests, closer to none other than the wedding party and the person performing the ceremony. And the ladies from the WI, who catered and helped Nicole with all those buttons. Buttons that he'd have to deal with later.

She didn't have a bridesmaid or a maid of honour. She insisted she didn't need one because she was getting the best part of the bargain. Him. Mitch went along with her wishes and rather liked her reasoning.

So much had happened since he came here with Nicole in mid-November, not all of it good. But they had faced it together. There were strange noises, unexplained shadows, and objects moving on their own. And if any other strange things happened in the house, they would do the same again.

As he waited for his turn to say his *I do*, Mitch pondered what strange things the house would reveal to them. He'd been out with his metal detector a couple of times. He had dug up some old coins, a belt buckle, and other things. Except for the coins, he found the other items in ashes, so likely from cleaning the wood stove or the location of the burn barrel. That was the logical answer to that.

But with Nicole and the old houses, there was no rational explanation.

"You may now kiss the bride."

Was the ceremony over that fast? He must have said what he needed to. Same with Nicole, but his thoughts were consumed by what other strange things might happen here. Would they find more mysterious artifacts buried in the garden? Would the house reveal more of its secrets? Only time would tell.

THE END

<<<0>>>

Also by Melanie Robertson-King

The Consequences Collection
Tim's Magic Christmas
The Secret of Hillcrest House
A Shadow in the Past (second edition)
Shadows From Her Past
YESTERDAY TODAY ALWAYS
Cole's Notes (Revised version)
It Happened on Dufferin Terrace
It Happened in Gastown
It Happened at Percé Rock
All Aboard the Canadian with Buddy and his Four Fantastic
Furry Friends!
It Happened at Lake Louise
WHISPERS THROUGH TIME
It Happened at Niagara Falls
(King Park Press)

Cole's Notes (A Short Story)
EFD1: Starship Goodwords – a cross genre anthology
(Carrick Publishing, 2012)

MELANIE ROBERTSON-KING

https://melanierobertson-king.com

Melanie Robertson-King has always been a fan of the written word. Growing up as an only child, her face was almost always buried in a book from the time she could read. Her father was one of the thousands of Home Children sent to Canada through the auspices of The Orphan Homes of Scotland, and she has been fortunate to be able to visit her father's homeland many times and even met the Princess Royal (Princess Anne) at the orphanage where he was raised.